'I don't really like dogs, but I absolutely loved this book.'—Jon McGregor, author of *Lean Fall Stand*

'*Dog* is a novel full of deft humour and escalating tenderness—a tale about misfits, human and canine, and the currents of hope and courage that bring them together.'—Ross Raisin, author of *God's Own Country* and *A Hunger*

'A deeply touching tale about the complexities of being human, and the journey we make to become our true self.'—Jon Ransom, author of *The Whale Tattoo*

'With humour and unwavering empathy, Rob Perry uncovers the imperfect specimens and misfits who survive on the edge of society, revealing the complexity of the human experience in even the bleakest or most circumscribed of lives. This novel is a picaresque delight.'—Karen Powell, author of *Fifteen Wild Decembers*

'*Dog* is both laugh-out-loud funny and quietly devastating. Heartbreaking, lyrical, and exciting, *Dog* will be your new best friend.'
—Owen Nicholls, author of *Love, Unscripted*

'Rob Perry is that rarest of breeds: not only has his writing the poise and beauty of a greyhound at full flight, it can also be riotously funny. A magnificent debut.'—Benjamin Johncock, author of *The Last Pilot*

'*Dog* is a delight. It's such a treat to meet a dog in a novel, especially one as touching and funny as this one.'—Andrew Cowan, author of *Pig* and *Your Fault*

'Scruffy, funny and tender, *Dog* is an edgily real adventure with a believable dog-hero that I read in one hit.'—Alice Hiller, poet and contributor to *Dog Hearted*

'This outsider fable of friendship and human-animal connection wields a comforting deadpan charm.'—Tom Benn, author of *Oxblood*

Rob Perry was born in 1987. He is a graduate of the UEA Creative Writing programme. In 2020, his novel *Dog* was shortlisted and highly commended in the Peggy Chapman Andrews First Novel Award. In 2019 he was selected for the National Centre for Writing's Escalator programme. He has been shortlisted for the Bridport Short Story Prize, the Bristol Short Story Prize and the Fish Short Story Prize. He won the Nottingham Short Story Prize and was first runner-up in the Moth International Short Story Prize and The Winston Fletcher Memorial Prize. Rob was a copywriter for several years, and has worked as a firefighter and a weightlifting coach. He lives in the Peak District.

Rob Perry

DOG

Europa Editions
8 Blackstock Mews
London N4 2BT
www.europaeditions.co.uk

This book is a work of fiction. Any references to historical events,
real people, or real locales are used fictitiously.

Copyright © 2024 by Rob Perry
First Publication 2024 by Europa Editions
This edition, 2024 by Europa Editions

All rights reserved, including the right of reproduction
in whole or in part in any form.

Rob Perry has asserted his right to be identified as Author of this Work.

A catalogue record for this title is available from the British Library
ISBN 978-1-78770-576-0

Perry, Rob
Dog

Cover design and illustration by Ginevra Rapisardi

Prepress by Grafica Punto Print – Rome

Printed and bound in Great Britain by Clays Ltd, Elcograf S.p.A

For mum, who planted the seed.
And Lucy, who watered it.

DOG

One

Benjamin Glass was on his way to see a dead whale when the dog started walking beside him on the sand.

'I'm going to see a dead whale,' he said out loud.

He didn't normally encourage dogs he didn't know, but this one seemed sad. It was dragging a red lead and looking around.

'You probably shouldn't come,' he said to the dog. He said that because he didn't know what a dog's grasp of death was—didn't know if it had the tools to cope.

Benjamin found out about the whale in a newspaper at work. When his supervisor Camille put him on tills, he used newspapers to obscure the scanner so it wouldn't make him go blind or mutate his cells. She jabbed her finger at a grainy picture on one of the front pages.

'You should go and see it,' she said, balled fist hovering over her heart. 'You should see how it makes you *feel*.'

Camille had already seen the whale, she said, as part of her complete and intrinsic connection to all the animals of the earth.

'I wouldn't like that,' Benjamin said, spraying antibacterial cleaner onto the conveyor belt.

'Maybe that's why you should go,' she said.

Benjamin stood upwind of the whale and took shallow breaths in case whatever killed it could leapfrog between species. He'd been worrying about airborne pathogens since he heard about a man who arrived at Gatwick airport with a highly contagious respiratory condition. Some of the newspapers said the illness came from East Asia because people were eating bats. Camille was standing by the vending machine with a diet fizzy in her hand when she heard that. She squeezed her eyes tight shut.

'Poor bats,' she'd said. 'Poor, poor bats.'

That afternoon she cleansed her chakras and increased her intake of certain homeopathic remedies.

'He's dead,' Benjamin said, pointing.

He was eyeing the whale's large mouth and blowhole. The dog sat down a few feet to his left. Even though the whale didn't seem particularly damaged, the sand underneath it had turned red. It made Benjamin think about blood slowing to a stop in veins the size of water pipes. He looked at its sad old eyes, dried out by the sun, and imagined the whale's internal organs all pressed up against each other as gravity weighed down on its body out of water.

'Where's your owner?' he said to the dog.

The dog didn't acknowledge him, just sat gazing at the whale, blinking and breathing. After a while, it walked over to the whale and licked the blubber.

'Fucking hell,' Benjamin said, glancing around to see if anyone had heard. When the dog came back, it pressed its wet nose against his hand. 'Fucking hell,' he said again.

Benjamin inspected the new patch of moisture just above his knuckles, the cluster of fine, red hand-hairs that had stuck to the skin. All the while, the dog watched him through distant, amber eyes. Slow blinks like it had just woken from a dream.

'I'm going to have to go home now,' Benjamin said.

Benjamin walked between the dunes with the saliva hand held out in front of him, the dog following loosely behind. As they made their way along a sandy track, snaking up the side of the California Sands Caravan Park, the dog stopped to sniff at vacant crab shells and bits of plastic washed up from the sea. They reached a hole in the mesh fence.

'I don't think you should come through here,' Benjamin said, pulling his sleeve down over the clean hand—the one the dog hadn't licked—for protection. It took a few steps forwards and shivered. 'If you get tetanus you'll get lockjaw,' he said. 'Which means you won't be able to eat.' He demonstrated a few chews. 'Your jaw will seize up.'

Then he squeezed through the gap. He didn't look back in case the dog got the wrong idea, just walked through the caravans—eyes forward, trainers slipping in the mud—past a flatscreen TV box sagging in the rain and a bike frame with no wheels.

At the caravan, Benjamin looked back along the track. There was no sign of the dog so he walked up and onto the wooden decking. When he turned to check again, the dog was there with its tongue hanging out. It stared, glassy-eyed and mouth ajar, as Benjamin slipped through the door and left it standing on the porch.

Benjamin leant against the wall and drew oxygen into his lungs. He slid off his jeans and put them in the washing machine, then thoroughly washed his hands in the sink. He crept to the window and peered out between the curtains. The dog was sitting on the decking, watching the caravan park's flag wobble on its pole. Every now and then it closed its eyes for just longer than a blink and swayed. When it looked at Benjamin again, he stepped away from the window and picked up the phone. He called directory enquiries to get the number for an animal welfare organisation and asked them to put him through.

As he waited for a call-centre specialist to become available, Benjamin took two puffs of his inhaler. He held his breath until he felt light-headed, listening to faraway-sounding pop songs crackling through the receiver like the signal was bad. Eventually a lady picked up the phone. She had a Welsh accent and a friendly voice. She said her name was Laura.

'Hi, it's Benjamin Glass,' he said.

'Hi Benjamin Glass. What can I do for you?'

'I'm calling because there's a dog that won't stop following me,' he said. 'I found him on the beach by a dead whale, which he licked. Then he followed me home.'

'A dead whale?' Laura said.

Benjamin felt like she'd missed the point a little. It wasn't the whale on the decking.

'Yes. On the beach. Do you think he could be infected?'

Laura didn't answer so Benjamin continued.

'I get wheezy when I'm stressed,' Benjamin said, hoping her silence was just the time she needed to come up with a solution. 'I've had to take my inhaler.'

'Let's start with what sort of dog he is,' Laura said.

So Benjamin thought about it. The dog was like other dogs, only his chest was deeper and his legs were longer.

'He looks like a racing bicycle,' he said.

'Right.'

'And he has an exciting coat. Like a tiger.'

'Okay. Anything else?'

'Some of his ribs are poking out,' he said. 'Not in a hungry way. I think they always look like that, don't they?'

'What do?'

'These dogs.'

'Possibly.' Laura said. 'Is he a greyhound, do you think?'

Benjamin could hear other telephones ringing in the background. Chairs knocking into desks.

'Yes,' he said. 'I think he is.'

Laura didn't respond immediately. It seemed to be her way.

'Does he have a name tag on his collar?' she said.

'I don't know. I'm trying not to touch him.'

'Where is he now?'

'I left him out on the decking.'

'Right. And he's still there?'

'I don't know. Shall I check?'
'If you could.'

Benjamin crawled to the door, stretching the cord as far as it would go, speaking louder because the handset didn't quite reach the side of his head. When he peered out through the letterbox, the dog was looking directly at him through the slot. It licked its lips and shivered.

'I found him. He's still there,' Benjamin said. 'He's shivering now.'

'Is there a chance you could let him in?'

'None at all,' he said. 'He's a germ factory. I just need you to come and get him.'

Benjamin opened the curtain. He felt bad saying things like that because the dog had emotional eyes and because it was cold, but he didn't want it rubbing its genitals all over the soft furnishings and spreading microbes around the caravan.

'Is he injured?' Laura said.

'Not really. His left eye is a bit bloodshot, I think. It's hard to tell from here.'

'Does he look like he's eaten recently?'

Benjamin examined the dog through the window.

'Other than the rib thing?' he said.

'Yes. Does he look hungry?'

Benjamin didn't like the pressure of having to decide on the spot. He wasn't a dog expert.

'Wait there,' he said, balancing the phone on the sill, running over to the cupboard.

He took the last slice of a white loaf from the bag and stuffed it through the letterbox. The sound of the dog sniffing was amplified by the slot as it investigated, but it didn't eat the bread.

'He's not hungry,' Benjamin said.

Benjamin could hear Laura explaining the situation to

someone in the background. While he waited for her to finish, he scratched an itchy bit on the inside of his forearm and made the skin go red.

'Benjamin,' Laura said eventually, 'are you still there?'

'Yep. Still here,' he said.

She hesitated.

'The problem we have, with this situation, that you're . . . *in*, is that we don't pick up healthy dogs.'

Benjamin didn't understand. It wasn't his dog. He thought maybe he'd misheard so he asked Laura to repeat herself.

'We don't pick up healthy dogs, Benjamin,' she said.

In the silence that followed, Benjamin thought about things. About the dog's tongue touching the blubber. About its uncovered feet leaving contaminants on the surfaces and about the fact that Camille believed animals were capable of complex human emotions like embarrassment and romantic longing.

'Have you ever heard of Toxicara canis, Laura?' he said eventually.

'I haven't,' she said.

'It's a kind of parasite that lives in dog faeces. It's basically a horrendous worm that grows behind your eye and makes you go blind.' Benjamin waited a few seconds for impact. The skin under his chin was itching. 'It can shut down your liver and lungs.'

Benjamin heard a phone ringing in the background. Waited for Laura to respond.

'There's a local dog warden I'm going to put you in touch with,' she said. 'I'm going to give you their number now.'

'That's great,' Benjamin said, relieved. 'Because I don't want to make a big deal out of this or anything, but he's already touched me a couple of times.'

'He's touched you?'

'Yes. On my hand.'

'I'm going to give you the number now Benjamin—'

He interrupted.

'Sorry Laura,' he said. 'It's once. It's actually only once.'

'What is?'

'The number of times he's touched me.'

Another pause. The barely audible sound of Laura breathing.

'The telephone number, Benjamin. It's—'

'I lied about how many times to make it sound worse. He's only touched me once.'

Laura read him the number. He wrote it down on an envelope with a shaking pencil, his skin white hot with the stress of it.

'I'm sorry I lied, Laura,' he said.

'Do you have a family member that might be able to help?'

'Normally my nan would know what to do,' Benjamin said.

'Great. Where is she?'

He faltered. He didn't like saying hospital. It felt as though he was speaking something sinister into being.

'She's at bingo,' he said.

'Fine . . . so she can help when she gets home?'

'It's a bingo holiday,' he said.

'I didn't know they did those. Where is it?'

'Tenerife.'

Benjamin wondered what his nan would have said if she could. He knew she would like the dog, because she liked animals, but that made him feel better and worse at the same time. Better because what he was doing was probably the right thing; worse because she wasn't there to say it.

'What about a neighbour?'

Benjamin automatically glanced outside. There *was* a neighbour, but not the sort that would help. He had unkind views concerning people from abroad and said inappropriate things about women. From Camille's limited interactions in the supermarket with him, she was convinced he'd been an advocate for leaving the European Union.

'It's out of season,' Benjamin said. 'There's no one about.'

'Okay. But the dog warden is closed now. Until Monday,' Laura said.

'I can't really leave him on the balcony until Monday,' Benjamin said.

'Not really,' Laura said.

Benjamin scratched his elbow. He looked back through the window at the dog, supping at micro-puddles on the decking. He put the phone down.

'Fucking hell,' he said for the third time that day.

Outside, the wind was picking up, blades of grass all leaning over. Benjamin pulled on a pair of washing-up gloves and went to the door. He opened it enough to peer out at the dog's slim body, shaking in the drizzle, ribcage pressed out onto tiger-print fur.

It squeezed its head into the gap.

'You're probably going to have to come in,' Benjamin said.

Two

Inside, the dog padded around, dragging its lead and smelling things. It was still shivering.

'You probably wouldn't feel the cold so much if you had a higher body-fat percentage,' Benjamin said, following it into the kitchen. Its nails tapped on the lino as it walked over to one of the cupboards and licked a spot on the door. 'I'll have to clean that now,' Benjamin said.

The dog walked over to him and stood with its front paws very close together.

'I don't know why you're still cold,' Benjamin said. 'You're inside.'

With the Marigolds for protection, he unclipped the dog's lead and put it on the worktop. Then he leant over and rubbed the thick bits of its back legs, running his hand along the bumps of its spine. With his flat palm on the dog's side, he felt the tremor of its heart pressing the ribs out and pumping blood around its body.

'Do you feel lost?' he said.

But that felt like a silly question. Because being lost wasn't always so clear-cut. He knew you could feel misplaced, even when your body was exactly where it was supposed to be. That, often, it had nothing to do with your location at all.

The dog walked over to the coffee table, brushing along the side of the sofa, then lowered its nose into a cold cup of tea. Benjamin picked up the cup and saw a dead moth disintegrating in the liquid, blurring across its surface. He made a mental note of where the dog had touched. As he poured the tea into the sink, the moth settled temporarily in the plughole before vanishing. Benjamin wondered whether the dog had been forced to drink saltwater and puddles while it was lost.

'I'll get you something to drink,' he said, filling a salad bowl at the sink.

He put the bowl down in front of the dog and it drank for what felt like a long time. When it lifted its head there were tiny beads of water balanced in the fine hairs of its nose. Benjamin watched one of them fall into the fibres of the carpet.

'I'm going to put you in the bathroom,' he said. 'Because I can't think while you're touching everything and wandering around.'

Benjamin shepherded it in, being careful not to make any actual, physical contact. As he closed the bathroom door the dog watched him with quiet eyes.

'I honestly won't be long,' he said, hoping the dog wouldn't urinate.

Benjamin used disinfectant spray on the areas the dog had touched, pausing as he walked over the peach rug to spread his toes in the thick pile. He picked up a cushion, pressed his face into it and shouted very loudly. When he had finished, he looked at himself in the mirror. His cheeks and neck were red. He stood in silence.

'I'm okay,' he said through the bathroom door, in case the noise had caused the dog any stress, in case its emotions were compromised.

At work, when a chicken packet split across the scales of Benjamin's till and dripped inside the circuitry, Camille had carefully explained to him the importance of venting your negativity. While Benjamin spent the best part of forty minutes washing the pink chicken juice from his hands and workspace, Camille expressed that the flow of energy was constant and unerring. She explained that you had to give it somewhere to go, like a river into the ocean. She said her way of doing that could sometimes be as simple as shouting into her coat after a difficult shift. She'd handed him one.

'I'm already very warm,' Benjamin said.

'It's not to wear. We're going to expel some negative sentiment,' she said, climbing up onto a nearby footstool. 'I find that a little elevation helps. To project.'

Up on the stool, Benjamin looked at Camille for a cue. When she pressed her face into the coat, he did the same. They shouted until their faces were bright red.

'Do you feel better?' Camille said. 'Freer?'

'A bit,' Benjamin said.

Except that, really, he felt much better. Partly because of the shouting, and partly because Camille made him worry less. She rarely let things bother her, and he found it comforting. She was trusting and kind and, basically, that was enough.

In the caravan, Benjamin rolled the Marigolds down his forearms, off over his hands, and hung them on the edge of the sink. He tore a sheet from a notepad on the table and wrote a list of places the dog had touched. *The wall in the hallway, the sofa (already wiped). All over the carpet.*

The list was a help. His memory was less reliable when he was worked up and it would stop him forgetting which items and areas the dog had smeared itself on.

In the bathroom, the dog was standing on the bathmat, exactly as he'd left it.

'Sorry I shouted,' he said. 'I was just venting.' Benjamin used his hands to gesture 'venting' by waving them around his temples. As he spoke, the dog adjusted its ears and head, as if a different angle might help him decode what Benjamin was saying.

'I've got a list now though,' he said, waving the piece of paper. 'So I won't worry as much about you contaminating my things. I can sanitise them later.'

The dog yawned, stretching out its neck.

'I'm going to have a bath,' Benjamin said.

Benjamin turned the taps on full, then folded his clothes and put them on the toilet seat. While the bathtub filled, he looked at his naked body in the mirror. As a child he'd always paid close attention to his pallor, because he'd learnt about the Black Death in history and lived in fear that he'd go grey then die like the poor people in the text book. His legs were covered in goose pimples. He automatically cupped his balls to check for lumps.

'You can lay down. If you want,' he said to the dog, motioning at the floor.

While the bath filled, the dog walked around in impractically small circles. After three or four rotations it lowered itself into a sphinx-like pose, stretching its front legs out, tucking the back legs under. Benjamin stood in the tub. As he descended, he felt the hot tide of cleanliness rise up and over his body, warming his skin. He slid down until the water reached the bridge of his nose and blinked a few times, then submerged completely.

Eyes open underwater, he watched his hair lifting up and away from his head, swaying like seaweed. He felt the ache for oxygen in his body, the adenosine triphosphate in his cells depleting while he tried to work out in days how long his nan had been in hospital. The light on the tiles wobbled in neat, bright diagonals.

The long, dark shape of the dog's head appeared above him, hovering over the surface of the water. When Benjamin sat up, it moved away, but he could still read the name tag around its neck.

The Mighty Gary, it said.

Three

Benjamin towelled himself dry as the water gurgled into oblivion between his feet. He wrapped the towel around his waist and stepped out onto the bathmat.

In the living room, he switched the storage heater on and took a handful of clean clothes from the drying rack. While he was pulling a jumper on over his head, Gary jumped onto the sofa and curled up like a prawn.

'Jesus,' Benjamin said, knowingly taking the Lord's name in vain, glancing at a watercolour picture of the Messiah on the mantel. His nan had never been particularly religious, but she had the odd trinket around because her father was a priest. Benjamin could see how appealing it might be— to believe in something greater, something *after*—it was just that he never could. The End seemed to him something final. The silence after a glass has been smashed. The blank pages at the end of a book.

Benjamin hoped his nan didn't feel that way, that she was able to believe that when the lights went out, she'd wake up somewhere different, in another body. In a different life. He picked up a pillow and used it to push Gary ineffectually towards the sofa's edge.

'You might have shit particles on your feet,' he said, pressing a little harder, forced to imagine the parts of a dog's paw that could harbour that kind of thing. He shook his hands in the air—fingers splayed—like someone drying nail polish, then leant in very close and scrutinised the dog's paws.

'I can make you something comfortable to lay on,' he said, grabbing a blanket from the armchair and putting it over the cushions at the other end of the sofa. 'This is really comfy and easy to wash,' he said. 'You don't even have to get down. I just need you to stop touching the sofa directly.'

Gary opened one of his eyes, then stood up and walked to the blanket.

'Thanks,' Benjamin said, adding *sofa—top cushions* to his list.

Benjamin sat down on the floor and turned on the TV. A blue glow spilt across the carpet as he flicked through the channels, landing on a nature documentary at the very moment a penguin was being eaten by a sea leopard. Gary stared at the screen, observing the sea leopard's jaws clamped firmly around the penguin, its tiny black eyes in panic.

'Sorry,' Benjamin said, turning it over.

After, he thought about the penguin floating in the heavy swell, its body being lifted up and down by the vast cold gut of the ocean. He thought about the sloshing water all around and the tragic permanence of what came after. He reached for a leaflet on the coffee table that said *Sunrise Take-it-away* and tried to distract himself with the *Chef's Specials*. The penguin's lonely struggle did not leave him.

'We should have some food,' Benjamin said, holding up the leaflet. He turned the TV down, picked up the phone and dialled the number.

'You probably always eat meat,' Benjamin said. 'But I don't like eating animals.'

He ordered a vegetarian set meal for two.

A car drove past outside and unsettled Gary. Its headlights lit the windows, casting long shadows that slid across the back wall. The dog looked like he was waiting for something to happen. When it didn't, he jumped down from the sofa and walked to the door where he waited, nose hovering four inches from the glass.

'What do you want?' Benjamin said, staring at the back of the dog's domed head.

Gary let out a long breath and shuttered his eyelashes.

'It's dark out there,' Benjamin said.

The dog fidgeted, moving his feet around on the spot. Benjamin didn't know how he'd clean up a piss.

'I'll let you out then,' he said.

Standing on the doormat, Benjamin squinted and listened. He tried to pick out Gary's shape from the heavy outline of things as he drifted around and worried about a lost dog like that on its own. About it accidentally eating rat poison or walking out into the road.

When it felt like Gary had had long enough to properly relieve himself, Benjamin called him, but the wind seemed to swallow his voice. When he said it louder, the sound of the waves heaving up onto land drowned him out. He felt the dark space around him like a physical thing. When he looked across at the lights of town, the houses and the people seemed distant in a way that had very little to do with geography. He thought about his nan. About the ambulance, its blue lights sliding silently over the outside walls of the caravan, and the dinner she'd cooked the night she'd gone into hospital—peas and a tiny pork chop—left cold on the lino beside an upturned plate. He remembered the sensation that had accompanied finding her on the floor, of barely being connected to his body. Like it could walk away and he might forget to follow. When he pulled her up, and as she was lying there blinking, she smiled at him on one side of her mouth. He tried to speak but the feelings wouldn't translate into words. He wanted to tell her it would be okay. That she meant something to him in a way that was dense and permanent, like stone, of the Earth, beyond delicate bodies. But he couldn't seem to get it out.

The seconds contorted. The longer Benjamin waited, the less sure he was about how long he'd *been* waiting, until eventually he wondered whether that was it. Whether what had just happened with the dog wasn't the beginning of something, but the sum of it. He was trying to figure out which it was he'd wanted when Gary loped back inside, breath drifting up in plumes, and a kind of relief swept over him that made his chest fill and his skin tingle.

Gary led him back to the sofa. The dog curled up on the blanket and closed his eyes and Benjamin watched. After a while, Benjamin flicked through the channels again, leaving the volume on low so he didn't disturb the dog. He stopped on the news. On the muted TV, a line of text at the bottom of the screen read:

'INTERNATIONAL STUDENT TESTS POSITIVE FOR BAT VIRUS.'

He didn't want to know any more about that, so he skipped back to the documentary. It wasn't much better. Now there were sharks spinning a shoal of fish into a frenzy then hammering into them from the side. The dog was awake again. He always seemed to be watching when something bad happened. His eyes lingered as Benjamin opened a drawer.

'We should probably just watch a film,' he said, moving his hand along rows of VHS tapes recorded direct from the telly. The labels were handwritten in block capitals. As Benjamin's eyes moved along the cassettes, he imagined his nan writing them, pressing the felt tip into the paper, a faint shake in her hand causing all of the horizontal lines to undulate like little waves. He was stuck on the image of her in a hospital bed when his hand brushed the dog's head. He pulled away for obvious reasons, but felt glad again that it had come back inside.

'This one's good,' he said, holding out a tape that read 'You've got Mail' on the label. He pushed it into the machine and pressed Play. The wheels inside turned and made a whirring noise, while lines of static stretched out across the screen then disappeared. Gary backed away.

'It's got Thomas Hanks and Megan Ryan in it,' Benjamin said. 'They start sending each other romantic emails but when they find out they're business rivals it all gets really awkward because he represents Change. It's not very good quality because it's VHS.'

Just at the point in the film when Tom Hanks has realised where his emails are going, a car pulled up on the grass outside. Gary stood with his ears pointed up, listening to the sound of the engine.

'It's just the food,' Benjamin said, pausing the film. He heard the driver clear his throat before he knocked.

'Two seconds,' Benjamin shouted, using his leg to keep Gary back from the door. He opened it enough to fit his head and arm out, allowing the lamp in the hallway to illuminate a triangle of the decking outside. The driver threw a cigarette over his shoulder and held up a takeaway in a white plastic bag.

'Chinese, mate?' he said, angling his head upwards to release a cloud of smoke. Benjamin tried not to breathe any in.

'Can you put it on the doormat for me please?' Benjamin said.

The man nodded, staring at Gary.

'That's a premium dog,' he said, leaning forward to put the bag down, 'like a miniature racehorse.'

The smell of cigarettes drifted inside the open door as he patted Gary's head.

'Probably wants a chicken ball, doesn't he?' he said, laughing. He held out his hand and let Gary lick his fingers.

'How much is the food please?' Benjamin said, trying to push Gary back with the side of his leg. But the man didn't hear the question. His eyes were still moving over the dog. Squinting. Working something out. Benjamin wondered if he always let animals lick his hands while he was delivering consumables and wished he would stop breathing so heavily, blowing smoke into the open door. The man squeezed his hand into the pocket of his jeans and took out a scrap of paper.

'It's eighteen-forty all in,' he said. 'Not including any kind of gratuity.'

Benjamin took out a twenty. He handed it to the man who put it in his pocket without offering change.

'Very distinctive markings he's got. They call it brindle, don't they?'

'I'm not sure what it's called,' Benjamin said. 'He's here temporarily.'

The man looked between Benjamin and the dog.

'Yeah. They call it brindle,' he said.

On the track behind him, the car was still running.

'Your car's still running,' Benjamin said.

The man straightened up.

'It won't always start, so I keep it turning over for drop offs,' he said. 'I usually do all my own maintenance, but I've been really putting in the overtime on deliveries.' He rubbed his thumb and first two fingers together to suggest he was well paid. 'I've fallen behind on some aspects of its upkeep,' he said.

Benjamin nodded.

'Thanks then,' he said, closing the door.

Benjamin peered through the curtains. He watched the man walk down the steps, briefly look around in the grass for the cigarette he'd thrown, then reach into his pocket to get another. He saw him get back in the car and take a box of matches from the glovebox. As he lit a cigarette, cupping it with his hand to shield it from the breeze, he stared at the front door of the caravan and Benjamin watched him. Then the man flicked the match from the open window and drove away, the car's taillights fading as he weaved his way back out.

Benjamin locked the door and dropped a couple of vegetable

spring rolls into an aluminium tray. He scraped in some rice, then put it on the kitchen floor in front of Gary. The dog leant over and picked up a spring roll. He bit it a few times then dropped it on the vinyl.

'It's probably hot,' Benjamin said, picking up the tray. He blew on the food to cool it down. 'You'll like it now it's the proper temperature,' he said. Gary had another go, swallowing it down without chewing. He walked over to the one on the floor and ate that too. Benjamin could see a flake of deep-fried pastry that was stuck in his whiskers.

'You do probably need the calories,' Benjamin said.

When they finished eating, Benjamin got his sleeping bag from the cupboard and pulled at the front of the sofa to turn it into a bed. Gary watched the transformation closely, backing away as it clunked into position, waiting to see if anything else was going to happen. When it didn't, he jumped back up and curled, croissant-like. Benjamin sat and watched as Gary closed his eyes, until the dog fell into a steady sleep, his side rising and falling with breath. In the quiet, he leant in to examine a scar that was drawn in pale pink tissue across Gary's chest and neck and wondered where it was from. It struck him as strange that things like that—what the dog had seen and heard and felt—were trapped inside or lost forever.

Benjamin drifted off sitting upright in his clothes, cocooned in the sleeping bag, waking only once to the liquid sound of Gary drinking water from the salad bowl.

Four

Outside in the darkness, a man moved across the wet sand, scanning the beach with a torch. He walked quickly, shoulders slumped forward, a plastic bag in his hand.

'Dog,' he said with an accent, his voice falling into the quiet static of rolling waves. He shook the bag, reached in and produced a dried sprat.

'I have fish,' he said, holding out the shrivelled fish body. He squeezed his free hand until the knuckles cracked.

'Fish for dog,' he said.

Five

Benjamin woke up and Gary's head was resting on the meat of his leg. It was almost lunchtime.

'Hi,' he said, lifting the sleeping bag so that the dog's chin slid off and onto the cushions. Gary opened an eye and yawned. His tongue was covered in dry saliva like a spider's web.

'Sorry,' Benjamin said, 'you were touching me.'

Benjamin transformed the bed back into a sofa and pulled the curtains, filling the caravan with a perfect light that warmed the surfaces and the bare skin on his arms. Gary stretched out and laid his face in a yellow slice of it, while Benjamin opened the door for airflow. He didn't know how long pathogens lingered and the delivery driver had been really craning his neck in.

The dog jogged down to the grass and urinated. On his way back up, Gary paused above an ant that was wandering across the decking. He watched it meandering between his front paws for a second or two, then pressed his tongue down on top of it. When more emerged from the cracks, he walked around, hoovering them up, making Benjamin feel bleak.

'I think that's murder,' he said from the doorway. 'Those ants are dying when you do that.'

The terminal aspect upset Benjamin. He didn't know how to explain it, but the powerlessness, the finality of what was unfolding, was overwhelming. Something was happening that couldn't be undone.

'If you stop eating insects,' he said. 'I'll make you some food.'

Gary lifted his head. The bright sun highlighted the hairs around his eyes and made them appear translucent. He licked up another ant and followed Benjamin inside.

Gary lifted his front paws onto the worktop and reached for the takeaway tray, so Benjamin grabbed it and held it aloft. 'We can't eat that,' he said, 'cooked rice grows Bacillus cereus at room temperature. It could give us food poisoning.'

Benjamin didn't know if dogs got food poisoning, but he remembered the day a Staffordshire Bull Terrier sicked up an entire robin on the doormat at the supermarket. Camille had been in a relationship with its owner at the time, a man who remortgaged his house to buy photos of feet. She said she always went for men that needed repair. When they broke up, Camille and Benjamin drank tins of sugar-free Lilt and shared a split bag of edamame beans by the delivery shutters. They sat on the wall, legs dangling, watching manky pigeons squabble over crisps.

Benjamin opened the fridge. The light inside flickered, intermittently illuminating the empty glass shelves. He picked up a pint of milk and held it up to read the date.

'This has yesterday's date on it,' he said, unscrewing the top and pouring it down the sink. 'I'm going to make porridge, but we'll have to do it with water which could be disgusting.'

While Benjamin stirred the oats, Gary stood near him, curving his velvet body around Benjamin's legs. Benjamin dropped the spoon and it clattered across the floor, flicking porridge onto the cupboard doors. Gary jumped like the caravan was falling down.

'It's okay, he said, leaning to wipe the door with a cloth.

Gary padded closer. He dragged his tongue across the lino where the porridge had been. When Benjamin told him to stop, he licked the cupboard instead.

Benjamin wrote *cupboard door* and *floor* on his list. Then he picked up the spoon to stop Gary indiscriminately licking the surfaces. He moved towards the back door, cold vinyl sticking to his bare feet, peeling away like plasters. Gary followed him out.

'When you eat outside it's called *al fresco*,' Benjamin said, putting one of the bowls on the decking.

As Gary ate, lumps of porridge clung to his whiskers. Once the bowl was empty, he licked his chops to find them. A cool breeze channelled through the caravans and made the dog cower. The wind died down and the bright sun warmed Benjamin's shoulders. He squeezed his eyes tight shut and saw orange through the thin skin of his eyelids.

'You can have mine too,' he said, putting his bowl down on the decking.

It felt nice to feed Gary. There was something vulnerable about him: in need of protection. It made Benjamin want to keep filling the bowl with food for as long as he would eat. He felt like he understood some of Camille's desire to care for damaged romantic partners.

When the dog was finished, he trotted over to a break in the hedge, to the path with the broken fence that led back down to the beach.

'Where are you going?' Benjamin said.

The dog walked a few more steps then stopped. He didn't turn back, but looked along the path, towards the sea.

'Let me lock the caravan,' Benjamin said.

Benjamin made sure the hobs were off so the caravan wouldn't fill with gas, then he followed Gary through the dunes to the beach. The dog jogged along in wobbly lines, pushed sideways by the wind as he went.

'Be careful of the shells,' Benjamin said, kicking one away. 'They're razor clams. They could cut you.'

In the distance, Benjamin could see the dark outline of the whale again, slumped on the sand. It looked like it was sinking, the boundaries between body and earth blurring. He stopped to take it in, struggling to get his head around the scale. How a brain could be forty or fifty feet away from the borders of its body, how nerves and tendons could stretch so far through flesh and bone. It was strange to him how something so large could just stop being, how something so complex could disappear forever.

'I don't want to see him today,' he said, turning his head away from the creature, like not looking could change the reality of it. 'Not up close.'

As they walked along the beach, moisture from the sand worked its way into the toes of Benjamin's trainers. His feet were cold, but it was nice to walk with Gary. Something about it felt vital, like the dog needed the breeze on his skin and the sun and the salt spray. Like he was being charged up by the noises all falling into his folded-over ears. Benjamin reached down and picked up a stone. It was smooth and grey and had a flash of white across it that looked like a cloud. He moved his fingers along one side and could feel the salt residue clinging to it. He slipped it into his pocket, then watched the turbines swinging lazily around on the horizon. Gary did a shit on the sand.

'I'm not picking that up,' Benjamin said. 'I don't mind temporarily making sure you don't die, but I'm not picking up your faeces.'

He stood staring at what Gary had done, surrounded by seagulls that were hovering a few feet above the ground. They were negotiating the invisible currents beneath their wings, lifted up and down by gusts of air coming in from the sea.

'I'm not your owner,' Benjamin said, trying to walk away, terrorised by the image of a child getting it on their hands and in their eyes while they made sandcastles or played football. He couldn't have that on his conscience. The sounds of the rolling waves began to feel very far away.

Benjamin looked across the sand to the long concrete path that ran along the front unbroken. He couldn't see a single person. He took a deep breath, then he used a sandwich packet from his pocket to dig out a shallow hole.

Gary's shit looked like a frankfurter. Benjamin scooped it up and dropped it into the hole. Then he kicked sand back over it.

'I can't believe you made me do that,' he said, walking to the water to drop the cardboard into the swell. It was drawn out with a wave, then slid back onto the sand.

'Let's go,' he said.

The beach turned into rocks and the rocks turned into cliff face. Benjamin and the dog followed a path that cut inland and led to a rugby field where he sat down on a multi-coloured climbing frame made to look like a helicopter. Gary walked along a hedge pushing his face into the leaves.

'Other dogs have probably pissed in that bush,' Benjamin said. 'The one you're putting your face on.' He pointed at the field. 'Why don't you go for a run?'

The dog walked over to the helicopter and stood in front of Benjamin. Even when he was still, the fibres in his thick back legs were flexing and twitching. The wind picked up and he cowered. He sipped at a puddle on the tarmac, then went back to the hedge and pushed his face into it some more.

'Come on,' Benjamin said, standing up. 'Like this.'

Benjamin jogged around. He made short bursts across the grass, encouraging the dog, but Gary barely had to run to keep up. He trotted in loose circles, wagging his tail until Benjamin stopped. The field was silent, except for the noise of Gary's breathing, heavier now as he filled his lungs, pulling his skin taut across his ribcage.

Benjamin watched the black tips of the trees swaying together, as if something large was working its way through the forest beneath. He remembered coming to the park with his nan when he'd first moved into the caravan. It was summer. They were sitting in the helicopter, looking out across the field in front.

'Do you want to talk about anything?' she said.

When Benjamin didn't reply she leant into his shoulder.

'I feel like Arnold SwarzenVinegar in here,' she said.

She gave him a sideways look.

'He's always in helicopters, isn't he? With his lumpy arms.'

Benjamin laughed.

'Get to ze chopper,' she said.

Benjamin didn't know what she said that for.

'Haven't you seen that film? It's fantastic. It's about an alien that hunts humans for sport. And also sort of a commentary on Toxic Masculinity.'

As a concept, that sounded quite violent, but also politically complicated.

'What age certificate is it?' Benjamin said.

She flicked her eyebrows up as if the *older* the certificate, the more *appealing* the film was.

'It's an eighteen,' she said.

'I probably shouldn't watch it.' Benjamin said.

She laughed.

'Oh, I don't know. That's just for guidance,' she said. 'You're very emotionally intelligent.'

When they got home, she put the tape in the VHS machine. When Arnold found three skinned dead men in a helicopter, Benjamin opened his eyes very wide.

'Maybe it is an eighteen for a reason,' she said, pausing it so the image jerked around on screen as though the men were also being electrocuted.

'Can we put something else on?' Benjamin said.

'Course, love.'

Benjamin didn't remember the gruesome bit in the film

now. What he remembered was the feeling of being included, of being seen by her. Welcome in the world she inhabited.

'Let's head back,' he said to the dog.

Gary followed Benjamin home along a track, avoiding a sequence of puddles until they came to one that stretched all the way across. There were tall weeds growing up on either side, so Benjamin edged his way around, muddying his shoes, lunging unnaturally to clear the water. When the dog approached, it stared at its own reflection wobbled by raindrops. Benjamin waited for it to jump. Instead, the dog fidgeted, looking at him like he might do something to make the puddle go away. The drizzle flattened Benjamin's hair and drops of water began to accumulate in blobs on the shoulders of his anorak.

'It's just water,' Benjamin said, gesturing at the narrow strip of sodden grass he'd used to skirt the puddle, 'Just walk around the side.'

The dog paced up and down and made an unusual noise, somewhere between a bark and a whine. When Benjamin lifted his collar up and started to walk again, the dog paced more urgently. He crouched several times like he was going to jump but didn't. Benjamin stopped at the end of the path.

'Come on,' he said. 'I can't carry you over it.'

The dog jumped. When he landed, he ran full pelt towards Benjamin, overshooting by a few meters before turning and running back. His tail was flicking from side to side and his mouth was open, tongue lolling about, more excited than Benjamin had seen him.

Benjamin smiled. He took in Gary's skinny body, cold in the drizzle, and wondered if the dog always avoided puddles. He thought maybe he did, but that it was okay, because he knew what it felt like to want to avoid things. Things like door handles and light switches, over-groped shopping trolleys and raw meat.

Six

At the caravan, Benjamin's neighbour stood inside his porch, aiming a hosepipe at a car on the driveway in a grubby white suit shirt and no trousers. He fish-eyed Benjamin and the dog as an arc of water ineffectually slapped the metal roof.

'There was some weirdo wandering around here earlier,' he said, adjusting the flow and diverting the stream to a hedge beside his steps. 'I think he'd been peeking in your windows while you were out. Your property was totally exposed. Lucky your nan wasn't in there with her bananas out.'

Benjamin stopped in the doorway.

'He sounded foreign, so I phoned the non-emergency number for the police,' the man said. 'The nutter had a carrier bag in one hand and was waving a fish about in the other.' He stopped to consider that. 'Don't know if it was a cultural thing or what,' he said.

Benjamin stared at the ground. 'Thanks,' he said.

The man turned off the hosepipe. As he went to go inside, he chirped up again. 'I hope you're picking up after that thing,' he said, 'probably does massive shits.'

Benjamin leant to undo his shoe laces and the dog took a step towards him. There were sand particles in the sleep channels beside his eyes and his legs were all covered in dirt. He smelt like mud and rain. When Benjamin stood up, he could clearly see the man watching through his front room window, clutching at the curtain to obscure half his face. He opened his own front door and the dog pushed its head into the gap, brushing his jeans.

'You're going to have to have a wash,' Benjamin said, pulling the Marigolds back on.

In the bathroom, Gary mistook a piece of potpourri for something edible. He ate it with frantic, exaggerated chews before letting it fall from his mouth and onto the floor.

'That's just for the smell really,' Benjamin said, throwing a handful of the petals into the bin and tipping in a few fresh bits from a bag under the sink. 'I'll get you more food when you're clean.'

Benjamin put his hands on either side of the dog's waist and walked him over to the bath. It was difficult because he kept curving off to the side, leaning away from the sound of the dripping tap. When they got close enough, Benjamin stood waiting, hoping Gary knew to jump in. He didn't, so Benjamin gestured.

'Please?' he said.

When Gary still didn't move, Benjamin leant over and put his arms around the dog's chest and back. He picked his front end up and put his paws on the side of the bathtub, smearing mud across the white plastic. Gary's front end was heavier than it looked. Benjamin assumed this was because his muscles were dense. He put him down again.

'You're very dense,' he said.

The dog waited while Benjamin worked out how to get him into the bathtub. He thought about using the ironing board as a ramp. About using bin bags as a body shield to pick Gary up and hoist him in.

Then he remembered the spoon. He daubed it in the pan, collecting lumps of porridge, then wiped it on the inside of the bath. When he laid the spoon by the plughole, Gary jumped straight in. Benjamin let him eat before he aimed the shower at the wall and turned it on. He ran it over his hand to make sure the water wouldn't burn Gary's skin, then did a demonstration, holding the shower head up so Gary could see how non-threatening the stream was as it sprayed into the white of the tub. The dog started shaking.

'It's honestly not that bad,' Benjamin said. 'It's nice to be clean.'

The dog rested its head on the side of the tub as Benjamin worked pink shampoo into its fur. The warm water felt strange through the latex gloves as Benjamin rubbed Gary's thick back legs and scratched the mud from his slim shins. Benjamin stretched out his arms so he could keep his torso away from the dirt, worrying that the shampoo might sting, blocking the suds from sliding down the dome of the dog's head and into his eyes.

Gary dripped, then he shook. He shook so hard his front paws slipped out from under him and he lumped into the side of the bath.

'Shit,' Benjamin said. 'Are you okay?'

Gary shook again, peppering Benjamin with warm droplets of water, but seemed fine, which led Benjamin to assume he had a very thick skull. Gary looked out over the edge of the bath but didn't move his feet. He looked down at them like he didn't trust them any more. Benjamin put a towel on Gary's back and dabbed him, thinking about the bathwater finding its way back into the sea.

'You know,' Camille had said, as they put the papers out one Sunday a few months ago: 'everything on Earth is united by a delicate framework of emotional and physical connectedness. Like the water in the oceans and rivers,' she said.

He imagined it. The bathwater moving over Gary to clean him—over his own arms—being sucked out through the pipes and drifting thousands of miles away, carrying particles and parts of them away to places they would never go. He thought about the sixty per cent of him that was water and wondered where that would end up when he was dead and whether somewhere far away it would be swirled up by a fish or dragged along in the flow until it met the sixty-per cent liquid portion of other people he had known. Like Eamonn Holmes from telly, or his nan. The thought was complicated. Sad on the surface, with a strange and hopeful layer somewhere deep beneath, until he realised that probably, statistically, it was unlikely. That Eamonn Holmes and his nan would be very distant for the rest of eternity. It made him feel far away from her, then and now. Less so from Eamonn Holmes.

'Can you get out safely?' he said.

Gary fidgeted. It took him a while to build up his confidence but before long he'd leapt from the tub and landed on the mat. While Benjamin rinsed sand down the plughole, the dog shook violently behind him, firing what water was left in his coat all over the bathroom. Some dribbled down the mirror. Once Benjamin had wiped it, he turned around to find the dog standing in front of him with a decorative lady in a satin dress in his mouth. She was hanging limply between his teeth, already slightly damp. He mouthed her gently, tail banging the storage heater as it flicked.

'Why have you done that?' Benjamin said.

Benjamin's nan used the satin lady to cover the toilet roll. He noticed one of her skinny material arms was already laying severed on the floor.

'You've mutilated her!' he said.

Gary dropped her on the carpet.

'You shouldn't have done this,' Benjamin said, picking her up between thumb and forefinger.

While his nan was away, Benjamin had been doing his best to uphold her domestic traditions. He'd spent weekend mornings putting toilet rolls under the frilly lady. He'd draped the rugs on the handrail out front and hit them with a wooden tennis racket, combed their tassels outwards once he'd laid them back on the floor. He'd refreshed the potpourri whenever the smell had faded, used foaming spray polish on the coffee table, and washed the whites with vinegar to keep them bright. All of it so that sometimes, for a split second, he could forget it wasn't her doing it. So that somewhere out of focus, it was as if she'd just nipped out for the morning, and she wouldn't be gone too long.

Benjamin dropped the lady on the floor.

'You might as well have her now,' he said. 'She's damaged.'

He wasn't angry. Even though he knew it would be difficult to find a replacement, he understood that being annoyed was pointless. That dogs didn't see things like that. It took them time to learn. It wasn't fair to project human expectations.

Gary fell on his side with the lady in his mouth, rolling around with his paws in the air. His front legs looked short and stumpy like the arms of a velociraptor. He rubbed his shoulder blades on the carpet, tongue hanging from his mouth. Benjamin watched him jump onto the sofa. The dog wriggled his head in between the cushions and closed his eyes. Although Gary's face looked sad, inside, Benjamin thought he might be quite happy. Benjamin sat down and put his still-gloved hand on the dog. He couldn't feel the fur, so he took it off. With his bare skin on Gary's back, he could feel how soft and shiny his coat was.

When Benjamin scratched above Gary's back leg, the dog stood up. He stamped his feet while Benjamin stroked him and laid down when he stopped. Small hairs fell from his coat and landed on the cushions. Benjamin moved his hand away and looked at it for a long time, then he walked over to the sink and washed his hands until he felt the untwisting inside that told him he could stop.

Seven

The man tied the bag of dried fish and dropped it into the glovebox. He dialled a number on his phone, then rested it on the dash where it buzzed on the plastic. While it rang, he ate pistachio nuts, levering them open with his nail.

'Have you found it yet?' the person on the line said.

There was barking in the background.

'Not yet.'

'Why the fuck not?'

The man adjusted himself in the car seat.

'There was a man,' he said. A man . . . with hose.'

A brief silence on the line. When the voice returned, it spat the words out, pausing between them.

'I—want—that—dog—back—Vasile. Do you understand?'

The man nodded, even though he was alone. 'Yes,' he said, putting a pistachio in his mouth. The line went dead. Vasile climbed back out of the car.

Eight

Gary woke up grumbling at the sound of someone banging on the door.

'I don't know who that is,' Benjamin whispered. 'We should sit in the bathroom until they go away,' he said.

He darted across and Gary followed, walking around, tapping the lino with his nails. Benjamin sat on the toilet seat. The doorbell rang repeatedly.

'Maybe I should answer it,' Benjamin said, peering back out. After a few more rings, wriggling digits pushed the letter box open.

'It's about the dog,' a voice shouted through.

Gary's ears were standing up on the top of his head.

'I know he's not yours.'

Benjamin walked heel to toe across the carpet without breathing. He watched as the fingers retreated, then stood perfectly still, listening. He heard the wind, the cable whipping the flagpole, the hum of the fridge from the kitchen. His hands were shaking. He moved closer to the window and hovered behind the curtains, gripping each side, then eased them apart to reveal the pale white face of the Chinese delivery man peering straight back at him through the glass.

'Let me in you twat,' the man said, waving at the door. 'It's Baltic out here you little sadist.'

The man stood just inside the doorway, rubbing his arms

and shoulders to warm up. He was wearing a green army jacket and a pair of blue jeans with white paint on the thighs. Gary came trotting over and dropped the one-armed toilet roll lady on the carpet at his feet. The man patted him on the head.

'I know he's not your dog,' he said again, pointing at Gary.

'I never said he was,' Benjamin said.

The man's face was tanned and well-worn. The wrinkles around his eyes were deep and heavy, but he could have been anywhere from thirty to fifty, it was hard to tell. He was skinny, too. Benjamin assumed he didn't eat enough calories to maintain a healthy BMI, or drink enough water to keep his body lubricated. He imagined his dehydrated brain and smoker's lungs.

'I'm returning him on Monday,' Benjamin said, opening a window.

The man ignored him. There was a breeze piling in.

'Are you mental?' he said, walking over and closing it. Benjamin eyed the rubber seal that was preventing fresh air from circulating. When he pulled his t-shirt up over his nose and mouth, the man gave him a puzzled look.

'It's for airflow,' Benjamin said, tilting his head at the window. 'For airborne pathogens.'

The man's forehead wrinkled. As he walked further into the caravan Benjamin tried to stand in his way but moved when the man didn't stop. He picked up a porcelain clown from the dresser, stared at it, then put it down on the coffee table with less care than Benjamin would have liked.

'Can you stop picking things up, please?' Benjamin said.

The man looked around the caravan. At the faded walls and carpets and the fold-out sofa. While he was distracted, Benjamin reopened the window to allow the air to circulate. He found the breeze reassuring and lowered the t-shirt to below his nose.

'Who do you live here with then? A Victorian family?' the man said flatly.

Gary sniffed the clown on the coffee table, touching it with his wet nose, and Benjamin added it to the list. *Smiling clown*, he wrote.

'What did you just write down?' the man said.

'I'm keeping track of the things he's touched,' Benjamin said.

The driver raised an eyebrow. 'Very organised.' He held his hand up over his nose. 'It smells a bit like an old people's home in here,' he said.

Benjamin didn't like that.

'It's my nan's caravan,' he said.

The man walked over to the mantel without taking his shoes off. Benjamin watched them pressing down into the pile and tried not to imagine the things he was cramming into the fibres with his soles. The driver picked up a picture and Benjamin took several deep breaths.

'You all right?' the man said.

'Yeah. I just—can you stop touching things?'

The man raised his eyebrow again like he was confused. Benjamin put a hand flat on his chest and tried to regulate his breathing.

'Do you have a condition?' the man said.

'I'm feeling tachycardic.'

The man turned to look at him, holding the picture. 'What does that mean?'

'It means my heart is beating fast.'

'Why didn't you say that, then?'

'I just did.'

'No. Why didn't you say, 'my heart is beating fast?''

Benjamin knew why. Medical terms were more accurate. He had a book on the shelf that listed them alphabetically. He liked the distance they put between a sensation or condition and its meaning. Like he preferred *dyspnoeic* to *she can't draw enough oxygen into her lungs*. It was easier to say *asystole* than the last beat of a human heart. Somehow better to say *palliative* than *end-of-life*.

'So your nan,' the man said. 'Where's she now?'

Benjamin looked around.

'Hospital,' he said.

The man leant in very close to the image in his hand. He nodded to show he'd heard. 'This her?'

'Yeah,' Benjamin said.

In the photograph, Benjamin's nan was standing on the sand in a swimsuit, matted brown hair lifting in the breeze, salt spray forever suspended in the air behind her.

'She was pretty nice,' the man said, offhand.

Benjamin reached out and took the photo. He put it back on the shelf, wishing the man hadn't sexualised his grandmother. He felt annoyed that he'd talked about her in the past tense.

'She was in the Commonwealth Games,' Benjamin said.

'You didn't get any of those genes then,' the man said. Not cruelly. Just as a statement of fact. 'You look like you could do with a bit of bodybuilding really.'

Benjamin shook his head.

'I'm not sure it would help,' he said. 'I'm a xenomorph. I have naturally long limbs.'

Benjamin looked the man over. They actually had very similar builds, but he chose not to say that. The man walked over to the window and looked out at the dark void of the ocean. He watched it sloshing up onto land, running along the beach like spilt ink. They didn't speak for a few seconds.

'Why are you here?' Benjamin said, his voice wobbling with stress.

'Because of the dog,' the man said. He slumped down on the sofa, putting his feet on the coffee table. 'Sorry if I didn't make that clear. I've had a few Kronenbourgs from the year 1664.'

He blew out, rubbing his paunch, then stretched out a hand

for Benjamin to shake. 'My name's Leonard,' he said. 'But don't call me Len.'

Benjamin looked at his grubby digits. At the callouses on his palm and the faded tattoos on his forearm. There was a yellow patch on the side of his right index from smoking. Benjamin didn't shake. He half-performed a wave before aborting it.

'I'm Benjamin,' he said.

Leonard took a comb out of his top pocket and pushed his hair to one side, scraping it into greasy channels. When he was finished, he put his hands in the air.

'Look,' he said. 'I can tell you don't want me in here. But what I've got to say, I think you should listen to.' Leonard raised both his eyebrows. 'Give me five minutes of your time. That's all I'm asking.'

Gary was back on the sofa now, wriggling his head in, closing his eyes to sleep. Benjamin didn't speak while his brain carried out its anxious calculations. Leonard pointed at Gary.

'All I'm saying is that it pertains to the safety of that animal.'

The dog adjusted itself, letting out a steady breath.

'All right,' Benjamin said.

Leonard clapped his hands together slightly louder than he needed to. The dog slid down off the sofa and padded over to Benjamin.

'Don't suppose you've got any snacks?' Leonard said. 'Before we get into all that.'

'Snacks?' Benjamin said.

'Yeah, you know. Crisps or whatever.'

'I don't think I have much in,' Benjamin said, walking to the cabinet with Gary by his side, the dog occasionally touching his trouser leg.

'Does he always do that?' Leonard shouted over.

'What?'

'Walk so close? Like he's superglued to your shin bone.'

'He seems to,' Benjamin said.

Leonard slid a packet of Benson's from his top pocket, tapped it on the table and took out a cigarette with his mouth. He let it hang limply there and lit it. 'He's quite weird, isn't he,' he said.

Benjamin shrugged. 'Please don't smoke,' he said, putting a tin of *all butter* shortbread down on the coffee table. He hadn't eaten the biscuits inside because of the saturated fat. 'I think he's just nervous,' Benjamin said, struggling to take his eyes off the glowing tip of the cigarette. Leonard raised his hands again and leant away from Benjamin.

'Not saying there's anything wrong with him. We're all a bit weird, aren't we?'

Smoke drifted up in plumes from Leonard's cigarette. He tapped the ash into the lid of the shortbread and Benjamin wondered where the particles were going as the smoke dispersed.

'Please stop smoking,' he said.

Leonard still didn't seem to hear him. 'Where'd you steal him from then?' he said.

'I didn't steal him,' Benjamin said. 'He followed me.' Gary squeezed his head into the gap between Benjamin's legs. 'I found him on the beach. Licking that dead whale.'

Gary walked over to Leonard and smelt his jeans.

'I know the one,' Leonard said, moving away like the dog was toxic, 'What a sicko.' He laughed, then leant over and ruffled the fur on Gary's back. 'Don't come near me you whale licker,' he said.

Leonard spent a few seconds picking a speck of ash from his tongue, then his face turned serious. 'You know who he is though, don't you? That dog?'

Benjamin shook his head as Leonard pulled a newspaper from his jacket. He slid it across the coffee table.

It was a copy of the *Anglia Racing Post*. There was a photograph of Gary on the front, tongue hanging out, the veins in his shoulders all full of blood and standing out from his muscles.

Dog that never loses is LOST was the headline.

Nine

Benjamin watched as Gary jumped back on the sofa. The dog looked at him—slow, intelligent blinks—then rolled over so his legs flopped about in the air.

'I wasn't going to keep him,' Benjamin said.

Leonard took a long drag on his cigarette.

'What's the plan then?'

Benjamin avoided eye contact with Gary. He shrugged, looked at his shoes.

'I don't know,' he said. 'The dog warden is on duty on Monday.'

'The old warden!' Leonard said, rubbing the top of the dog's head, nodding. 'The canine Gestapo. They'll get him back to the track, I'm sure.' He scratched the stubble on his chin. 'I suppose we just need to hope that slender Gaz over there can keep his speed up for another couple of years. Get a decent run, if you know what I mean.'

'A decent run?' Benjamin said.

'You know how it is mate. They're only really good for one thing, aren't they.' He pointed at the dog. 'Once they run out of juice . . . ' Leonard drew his thumb across his own neck. 'They tend to give them the old—'

Leonard acted out a very dramatic execution, including a simulation of spurting blood, and Benjamin felt as though there wasn't enough air inside him. Like his breaths were being cut short.

'Don't they just get rehomed?' he said.

'Yeah, yeah, rehomed,' Leonard said, holding his fingers up in inverted commas. 'Dead in a wheelbarrow, more like.'

Leonard raised his eyebrows and scanned the room while Benjamin watched Gary licking his paws. He remembered the way the dog had hung his head while he scrubbed suds into his scalp in the bath.

'I can just phone the dog track now for you if it helps?' Leonard said. 'I'm sure they'll know who the owner is.'

Benjamin looked at Gary very closely. At the short grey hairs in his lashes and the downy bits behind his ears, at his perfect left eye and the pink bump below his right that contributed to him looking sad—on the outside—a lot of the time.

'Wait a minute,' Benjamin said. 'How much do you think is left in his legs?'

Leonard laboured an inward breath, like a dodgy mechanic appraising a job. He shook his head.

'He's run a few seasons from what I can remember. But he'll probably be okay.' He tried to sound more optimistic. 'He'll be fine,' he said.

Benjamin felt peculiar. It was as though his limbs were swollen and his body was expanding like a balloon, his particles drifting out and away from his centre of mass. He looked at Gary and wondered if he had any concept of what they were talking about. He imagined his limp body being moved about in a wheelbarrow, bouncing over clumps of mud in a field somewhere. Then, before he could stop it, he imagined his nan's hand closing on the tablecloth as she slipped from her chair. Peas rolling from her plate to a gap just below the fridge. Leonard sounded distant as he spoke, like his voice was coming from another room.

'I can help you,' he said. 'If you're worried.'

Benjamin's eyes met Leonard's.

'I've got some contacts. Some ideas,' he said.

Benjamin opened his mouth to speak. He didn't know what to say.

'Does anyone know he's here?' Leonard said, cutting him off. He walked to the window that faced the track outside and used his index and middle finger to move the blind. He scanned around, then turned to Benjamin.

'I walked him earlier,' Benjamin said.

'Did anyone see you?'

Benjamin stood silent. His breathing felt abnormal again, like something was pressing in on his chest. 'He saw us,' he said. 'When I walked him.'

'Who?'

Benjamin pointed in the direction of the caravan opposite and tried to recall exactly what the neighbour had told him. Leonard raised one of his eyebrows and shook his head.

'He said someone strange was here,' Benjamin said. 'With a plastic bag and an accent.'

Leonard was getting worked up. He moved towards Benjamin and stared at him, his bright blue eyes like the lit flame of a boiler.

'Someone strange?' Leonard said.

Benjamin nodded. His hands felt like they were tingling, so he shook them in the air. 'He needed to stretch his legs,' he said.

Leonard looked shocked. He shook his head. 'These could well be very serious people, Benjamin. That dog is a very valuable asset.'

Benjamin felt a sinking feeling in his gut as he struggled to remember the details. He felt like he couldn't hold on to information, like it was slipping away from him. Everything was happening very quickly.

'I don't think we should stay here,' Leonard said. 'We should go somewhere else to talk. If you're serious about helping him.'

'Where would we go?' Benjamin said.

Leonard nodded like it was all very simple and Benjamin was making the right decision. 'We should head to the snooker club,' he said. 'Just while we work out what to do.'

Benjamin tried to think. He imagined the dog warden picking Gary up and taking him away. Imagined Gary walking down the steps and climbing into the boot of a van, his simple brain processing nothing more than the absolute present. Wind on his side. The smell of diesel, the sound of the engine running. Gentle thoughts, each one following the last. Happy or sad or warm or cold. He imagined the warden giving Gary back to his owners. Imagined them letting him run until he slowed and then one day, in a field somewhere, or a lay-by, or behind the outbuilding of a farm, switching him off. Putting out the spark that made him alive.

Benjamin felt a vagueness in his body again, like there wasn't much holding it together. He looked outside. At the overcast sky, clouds full of rain and threatening to burst, then at Leonard smoking and touching things in the caravan.

'Okay,' he said. 'Let's go.'

Benjamin opened the door and Gary padded outside onto the decking. Leonard took a long drag on his cigarette, filling his lungs, then exhaled and walked out. Benjamin thought about cancer.

'Does he need a lead?' Leonard said, gesturing at the dog.

Benjamin remembered the red one inside, lying on the kitchen counter.

'I don't think so,' he said.

Leonard shrugged. As he walked to the car, Benjamin looked at the collar—at the golden name tag that said '*The Mighty Gary*' on it. He undid it and slipped it into his jacket pocket as Leonard unlocked the passenger door, climbing over several empty tins of Kronenbourg and across to the driver's seat.

'Lock's fucked,' he said, frustrated by the effort.

Gary urinated on the corner of the caravan and some of it went on his legs.

'He's pissing on his own legs,' Leonard said, waving with his cigarette hand, hard enough that lit embers spun downwards, landing in the footwell and on the plastic bits around the gearstick. Leonard blew on them. Then he leant over to open the glove box and produced a t-shirt, dragging several screwed-up lottery tickets with it.

'Give his legs a wipe with this then,' he said, 'so he doesn't get it on my seats.'

Benjamin stood. He looked at the shirt, then the dog, then the shirt. At the dirty seats already covered in cigarette burns and water marks.

'Why are you eyeing my general-purpose cleaning rag like that?' Leonard said. 'Like it's going to give you Ebola.'

'It doesn't look very clean,' Benjamin said.

'It's not. That's the point of a general-purpose cleaning rag.' Leonard threw the T-shirt at Benjamin and it hit him in the chest. Benjamin recoiled like it was an actual bullet. 'Give him a wipe,' Leonard said.

In the caravan across the way, Benjamin's neighbour was watching from his window, peering over the top of a newspaper. Leonard opened his eyes wide like it proved something—to suggest they hurry up—so Benjamin crouched, hand hovering near Gary's wet front leg.

'Mate,' Leonard said from inside the car, looking back at Benjamin's neighbour, 'we shouldn't hang around here.'

Benjamin dabbed at Gary's shins, wiping the droplets of urine into the t-shirt and Gary stared in a distant, peaceful way. He licked the air and yawned.

'Just chuck the rag down there,' Leonard said, pointing at Benjamin's decking. 'We'll let the rain wash it and collect it later.'

Benjamin did what he was told. He knew the longer he held the rag, the more likely it was that the liquid would seep through the material and onto his hands. He thought Leonard would get funny about going back inside to wash them, so he squirted a little blob of sanitiser from a bottle in his pocket onto his palm and rubbed it around, interlocking his fingers.

'Encourage pencil legs to jump in there,' Leonard said, using his thumb to point at the back seats, 'You may have to recalibrate the'—he waved his hand around in the air—'stuff in the back.'

Benjamin looked in. The back seats were almost completely obscured by boxes covered in Japanese writing.

'Expensive produce, that is,' Leonard said absently. 'Vintage *sake*. Been sitting on it for a while, waiting for the prices to go up.'

Benjamin moved the boxes to one side and used an open arm to show Gary where to jump.

'Up,' he said.

Benjamin's neighbour was still at the window. He had a telephone pressed to the side of his pale, fleshy head. Leonard unbuckled his belt and climbed across the passenger seat, with his cigarette in his mouth. He used both hands to shove Gary's bum towards the car, pushing until Gary's front feet were up on the seats. The dog continued to resist.

'He's not very well trained, is he?' Leonard said, holding the cigarette away and tapping the ash so it fell into the grass before putting it back in his mouth. He picked up Gary's back end.

'Still got his balls I see,' he said, as he shimmied him in.

Benjamin looked at Gary's testicles. 'Why wouldn't he?'

'Good for him, that's all,' Leonard said. 'Good for him.'

Leonard lifted the last bit of Gary's rear end into the car and Benjamin looked back at the caravan. For a few seconds, he stood wishing his nan was there to tell him what to do. He remembered a time when he was little, when he hadn't been living with her long, that she'd marked active volcanos on a map (because it was keeping him awake), with distances from B (Benjamin), so he wouldn't worry.

'It's all so far away from us Benjamin,' she said holding up the map. 'Thousands and thousands of miles.'

He longed for the way she could alter the weight of things

like that, make the world less toxic, just by being in the same room as him. Occasionally just by existing.

'You've got to be assertive,' Leonard said, pushing the car door closed. 'This dog is calculating the power dynamic. I think he probably knows I'm hot shit.' He slapped his own chest. 'Like a grizzly bear with a massive boner.'

Ten

Leonard slapped the roof of the car and climbed back across to the driver's side. Gary was standing on the back seats, angled towards Benjamin. His nose touched the window and left a wet smear on the glass.

Leonard crossed his fingers and turned the key. The engine turned over a few times and stuttered, the electric sound of the starter motor falling away just before it roared into life. It sounded powerful but poorly maintained, the revs intermittently increasing and decreasing. Leonard shouted over the noise.

'You ride in the back,' he said, 'stop him assaulting me while I drive.'

'It's quite enclosed,' Benjamin said.

'We'll be driving with the windows open,' Leonard said, rolling his down. 'So you don't need to stress.' Benjamin reached into his pocket. He fished around then held up a ziplock bag with two surgical masks inside.

'I have these for hospital visits,' he said. 'Japanese people wear one when they have a cold.'

He held a mask out for Leonard who grabbed it, dangling it by the string like dirty underwear.

'We're not in Tokyo mate,' he said, putting it on top of his head like a hat.

Benjamin didn't think geography stopped it being a considerate thing to do.

'I'm definitely not wearing this,' Leonard said.

'I just thought we could both wear one. For mutual safety.'

'Yeah. No. You can wear it in the car, but you'll have to take it off at the club because you'll draw attention to us. We need to keep a low profile. Slink under any radars that might be perving.'

Benjamin put his mask on and got in. He buckled the belt on Gary's side, then lined it up in front of the dog's chest. It kept sliding onto his neck so Benjamin held it in place for him. Leonard handed back the contaminated mask and grinned at the arrangement. He nodded very formally at the dog.

'Got a head like an umbrella, hasn't he?' he said.

Benjamin didn't respond.

'He looks a bit like Dobby the house elf as well,' Leonard said.

'I don't know what that is.'

'He's like an imp. He tidies wizards' houses,' Leonard said.

Benjamin looked at Leonard.

'Are you sure you're safe to drive?' he said.

'It's from a book,' Leonard said. 'It's from *Harry Potter*.'

'I don't read children's books,' Benjamin said.

As they pulled away, the sun slipping behind the horizon, the engine spluttered like it was struggling to breathe. Leonard turned the fans on full to clear the fog of their breath.

'This car sounds broken,' Benjamin said.

'You've obviously never heard a high-performance engine before,' Leonard said, hair flapping about in the wind from the open window. 'Plus, some absolute troglodyte stole my catalytic converter.'

'What's one of those?'

'A troglodyte or a catalytic converter?'

'Both,' Benjamin said.

A troglodyte is someone who lives in a cave. A catalytic converter is something that reduces the toxic gases a combustion engine produces.'

Benjamin nodded. 'Why would they steal that?' he said.

'Precious metals I think, good money on the black market.'

'Don't you need one?'

Leonard waved around the cab like it was proof of something satisfying.

'Apparently not,' he said. 'You just have to leave the windows open, so the fumes don't kill you.'

Benjamin watched Leonard's face, hoping for a change in expression that would tell him he was joking.

'That's why it's a win–win that I'm allowing you to temporarily wear that mask,' Leonard said, beaming.

Benjamin wound his window down. He sat with his hands in his lap with Gary wobbling on the seat beside him, watching Leonard's eyes in the rear-view mirror. He felt the pressure change in his ears as the lampposts whipped by, listening to the sound of the engine bouncing between rows of pale-brick, double-glazed houses. Benjamin scratched the bit of Gary's neck that was normally covered by his collar and Leonard turned the radio up. He drummed along on the steering wheel to hair metal and coughed. He thumped his chest with a fist, then looked back at the window. Benjamin clamped his hand down over the mask.

'Have you had a temperature recently?' Benjamin said, trying to sound relaxed.

'A temperature?' Leonard said.

'Yeah.'

Leonard thought about it carefully.

'No,' he said. 'Why?'

'What about your sense of taste and smell?' Benjamin said.

'What about them?'

'I'm just wondering, because, you know. That thing on the news?'

Leonard raised an eyebrow.

'I probably need slightly more information to know what you're talking about.'

Leonard turned to look at Benjamin.

'The thing with the bats,' Benjamin said.

'Oh! That! I wondered why you were being weird at yours.' Leonard pushed his hair back. 'All that will one-hundred per cent definitely blow over within about three weeks,' he said. 'Absolutely guaranteed. If it's even real.' He held up his cigarette. 'The cough is more to do with these, I'd imagine.'

Benjamin studied his features, feeling the chill from the open windows. 'Why do you think it will all blow over?' he said.

Leonard pushed his hair off his face.

'Not based on any scientific fact or anything, I just know it will. I have a feeling for these things.'

Benjamin sat there thinking, watching the dog, the dog watching him back, until they pulled into an industrial estate and stopped outside one of the units. It had a large *Snooker and Pool* sign across the front.

'This is an important venue,' Leonard said as they parked diagonally across two spaces. 'Borderline spiritual.'

Benjamin looked out across the car park, at a streetlamp spotlighting a stained brown mattress hanging limp from the side of a skip. He took the building in with a feeling of dread which he struggled, apparently, to avoid displaying on his face.

'No need for the judgements mate,' Leonard said. 'We're here to figure out how we can best serve this animal.' He pointed at Gary in the back and tapped the side of his head. 'I need my best brain. And this is where I'm able to access it.'

'Will it be busy?' Benjamin said.

Leonard weighed it up.

'It used to be,' he said. 'But no, it won't be busy. Not so much these days.'

Leonard pretended to peek up over an imaginary object like a mime.

'You need to take that mask off mate,' he said.

Benjamin re-squeezed the wire tight across his nose. Leonard exhaled.

'I do hate to be a drag,' he said, 'but this is quite serious stuff.' He turned his body to point at the dog. 'In terms of his life and wellbeing.'

Benjamin looked at Gary and Leonard waited for him to turn back.

'You want to take care of him, don't you mate? Keep him safe?'

Benjamin nodded. He took the mask off.

'Good lad,' Leonard said. 'Your cooperation is appreciated.'

Leonard reached under the seat and produced a thermal bag. 'We'll have to leave old sniper rifle in the car because the club's not canine-friendly from what I can remember, unfortunately. He can have this to cheer him up though.'

Leonard peeled silver foil away from some sweet and sour chicken balls and handed Gary a chunk. The dog licked it tentatively at first, then took the whole piece from Leonard's hand.

'I stole it from Mr. Chen,' Leonard said, 'my corporate oppressor.'

While Gary sat licking his lips and whiskers, Benjamin panicked about leaving him in the car. He wound his window back up and Leonard did the same.

'He likes that,' Leonard said, laughing.

They got out. Leonard took his comb from his inside pocket and fixed his hair, raking it over sideways across his scalp.

'He'll be fine,' he said. 'We won't be long.'

'Have you locked the car?' Benjamin said.

'Course I have.'

Benjamin peered down into the closest window at the plastic lock knub. 'It's unlocked,' he said, grabbing the handle. The door swung open and Gary jumped down.

'Piss,' Leonard said, running back. He shooed Gary back in. 'Sorry, I was sure I had,' he said.

Leonard made a show of pressing the central locking button on his key fob and trying the handles.

'All good?' he said.

Benjamin walked around the car, checking the doors. His eyes lingered on Gary, curled up on the back seat, and he nodded. Then he followed Leonard into the club, wondering if breathing exclusively through your mouth reduced your chances of contracting a highly contagious airborne virus.

He decided it probably didn't.

Eleven

There was a lamp on in the caravan. It illuminated the kitchen, so that when Vasile peered through the glass, he could see Gary's red lead lying on the counter-top. He made his way around to the back where he leant against the wall and pulled on a pair of leather gloves, interlocking his fingers to get them snug. He tried the door, but it was locked, so he pushed on one of the panels to feel out its strength. It gave a little. He stepped back and looked around, then he kicked it open, smashing it into the wall. The door wobbled back towards him in the dark.

Twelve

Benjamin and Leonard walked along a corridor and into the muted light of the snooker club. Through a set of saloon doors, there was a man watching TV from behind the bar. He had long curly hair like a footballer from the eighties and his skin was unhealthily tanned, like animal hide. In front of him, there was a cigarette propped in a glass ashtray, adding to the smell of smoke in the room. Benjamin fought the temptation to pull his T-shirt back up over his nose.

'All right Leonard,' the man said flatly, walking along to where the cues and balls were. He took a tray down from the shelf. When Leonard put his hand out, the man didn't take it.

'Don't suppose my cue's still here, is it?' Leonard asked.

The man shook his head. 'No, it's not Len,' he said. 'We had a clear-out. Got rid of a lot of old shit.'

Leonard tried to laugh it off.

'Probably need a new one soon, anyway,' he said, looking around at the pictures on the wall. 'We'll just have a couple of rentals then please, Terry.'

The man reached behind the counter and took two from a rack. He laid them down.

'Benjamin, this is Terry. Terry, this is Benjamin,' Leonard said.

While Terry took him in, Benjamin tried to breathe as little as possible, to limit the amount of smoke and particulates going in.

'Hi,' he said.

Terry nodded and said 'all right,' but it wasn't a question.

'We'll just have an hour, I think,' Leonard said, reaching for the balls.

Terry gripped the sides of the tray. 'Pay up front,' he said.

Leonard patted his pockets down theatrically. 'Can you cover this?' he said to Benjamin, watching the TV on the wall as he said it. 'I don't really carry cash, *per se.*'

Terry laughed at Leonard as Benjamin took his wallet from his pocket, but it wasn't a kind laugh. Benjamin used his thumb to separate off one of the notes.

'We'll have a couple of pints, too,' Leonard said as Terry slid the balls and the cues over the counter. Terry pulled one of the pints.

'I'll just do you an orange juice, shall I?' he said to Benjamin, who didn't bother telling him he was old enough but didn't want a beer anyway because alchohol kills your brain cells.

'Yes please.'

Terry slid the drinks over and Leonard picked up his pint. He walked a few paces then spoke without turning back.

'Sally been in much at all?' he said.

'No, Len,' the man said. 'Of course she hasn't.'

They walked towards a door in the corner, past a man leaning on a fruit machine. He looked like he was melting into it, his forearms pressed onto its sides, face inches from the flashing buttons of the display.

Leonard casually prised a dart out of the dartboard and threw it, missing so badly it stabbed into the plaster. He gave Terry a sideways look as he wriggled it out.

'Get the door will you,' he said.

Benjamin pushed it open with his elbow. The room was empty. He felt glad there wasn't anyone else in there to share oxygen with. The bulb above their table made a noise like tapped glass then flickered into life.

Benjamin watched while Leonard placed the balls on their spots, his face mostly obscured by the long lampshade over the table. He seemed to think each ball had a definite top and a bottom, moving them with his thumb and index finger a fraction at a time until he was completely satisfied. Benjamin pictured Gary in the car, stood on the backseats, waiting for him.

'So, are you some sort of germ spaz then?' Leonard said.

'What?' Benjamin said.

'You know,' he pointed back at the door, 'opening doors with your elbow and all that?'

'Lots of people touch doors,' Benjamin said, looking at his shoes.

Leonard narrowed his eyes.

'You're probably really good at maths or something though.'

'Why would I be good at maths?' Benjamin said.

'I was under the impression that was how it was—you know—with people like you. You're not good, socially, are you? But you're good at maths.'

'I wasn't very good at school,' Benjamin said.

Leonard did an upwards nod to show the information was surprising to him, then put the empty tray on the shelf below the scoreboard. He picked up his cue and chalked it, leaving a tiny cloud of turquoise dust hovering in the air. He flexed his skinny arms. 'You don't need it anyway,' he said. 'I was shit at school and look at me now. A fucking megalith.'

Benjamin was fairly sure megaliths were big stones but didn't say anything. Leonard leant over the table. He pushed his chin into the cue and fired the white towards the triangle of reds. He watched the balls settle. 'What are you afraid of then?' he said, eventually.

Benjamin took a gulp of orange juice from his glass. He didn't say: volcanoes, human blood, animal blood, the dark, or essentially, every human disease that could kill or degrade you he'd ever heard of. Instead, he just said: 'quite a lot of stuff.'

Leonard scratched his chin. 'To be honest, it just feels like a classic case of fear,' he said, dropping a red into one of the corner pockets. 'A generalised fear of demise, most likely.'

Leonard surveyed the table, looking along the line of his cue towards the options. After careful deliberation, he fired the pink along the cushion and into the pocket. 'That's all this is though, ultimately,' he said, gesturing very generally at everything around them—peeling wallpaper, worn carpets, his pint—as the pocket swayed to a stop. 'The slow trudge to annihilation.'

Benjamin looked around at the things Leonard had highlighted.

'That doesn't really help,' he said.

'I just mean that, when the sun explodes in 5 billion years, your long-dead body will be fired into oblivion anyway. You know, with the mud and whatever it's mixed up in.'

'That doesn't either,' Benjamin said.

Leonard walked around the table and looked at Benjamin for the first time in a while.

'It's not really supposed to,' he said. 'It's just cosmic inevitability. You might become part of another solar system though? Which I think is filled with a sort of tragic hope.'

Benjamin had more orange juice. 'You don't get to choose what you worry about,' he said.

Leonard picked up his pint and raised his glass. He swept his hand across the green felt of the table. 'Fair,' he said.

Leonard seemed transfixed by the table's surface, his eyes a little glazed. Benjamin thought he could see the tiny reflections of the balls in the wet bits of his eyes. After a pause, Leonard looked at Benjamin.

'You played snooker before?' he said.

Benjamin shook his head, no.

'You should think about it,' Leonard said, tapping his temple: 'excellent for stabilising the primary organ.'

'The primary organ?'

'Yeah, the mainframe. The central cortex.'

Benjamin didn't know exactly what Leonard was getting at.

'It's good to have a hobby that gets the chemicals in check, is all I'm saying.'

Benjamin imagined having a hobby. One that needed specialist kit and regular practice. He'd thought about fencing before but there was nowhere to do it and it seemed quite physical. Ping pong was an option.

'Doesn't it affect your eyesight?' he said.

'My eyesight?'

'Watchmakers lose their eyesight much earlier than most people,' Benjamin said. 'Because they have to look at the tiny components all day. I thought this might be similar, because of the focus.'

Leonard potted a ball and shook his head. He used his fingers to open his eyes to maximum aperture. 'Not as far as I know. My vision is 20-20 like a fighter pilot. Maybe you're confusing it with wanking?' he said, deadpan.

Benjamin took a long gulp of his orange, wetting the patchy hair of his top lip. Comments like that made him feel awkward. The kind of comments that men often made to each other when they were unobserved.

'It's a game of angles,' Leonard announced. 'Like everything, really.'

Benjamin tried to see him under the long shade again, but his head was cut off.

'It's all about choosing the correct angle at the appropriate time,' Leonard said. 'Putting yourself in positions of *opportunity*.'

Benjamin didn't really know why Leonard was talking about angles. It seemed like he was just potting balls. Sometimes when people tried to overcomplicate things Camille said they were chatting shit.

During a stock-take at work, Andy Nelson (the area manager) had spent a long time talking about sales forecasts and shrinkage in relation to 'the bottom line.' He said his mastery of this as a manager had enabled him to purchase a vehicle made by Audi, with the metallic paint add-on.

Camille said metallic paint add-ons weren't emotionally enriching. She said she'd recently learnt that the beautiful and soulful people of Bhutan recognised happiness as the only relevant metric. They used 'the Gross National Happiness Index' to make decisions about policy and national projects. She said she was considering moving there, or at least organising some responsible tourism.

The idea concerned Benjamin. Camille was a human filter for all the things he found difficult to deal with at work, and she always emptied his waste bin at the end of a shift so he didn't have to touch it.

Benjamin thought about how much better Camille sometimes made him feel while Leonard played more shots. He walked around the table, looking along the cue like it was the sight of a gun and potting balls. Some he dropped in dead weight, others he fired in hard enough that they pummelled the leather backs of the pockets. It was hypnotic. Benjamin's mind wandered outside to the car. It was probably dark now. He didn't know whether that would bother Gary, but he worried that it might. Worried that there was an unease built into him like the one Benjamin felt. Something installed in him by echoes in his DNA, from relatives that sheltered in caves and ate raw meat off the bone.

Steadily, more of the tables illuminated. People moved around in the shadows and on the periphery, playing shots and talking quietly. By the bar, Benjamin saw Terry watching them through the glass.

'So where exactly did you find him then?' Leonard said eventually. 'The dog.'

'I told you. He was licking the blue whale on the beach. The dead one that's in the paper.'

'Well, he definitely wasn't,' Leonard said.

Benjamin didn't know what to say other than the truth

which was exactly what he'd said. It made him feel awkward. He scratched the inside of his arm.

'The whale on the beach is a fin whale,' Leonard said. 'The blue whale is the largest whale on the planet and the fin whale is the second.' He potted another ball. 'They're easy to mix up. Sometimes people call fin whales the greyhounds of the sea, actually. Which is funny,' he said, pointing the cue back towards the car park. 'What with him in the car.'

Benjamin craned to see Leonard's face around the shade again. He didn't seem the type to watch nature documentaries.

'He was licking the fin whale then,' Benjamin said.

Leonard nodded.

Benjamin thought about the penguin on TV. It was so helpless, at the mercy of something so overwhelming. Not just the sharks, but the ocean itself. He almost felt the weight of it bearing down, squashing his body and organs for a moment, before he was dragged inland again in his mind, along the beach and towards his nan's ward. He resisted the blur of memory and imagination, the thoughts forcing their way in, and dragged himself back to the envelope of light surrounding the snooker table. He needed a wee.

'Can I use the toilet?' he said suddenly.

Leonard laughed. 'Why are you asking me?'

'I don't know. I don't know what the rules are.'

'You're allowed to piss without asking.' Leonard said. 'You're not under duress.'

Benjamin stood still for a minute. He felt a bit like he was under duress. He wanted to ask Leonard why he was helping him—to clear things up and establish motivations.

'I'll be back in a minute,' he said.

Benjamin walked along the dark edge of the room towards the toilet. He looked back to see Leonard bobbing to the quiet music drifting through from the bar, then at Terry who was standing in the window again with his arms crossed. Benjamin stopped in front of a wall covered in black and white photos. They were mostly of snooker players in waistcoats, leaning over tables, holding trophies and shaking hands. Benjamin scanned the images. One was of Leonard holding a trophy up over his head. There were several more of him too, looking much younger, but when Benjamin turned to show Leonard he'd seen, there were three men at their table, distracting him. Leonard was gesticulating with his hands and looking apologetic when one of them grabbed him by the neck and pushed him into the scoreboard. Leonard nodded like he was agreeing, exaggerating his submission until the man loosened his grip and Leonard tried to punch him. He missed and the man exploded back, hitting Leonard in the middle of the face, disturbing his brain enough that his body crumpled to the floor. No one else in the room seemed to be paying much attention to what was happening. Or they were ignoring it. While the man rubbed the hand he'd used to punch Leonard, another stepped forward and sunk his boot into Leonard's ribs. Benjamin slid backwards into the gents.

Predictably, the toilets smelt faintly of urine. The room was dimly lit by a low-watt strip bulb and had a stainless-steel urinal running across the back wall under a cracked window. Benjamin could hear the rain outside. His body pulsed, or the blood inside it did, forced around by the sped-up beating of his heart. There was too much happening to fit in his head. He was pacing up and down the tiles and avoiding the wet spots when the man from the slot machine walked in. He stood swaying and squinting, steadied himself when he saw Benjamin.

'You on drugs or something?' he said.

Benjamin stopped.

'I need to go home really,' he said, walking over to the window. The ledge was covered with damp and cigarette ash and there was a glob of dark blood on the shiny top of the urinal. The man from the slot machine composed himself.

'There's a door out there you can use for that,' he said, grinning. Pleased with his joke.

'Did you see what was happening out there?' Benjamin said.

'I did,' the man said. 'Is he your mate then?'

Benjamin shrugged his shoulders. 'I don't really know him,' he said.

The man walked unsteadily forwards. He had a sweaty smudge of a face.

'Even if he was your mate,' he said, 'I expect you'd still be looking at that window, wanting to climb out.'

Benjamin didn't respond.

'Do you know what I'm saying?'

Benjamin did.

'I'm saying he's a wanker,' the man said, reaching past Benjamin to shunt the latch. It popped wide open, letting fine rain land on the sill, punching holes in the layer of dirt there.

'I wouldn't worry too much,' he said. 'He probably deserves it.'

With that, the man walked to the urinal and unzipped his flies. Benjamin took a last look at the dirt on the sill before he climbed up onto it and squeezed his torso out. He tried to stop his hands from touching anything as he eased himself down the outside of the pane, worrying about it cracking under his weight, about severed arteries and profuse bleeding and the dirt from the sill going in. Carefully, he managed to squeeze a leg out, then another, before being birthed into the drizzly night outside.

Thirteen

Benjamin ran along the alley, the heat of a graze on his chest, the cool rain on his face. When he got to the car, Gary's nose was pressed to the window. He'd pulled the cooler bag out and torn the foil to pieces.

'I'm going to get you out,' Benjamin said, trying the handle. Everything felt incredibly stressful and high-stakes—Benjamin didn't know how long he'd have before someone came out—so it felt appropriate to hold on to the mirror and kick the window. His foot slid off and he fell on the floor. He cut his elbow.

'Give me a second,' he said, hunting around for an object to help him gain access. He found a brick at the foot of the collapsing car park wall and passed it between his hands to feel its weight. It was crumbly, but there was a clump of cement still attached to its side which gave it some heft. He walked around the car to the driver's side and he slammed it into the window with every fibre of his being. The angle was wrong. The brick bounced off and out of his hands, its uneven surfaces cutting into his skin as it followed the adjusted trajectory. Gary launched himself into the back seats of the car. He looked very concerned.

'Sorry,' Benjamin said, exaggerating with his lips so he could keep the volume down. 'I'm sorry.' He tried to show Gary he wasn't panicking by looking calm, but he could feel his features being pulled out of shape involuntarily. 'Stay where you are,' he said. 'I'm going to get you out.'

Gary seemed reassured. He jumped through to the front seats.

'You have to stay back,' Benjamin said, bouncing on the balls of his feet with fear and frustration and dirty hands. 'I'm going to smack the window.'

This time the corner punctured the glass. Benjamin used it to hit the hole more carefully until it got bigger, until he could pull at the shards. He cut his fingers but couldn't stop. Even though he was thinking about the germs from the toilet sill entering his blood stream, feeling sick with the stress of it, he eased his arm through the gap and pulled up the lock and the door swung open.

Gary jumped down. He half-thought it was a game, circling Benjamin as they ran towards the sea. The dog's long black shadow stretched out across the concrete as they moved under the streetlights. With each stride Benjamin felt a little less like the world was ending.

He ran until his lungs hurt. When he stopped and listened, all he could hear was the waves and his own breathing. All he could see was the flashing beacons of the fishing boats, bobbing around offshore.

He made his way down to the ocean and plunged his hands into the icy saltwater. It stung, but there was something calming about the lack of detail in the dark, just the knowledge that the sea was cleaning his cuts. He used the sand to rub away the dirt and could feel the pulse of his heart in the veins of his hands. The thought of pipes ejecting waste into the sea crossed his mind, but its association with his nan, of her swimming there, seemed to diffuse it. The worry ebbed away as he imagined the grime from the toilet windowsill floating out into the deep. He wondered about the men who attacked Leonard in the club, trying to remember their faces, trying to establish why they had been very recklessly attempting to kick his head. It was the kind of violence that landed you in prison. The kind that people didn't carry out for no reason. The heavy sound of the water brought Benjamin back to the sand. It made him think about his grandmother, swimming out in the swell, pushed this way and that as she cut a jagged line through the water, moving further and further away. He shivered. He felt the sea pulling the sand away beneath his shoes; the ground slipping out from under him like it had with the whale. When he looked at Gary, he felt a little less alone.

The rain picked up as they walked, and Gary shrank more and more into his own body the heavier it fell. In the distance, the shadow of the pier loomed out of the dark, growing larger, until Gary walked under it and Benjamin followed. His eyes adjusted enough that he could make out the silhouettes of the beams running in even parallels above them. The sound was different underneath. It wasn't the isolated crash of waves, but the rips of water hitting wood. Benjamin sat down because his legs felt as if they were empty, and Gary sidled up next to him. The dog leant heavily on his side, looking around, and Benjamin listened for the sound of people following. No one came. After a while, the fear began to lift, replaced by a chill that was bone deep.

They shivered, both of them together, under a fat moon that sat low in the sky and gave everything a cool white glow. Benjamin's shoes were soaking wet, and his feet were cold. He put his arms around Gary's middle and felt the band of muscle that ran along the lower part of his ribs and his slick wet fur, felt the crisp nighttime air in his throat. When Gary pushed his head in against Benjamin's side, it was hard to tell which of their bodies the shivers came from.

Benjamin felt the dog's steady breath on his skin and, after a while, Gary trembled less.

'We should go home,' Benjamin said.

Fourteen

When the caravan came into view, the curtains were closed and the lights were on. It threw Benjamin because he normally turned everything off to save on bills and to avoid the unnecessary risk of fire. Sometimes, at the till, he would imagine hot bulbs exploding and setting light to the rugs while he was out, licks of flame running up the curtains and turning the caravan into a bonfire. He tried to remember how they'd left things when they departed for the club but the cold was distracting. He hugged himself and rubbed his arms. The curtains twitched. He felt fear like a loud noise and leant up against a nearby fence. He was looking for somewhere to hide, but Gary had already run onto the decking. The dog sniffed the air by the steps, his claws tapping on the wood as he paced around. He whined inconveniently. Benjamin loped forwards and used his hands to carefully shut Gary's mouth. Gary pressed his nose in further. The decking creaked.

'Shh.' Benjamin said, not wanting to move, feeling like his feet were stuck. He pressed his ear to the door and heard the liquid surge of heartbeats in his head, felt the cold plastic on his ear, and listened. Minutes passed. The chill worked its way further into the lean meat of his body, until the discomfort forced him to move. He pushed the key into the lock and turned the handle.

The caravan was freezing. The back door was wide open and so were most of the cupboards, their contents turfed out onto the living-room floor. The satin toilet-roll lady was still lying damaged on the welcome mat, her severed arm beside her. Gary sniffed her dress as Benjamin kicked off his shoes and stepped inside. He examined the splintered wood around the lock and a muddy boot mark on the door. He tried to close it, but it didn't line up with the frame, so he used his shoulder to jam it into the gap. Rain had soaked the mat. There was smashed glass on the carpet and several broken frames scattered around. Gary jumped up on the sofa.

'Be careful,' Benjamin said. 'Glass is extremely sharp.'

It wasn't the first time he'd worried about the soft skin on Gary's paws. As he drifted between rooms, he imagined someone rifling through, pictured them picking things up and putting them back in the wrong places. Contaminating them. He also thought about their personal hygiene and whether they'd washed their hands after they last handled their genitalia. Before they'd touched all his personal items.

It made the caravan feel far away and unfamiliar, like it belonged to someone else. He felt the weight of it in his chest, took two puffs of his inhaler and waited for the salbutamol to open up his bronchioles.

When his breathing steadied, he pushed the sofa to the damaged door. It left rectangular indents in the carpet that made him think about his nan's feet sinking into the pile when the caravan was new, when her body was younger. He thought about the hospital room she was in now, machines beeping around her in the dark, cells starting slowly to forget their own jobs. It hurt to think of her seeing the caravan like this.

He went to the bathroom to scrub his body with soap and washed the parts of him that had touched the windowsill, then the graze on his chest until it bled. He watched the blood mingling with the suds and remembered his nan slicing her finger in the kitchen chopping carrots.

'I ain't got time to bleed,' she said, squeezing it above her head.

That seemed like a very strange thing to say.

'What?' Benjamin said.

'It's from *Predator*!' she said. 'Sorry. I always forget we didn't finish it.'

She held up her hand and a single drop of blood fell to the floor and splattered outwards.

'What have you done?' Benjamin said, rushing over, terrified she'd hit an artery.

'It's okay—it's just a little nick,' she said, smiling. 'It's nothing.'

With his body clean, Benjamin wanted to lie down. To close his eyes and sleep. In another memory he didn't have the energy to resist, he saw his nan leaning against a cupboard in the kitchen. Her skin was pale, each breath shallower than the last. She didn't have the strength to speak, but she smiled. Benjamin felt himself drifting again. He wanted to feel something different. Less hopeless, less like the core of him had been taken out and he was collapsing inwards. He started cleaning.

He pulled on his rubber gloves and scrubbed the sink with bleach, used antibacterial spray on all the surfaces. He put the photos on the mantel and used a gardening glove from the cupboard to pick up the glass without cutting the soft skin on his fingertips. He stacked items into piles. Gary watched from the sofa as he mopped the floor.

When he was finished, Benjamin moved the armchair to face the broken door and sat in it. With his eyes closed, he felt light-headed. Like gravity had been adjusted and he was slipping into infinite space. Gary jumped down from the sofa and stretched out on the carpet beside him and they sat waiting in the dark. No idea what for.

Fifteen

Benjamin woke to the smell of cigarette smoke. He squinted into the semi-dark, towards a banging noise that was coming from the decking. There was someone outside, pushing at the broken door. Benjamin put his hand on the lamp, hovering over the switch, and waited. When a head forced its way through the gap, he flicked the lamp on and illuminated Leonard's bloodied face.

'Jesus. What are you doing?' Benjamin said.

Leonard tried to speak but coughed into his sleeve. He dragged his torso and an arm into the room. 'Things are more serious than I thought,' he said, hitting his own chest like it might dislodge something. 'Fucking brown shirts gave me a right decking.'

He was wearing aviator sunglasses. When he lowered them down his nose with a finger, Benjamin could already see the dark bruising that had appeared around both his eyes. His top lip was swollen. He coughed again and Gary stared at him.

'You going to let me in then?' Leonard said, raising an eyebrow. Benjamin pulled the sofa out of the way.

'What time is it?' Leonard said, stepping in.

Benjamin looked at the clock on the wall.

'It's three in the morning,' he said. 'Why did you come here?'

'That's charming,' Leonard said, rubbing his jaw.

Benjamin looked around the room, seeing it after the fog of sleep as something new. A fresh wound.

'Don't worry about my injuries,' Leonard said. 'They're very superficial.'

'Have you been to a hospital?' Benjamin said.

'No. They'd ask too many questions.'

'The man in the toilet said you probably deserved it,' Benjamin said.

Leonard shook his head. 'Which man in the toilet?'

'The one from the slot machine.'

'Tony?' Leonard said. 'Tony Langley?'

Benjamin shrugged his shoulders.

'Another example of a troglodyte, Benjamin,' Leonard said, getting so animated some spit came out. 'A few years ago, he got so drunk he fell off his stool and hit his head on the machine. He woke up and claimed he could see what the universe was made of.'

Leonard took a long drag on his cigarette. As he lowered it again, smoke drifted up and away, curling in the lamplight. Benjamin wished he wouldn't smoke in the caravan, but it felt like there were more pressing considerations. He wondered what Tony Langley had seen, imagining minuscule blobs of colour with indistinct edges that pulsed and glowed, drifting around like pollen.

'Got any paracetamol?' Leonard said, stretching and groaning in an exaggerated way whenever he hit the limits of his movement. He walked into the kitchen and opened a cupboard. Took out a tube of effervescent vitamin tablets.

'These will help,' he said, shaking the packet. He filled a mug at the sink and tapped in three or four, tipping his head back to drink them before they'd fully dissolved.

'You're only supposed to have one of those,' Benjamin said.

'You leave my vitamin intake up to me,' Leonard said, hitting his own chest again. 'My canals are my business.'

Benjamin felt Gary's weight leaning into the side of his leg. The proximity was comforting.

'What happened to the door then?' Leonard said, surveying the room, noticing the glass and the dragged-out items all stacked up by the cupboard.

'Someone broke in,' Benjamin said.

Leonard nodded. He puffed on his cigarette a few more times.

'I think there's some quite serious shit going on here, Benjamin,' he said.

Gary forced his nose in under Benjamin's leg like a scoop and Leonard shook his head.

'He's wet, that dog,' he said.

Benjamin signalled in the direction of Leonard's damaged face. 'Do you know who they were?'

Leonard took a deep breath. He looked back at the door, hanging open with its hinges bent, then walked over and put his hand on Gary's head. He crouched down to look at the dog's face.

'They're not nice men, Benjamin,' he said, rubbing the back of his own neck. 'And they know about him, obviously.'

Benjamin paced. He headed for the rug and dug his toes into it, then gazed around the room taking shallow breaths. His skin turned cold. He picked up a pillow and pressed his face into it. It felt like the caravan was spinning around him. Leonard shifted his weight uncomfortably while Benjamin muffled an animal shout with the bedding.

'I don't know what to do,' Benjamin said, looking at Leonard, waiting for him to speak.

Leonard moved his hand up to his face. He picked at a bit of dry skin on his palm.

'I don't know what that particular display was about, with the pillow, but I don't think you should stay here,' he said.

Benjamin put his hands on the sides of his face and stared at the carpet, bouncing his heels. He scratched his forearm. Gary was curled up on the dirty T-shirt Benjamin had thrown on the floor the night before.

'Do you think they'll come back?' Benjamin said.

'I think so,' Leonard said.

Benjamin sat down near Gary. The dog lifted his head from

the ground and opened one of his eyes. His tail flicked almost imperceptibly as Benjamin looked at him, remembering now the way he'd stood beside him under the pier, how the dog had stopped trembling when he was close to him.

He looked at the bruises on Leonard's face.

'I don't want to give him back,' he said.

Leonard looked between the dog and Benjamin.

'Not returning him might not be an option,' he said.

'But I don't want them to . . . ' Benjamin grimaced. '—you know. What you said. When his legs are done.'

Leonard tried to rub his chin with his hand. The pain made him flinch.

'I get that,' he said.

Benjamin looked at him, eyes wide. 'Will you help us?'

Leonard thought about it for a while. He gestured at his face, then tried to smile.

'I think I'm sort of implicated now anyway,' he said.

There was a sound outside. A door slamming or a bin falling over. Leonard squinted at the window. 'We can't stay here, though,' he said.

Benjamin swallowed.

'Where could we go?'

Leonard walked to the pile of things that had been pulled from the cupboard. He picked up a tent that was perched on the top.

'Maybe we could camp out in the woods,' he said. 'We could eat rabbits and drink from the stream. Like Ray Mears.'

Benjamin didn't eat animals in general, but the idea of eating a rabbit was particularly sad. He didn't know who Ray Mears was.

'I definitely don't want to go camping,' he said.

Leonard laughed. The effort pained him, pulling on the damaged parts of his face.

'Don't rush a decision,' he said, grimacing. 'I actually did some of the groundwork when I had this thing going on a while ago,' he said. 'I thought I might have to disappear or whatever. There's a part of the woods I know. It runs along the beach not far from here and it's all fenced off. I think people meet up in the car park sometimes, wife-swappers or whatever, but if you made it to the woods you could hide out for weeks before anyone found you.'

Benjamin wasn't sure what Leonard meant by a "thing going on," but didn't dwell.

Leonard waved the canvas tent in his hands. 'There's a carp lake nearby as well,' he said, sounding optimistic. 'Not that you can really eat carp because they taste like mud. But for recreation. Plus, fresh air. Which you love.'

Benjamin looked at the tent. It made him think about a trip he took with his nan, not long after he'd moved into the caravan. He'd come home from school to find her waiting in the doorway with her hair tied up on top of her head, beaming. It was the smile he remembered the most. How happy she was that they were going.

Benjamin had never been camping. After they'd set everything up, he touched a sausage packet while she was cooking on a disposable barbeque. He sat on a camping chair, watching the pale pork chipolatas turn brown one side at a time, thinking about the point of contact between him and the cling-film, the invisible trace of blood that had coated his finger.

It was the first time he could remember feeling as though his body was bloated and covered in wrinkles, that everything was spoilt in some indefinable way. He couldn't focus on the words she was saying or even explain it to her.

He just said he needed to go home.

As they drove, his hands hovered in the space above his thighs, loose fists to avoid further contamination.

'I really don't want to sleep outside,' Benjamin said again.

'We'd make a shelter and a dump hole, if that's what you're worried about,' Leonard said.

'That's not what I'm worried about.'

'What are you worried about?'

Benjamin shook his head.

'I just don't want to do it,' he said.

Leonard shrugged, 'okay.' He stood pondering, probing bits of his face to see what hurt. 'I suppose we could head to my holiday home,' he said.

A holiday home sounded more sensible. More hygienic.

'Where's your holiday home?' Benjamin said.

'It's a bit further round the coast. Up on the cliffs.'

Benjamin watched Gary adjusting himself on the floor, shimmying his nose into the carpet to scratch an itch.

'How long will we have to go for?' Benjamin said.

Leonard blew air from the side of his mouth, simulating the sound of a tyre deflating.

'It could be a while mate. We've got a lot to figure out.'

Benjamin looked around at the mess in the caravan.

'We can't leave it like this,' he said.

Leonard pushed at the sofa until it was back blocking the broken door. He ferried books from a shelf to its cushions, stacking them up until they were squashed and mangled under the weight.

'We'll fortify the defences,' he said.

Benjamin let his shoulders hang loose in their sockets, relaxing his eyes until he saw the blur of his eyelashes. When they refocussed, he looked around at the cupboards, the doors all hanging open, the broken picture frames on the mantel, and then finally, at the dog, who was staring at him, big amber eyes wide open.

'Okay,' he said.

Benjamin dragged an old leather duffel from under his bed. He filled it with clean clothes then brought it back to the sitting room where Leonard was holding a squat porcelain fisherman he'd found on the shelf.

'That's my nan's,' Benjamin said, wondering why Leonard always had to pick everything up.

'It's a nice artefact,' Leonard said.

While Leonard moved the object around in his hands, Benjamin clenched his fists.

'Are you okay?' Leonard said. 'You look like you need to go to the toilet.'

'I don't,' Benjamin said.

'What is it then?'

Benjamin didn't reply.

'Let me know if I'm overstepping, but I think you could work on your communication skills. Mostly just saying what's on your mind.'

'I want to go and see her,' Benjamin said.

Leonard looked up.

'See who?'

'My nan.'

Leonard grimaced and shook his head. 'I'm not sure. She's at the hospital, isn't she? We need to avoid busy places really.'

Benjamin thought about all of the things he needed to say. What he hadn't said before.

'You told me it could be a while?'

'Yeah, but not months. We're not going to sea,' Leonard said. 'Unless she's likely to croak.'

Leonard laughed but stopped immediately when Benjamin shot him a look. Benjamin didn't blink.

'We have to go,' he said.

Leonard dipped his head.

'Oh Christ,' he said. 'You've twisted my arm. But we can't stop long.'

Benjamin put his back-up inhaler inside a ziplock bag and stuffed it into his pocket. Leonard picked up the duffel. He contracted his bicep and tensed his skinny arm like a bodybuilder doing curls, so the veins showed. The sun was coming up outside.

'We really need to get out of here,' he said. 'They could come back at any time.'

Leonard lingered by the door.

'You got any cash?' he said.

Benjamin nodded. He glanced towards the cabinet where he hid his supermarket money.

'I'll get some if you don't look,' he said.

Leonard made a show of squeezing his eyes tight shut.

'Can you turn around please?' Benjamin said.

Leonard spun on the spot and put his hands over his eyes in a pantomime way. 'Promise I won't look,' he said.

Benjamin slid a biscuit tin out from a drawer, then carefully removed the lid to stop it making a sound. He took out a handful of notes. When he put the tin back, he saw that Leonard was watching him in the reflection in the TV.

'I've got some,' he said, turning off the lights.

The morning was cool and bright. On the way to the car, Leonard reclaimed his general-purpose cleaning rag and slapped it on the decking. Gary stayed close to Benjamin.

'I'm just dislodging the piss particles,' Leonard said, stuffing the rag into his pocket.

At the car, Benjamin avoided staring at the window he'd broken the night before, at the black bag Leonard had taped over it being pressed in by the wind. He opened the door to see that Leonard had left the smashed glass in the footwell. There was still a lot of *sake* on the back seats. Gary walked forwards and stood with his nose hovering above the leather while Benjamin placed one of the boxes on top of the shards. He put Gary's front paws on the seats and lifted his back-end in.

'We might have to talk about that at some stage,' Leonard

said, nodding at the window as Benjamin climbed in. 'Not saying you'll have to pay for it all in one go.'

As they pulled out, a warm orange sun was emerging above the flat line of the horizon. Benjamin felt the cool air on his face as it channelled through from the front, pressing on the fabric of his T-shirt, reminding him of the cuts on his chest. Gary settled down on the seat.

As soon as the caravan was out of sight, Benjamin started to feel a little better. The further they drove, the less acutely he felt the unpleasant electricity of worry, moving through his body.

Sixteen

Whenever Benjamin thought Leonard's attention was fully on the road, he stole glances at him, watching the shiny bits of his eyes darting around in the mirror.

'She'll warm up in a bit,' Leonard said, slapping the dash, trying to grin but clearly in pain. The cold was making its way into Benjamin's bones, drawing the blood inwards, away from his skin and to his organs. He took a jumper from his duffel bag and draped it over Gary. What little spare there was he pulled over his legs. He lifted the collar of his anorak higher, then sunk down into the passenger seat. There were plumes of breath coming from all their mouths. Leonard swung into the hospital car park and skidded to a stop in a space.

'I'm not sure you can visit at 5 A.M.,' he said.

Benjamin sat staring forwards. 'We can just wait,' he said.

"That reminds me—' Leonard said, leaning across Benjamin to open the glove box. The inside was sloppily and liberally lined with tinfoil.

'Have you got a mobile?' he said, waving at the bizarre cubby-hole like he was very proud. He tapped his own temple. 'Put it in here if you have.'

'What's that?' Benjamin said.

'It's to stop them tracking our signals.'

'I don't have a phone.'

Leonard looked surprised. 'Because of the 5G? Very wise, mate.'

'No. I just don't really need one.'

'Any other trackable devices then? Do you have a pager? An iPad? What do you do about 'sexting?'' he said. 'How do you send your sexts?'

'I don't do that,' Benjamin said flatly. 'Who do you think would be tracking us anyway?'

'The dog's owners, or the fuzz. Anyone these days,' Leonard said. 'If you don't think about these things, the next thing you know they're in your studio flat, standing on the back of your head, telling you not to hang around in your ex-wife's new boyfriend's garden with an album full of wedding photos.'

'Right,' Benjamin said.

'Anyway. I'm going to catch up on some sleep,' Leonard said, crossing his arms and sinking down into the seat. Leonard closed his eyelids and Benjamin carried on watching. He still didn't know what he was looking for. A twitch or a sign maybe, that he could relax, that he could trust him. Or something that indicated he couldn't. Leonard snuck a look out of one eye, then snapped it shut when he saw Benjamin staring.

'That's quite off-putting,' he said, scratching his stubble.

'Sorry,' Benjamin said.

Gary stood up and put his head over Leonard's shoulder.

'He smells a bit funny,' Leonard said.

'He got rained on last night.'

'It's activated something. He smells like chopped vegetables.'

While Leonard slept, Benjamin watched the hospital staff arriving for work or finishing their shifts. Most of them had red eyes regardless. They carried thermal cups and had passes swinging around their necks. To kill the time, Benjamin watched Gary sleeping, waking occasionally to clean his paws, his pink tongue dragging along his foreleg and wetting the fur. Benjamin studied the black stripes across the dog's back and the white one running along his nose, the separate segments of muscle along the side of his stomach. Gary lifted his head, in a place not far from sleep, and looked at Benjamin. Benjamin wondered about the spongey lump of his brain, whether he had an awareness of anything beyond the moment they were in. He wasn't sure. But the longer he looked at him, the more he became convinced—knew—there was feeling in there that was deep and complicated, a kind of gentleness that ran through every cell in his body. Something good and pure that needed looking after. Benjamin didn't know if he'd ever seen anything like that before. Or maybe it was just the first time he'd been responsible for it.

When his nan first went in, Benjamin would imagine finding her sat up and talking, the doctor telling her she could come home. He wished again that that would be the case, even if he knew that most likely it wouldn't. He imagined getting a taxi and telling her about Gary, the two of them at the table eating toast and marmalade, her speaking to the dog like he was human. She always did that to animals. After they'd eaten, Benjamin would tell her about the whale—about its lumbering consciousness gliding through deep, heavy water and the fate it was swimming towards on the beach; the moment that waited for it there.

'I don't mind dying,' she'd said, once. 'I just don't want to be there when it happens.'

Benjamin wished he felt like that, but the idea of it terrified him. He was so often overwhelmed by the frailty of his own body, the tenuousness of his existence. He worried about ominous things occurring internally, and the gradual decay of his organs even if he ate very healthily. The last moments before a forever-silence.

It was fully light by the time visiting started. Benjamin used his elbow to nudge the fleshy part of Leonard's arm to wake him.

'I'll sort it,' Leonard said, trying to go back to sleep.

Benjamin nudged him again.

'I'm sorting it,' he said more aggressively, with an edge Benjamin didn't recognise.

'Leonard?' Benjamin said.

Leonard opened his eyes very slowly, like he was afraid of what he might see.

'I'm going to go in now,' Benjamin said.

Leonard nodded. 'I'll wait out here with pencil neck,' he said, closing his eyes again.

As Benjamin reached for the door handle, Gary climbed the front half of his body through between the seats and pushed his cold wet nose into the side of Benjamin's head. Leonard pushed him into the back with an arm.

'I wish you'd stop being so dynamic on my seats,' he said to the dog.

Benjamin turned to Gary, then back to Leonard.

'And you'll wait here?' he said.

'Right here,' Leonard said.

Benjamin looked at Gary again, then at the keys dangling by the steering wheel. 'Can I take those with me?'

Leonard raised an eyebrow.

'What?' he said.

'The keys. Can I take them?'

Leonard smiled.

'What do you need them for?'

Benjamin felt stupid for asking. His skin was tingling again. Gary was settling in the back, sprawled out across the seats.

'I just—I don't like leaving him,' he said. He considered it a few seconds. 'Maybe you could wait out front?'

'I can do,' Leonard said, opening his eyes wide to take Benjamin in. 'I suppose I should get us combat parked anyway.'

Benjamin raised his eyebrow. He didn't understand the terminology.

'You just park according to the direction of exit. For when you need to GTFO,' Leonard said.

Benjamin was still confused.

'For when you need to Get The Fuck Out,' Leonard said.

Leonard reversed out of the spot and drove towards the plate glass of the hospital entrance. He pulled into a loading bay, just along from a big set of automatic doors. There was an elderly couple working together to lift a wheelchair into the back seat of their car.

'It's not perfect,' Leonard said, 'but we should be able to extract at pace, if needed. Now go and see your nan. Just don't tell anyone about the dog. Or me.' He tapped the side of his nose.

Benjamin pushed the door open and stepped out onto the pavement. He pulled the elastic straps of a surgical mask over his ears and walked into the hospital, into the cool breeze of the foyer's aircon. He turned to see Gary sat bolt upright in the back of the car watching him go, one ear pointing up, the other falling over sideways.

Benjamin walked along the dimly-lit corridor, sticking to one side as he passed the morgue and its damaged oxygen. He paused while a very large man on a ride-on cleaning machine whizzed past, buffing the lino floors and making them shiny. At the entrance to the ward, he pumped clear sanitiser onto his hands that made the cuts sting. He dabbed some on his neck where Gary had licked him, then gritted his teeth and rubbed his hands together until the alcohol evaporated.

There was no one at the nurse's station so he walked straight to his nan's room. From the doorway he watched her shrunken outline rising and falling under the crisp white sheets, and listened to the beeping machinery around her. He filled a plastic cup at the sink and poured it into a plant pot on the windowsill, then sat down on a turquoise leather chair covered in easy-wipe plastic. He looked at her face. The same plain expression of sleep she'd had since they'd moved her back to the ward. He lowered his mask to talk to her.

'I found a dog,' he said, keeping his voice down. 'I've had to look after him. I think he might have been run over or poisoned otherwise.'

Benjamin leant forward to touch her hand.

'You can see all his muscles through his skin,' he said. 'His name is Gary.'

A nurse that Benjamin knew appeared at the door. His name was Mike. He had long brown hair pulled back in a ponytail and a habit of stooping like he was sorry for being tall. Benjamin pulled the mask back over his face.

'Morning,' Mike said, smiling.

'Hi,' Benjamin said.

The last time she was in, Benjamin's nan hadn't seemed so sick. She was awake most of the day so Mike would wheel her out to the car park and Benjamin wouldn't have to go inside. Mike would stand hunched, fifteen or so feet away, smoking a cigarette while Benjamin and his nan talked.

Benjamin saw Mike in town once. He was outside the supermarket, wearing a Hawaiian shirt. He was smoking then, too, but the cigarette smelt different. He told Benjamin he was bunning a zoot and politely requested he keep it to himself. Benjamin did, but he also printed out some guidance he found on the public library computer about the connection between marijuana and mental health problems.

'I thought I saw you, cruising the corridors like a panther with a Masters in Business Studies,' Mike said, smiling. He often said slightly abstract things like that. 'What are you two discussing?'

Benjamin liked that Mike put it that way, that they were having a dialogue. That she was involved. Even though she hadn't been able to reply properly since Benjamin had found her on the kitchen floor with her dinner beside her. He wondered how long it took to forget how somebody sounded.

'I was just telling her about something I found on the beach,' Benjamin said.

'Oh nice. Was it six duffel bags full of co-cay-yena? I watched a documentary about that recently.'

'No, it wasn't that.'

'Shame. If I found that sort of shit, I can't tell you the kind of debauchery I would indulge in. I'd read Game of Thrones in a silk dressing gown. Eat pizzas astride a replica zebra.'

Benjamin liked Mike but it didn't feel like a good idea to tell him about Gary. He put his hand in his pocket, found the cool surface of the stone from the beach.

'I just found a stone,' he said, producing it.

Mike reached over and Benjamin dropped it into his hand.

'Nice,' Mike said. 'I could have sworn I heard you talking about a dog.' He shook his head. 'But rocks are legitimately the tits, also.'

Benjamin nodded.

'The rock cycle is intense,' Mike said. 'It's like, the more heat and pressure you add—' he pressed his palms together '— over, millions of years or whatever, the more a rock *becomes*. Via Metamorphosis.'

'How do you know about that?' Benjamin said.

'I guess I just feel an affinity. I'm mega into the idea of being *developed* by pressure and stress. I researched it once after I'd consumed a significant volume of enchanted mushrooms.'

Mike put his arms in the air and mimicked the voiceover from a film.

'THE MAN BECOMES MARBLE,' he said, chuckling.

Benjamin smiled.

'I thought about getting a tattoo of a kitchen worktop at one point,' Mike said. 'Granite etc. For, like, comedy. And philosophy. Plus, it's more nuanced than just getting a boulder on your chest which was my first thought.'

Benjamin winced at the idea of jokes that could be indelibly marked on your skin.

'You don't like tattoos?' Mike said. 'That's cool. I get it.

Keep it pristine.' He held his hand out for a high five and remembered Benjamin tended not to reciprocate, mid-gesture. He checked the numbers on one of the machines.

'I was going to say to you, man. Make sure you keep talking. Like, anything you might want to say to her.'

Benjamin looked out of the window.

'I know you probably do. But anything significant or whatever?' Mike added. He looked around, checked a clipboard on the wall. 'I don't want to be a bore, because I know I mentioned it last time, but the doctors really need to have a chat with you?' he said.

Benjamin didn't reply.

'It's important,' Mike said.

Benjamin nodded. He didn't always like hearing what people said to him here.

He often tried to let the words float by, shapeless and light. When Mike left the room, Benjamin looked out the window for the entrance doors where Leonard was parked, but there were trees and buildings in the way. He turned back to his nan and thought about the last time he'd seen her eyes. A sadness moved through him then. He was sad because certain words had been so hard to find when she first got ill. Sad that sickness added a weight to everything, the stakes of breaking the silence so high, he ended up not saying much at all. Sad that he found it easier to talk to her now she didn't say anything back. He was aware of all the words just under the surface, hundreds if not thousands of them, that he wished he'd said. His mouth was dry. He walked over and stood in the doorway, watching a crowd of people in scrubs wheeling a patient along the corridor, holding his breath as they rolled past.

'WHO have declared a public-health emergency now,' one of them said. 'They're talking about containment.'

Benjamin didn't know what that meant, but it made him feel uncomfortable. It also made him even less inclined to wait for

Mike, or the doctor. To wait for another set of difficult words. Difficult, because once he'd heard them, he knew they couldn't be changed or unspoken. He turned to his nan.

'I'll come back,' he said, placing the new stone he'd found on the windowsill next to a handful of others. It cast a shiny shadow in the gloss paint. 'I'll come back.'

Leonard was waiting in the drop-off zone. The old couple were still parked in front of his car, and an ambulance had pulled up tight to his bumper at the back. From the walkway in the atrium, Benjamin watched him through the sheet glass, manoeuvring forwards and backwards, trying to wriggle the car from the space with a visibly red face. Benjamin ran down the stairs and out of the double doors to the car. When he spoke, he felt his own voice wobble.

'What are you doing?' he said.

Leonard pointed at the old couple in front.

'I was just lining us up for a swift getaway,' he said. 'This pair of codgers got in the way though.'

Benjamin looked at them. He imagined himself in an old body. His skin loose over his bones.

'It looked like you were trying to leave,' he said.

'Why on Earth would I do that?'

On their way out of town Leonard pulled over at a petrol station. He tapped the fuel gauge and feigned shock, his face like a resus dummy, mouth in the shape of an 'O.'

'The petrol light is on,' he said, jumping out. 'I'll refuel and you go in and pay.'

While Leonard was filling up, Benjamin looked at the pet food. He inspected a yellow tin with a collie on the label. Although Gary wasn't a collie, Benjamin assumed they'd eat very similar food. He selected one tin of fish-based chum—because fish have quite soulless eyes—and a chicken—because chickens have the smallest brains of the dog-food animals. He took the tins over to where the magazines were and waited for Leonard.

The garage had two shelves full of half-covered adult magazines—the ones with cellophane wrap midway up to stop you seeing the erotic bits. Benjamin looked at the people pulling sexy faces under the titles and imagined them in other, more domestic settings. Not in a way that assumed they were made unhappy by their work, just squinting at a bus timetable in the rain or eating Weetabix. He did that sometimes, fleshing out the lives of people he saw.

'It's called empathy,' Camille had said. 'It's a superpower.'

He didn't know why he did it, just that it made him feel warmer towards people. Which made him feel more connected. More affectionate. Less lonely.

Over at the till, a man and a woman in matching yellow polos leant in conspiratorially and whispered to each other. They looked almost identical, like twins. Benjamin thought about telling them he was imagining one of the ladies from *Bored Housewives* stirring pasta and listening to the radio when they both laughed out loud. He turned away and looked at the newspapers. His cheeks felt hot as he scanned the headlines, barely reading the words until one of the front pages caught his eye. It was a picture of a military aircraft being loaded up with people.

RAF EVACUATES BRITONS FROM VIRUS GROUND ZERO, it said.

Outside, Leonard was filling the car's tank to the absolute brim—dribbling more in each time the pump cut off. He stood upright and gave Benjamin a wave, but Benjamin barely registered it. He was too busy imagining the airborne particulates inside the plane as they moved in and out of two hundred sets of lungs. It made him wish he'd put his mask on when he came into the garage. On the way to the till, he stopped by a badly-stocked shelf of medical supplies. He picked up a thermometer and more sanitiser, then slid the tins across the counter to the almost-twins without making eye contact. He gestured towards Leonard to indicate that he wanted to pay for the petrol.

'Just these and the fuel?' the man said, smirking. 'Sure you don't want anything else?'

Benjamin shook his head. The man looked at his colleague.

'A magazine or anything?'

They both laughed.

'No,' Benjamin said.

'£64.75 then please.'

Benjamin took out the roll of cash. While he was separating the notes, he thought about Angelina Jolie snorting cocaine in a film he'd seen on TV, his subsequent internet research into the dangers of the practice at the library, and the resultant statistic that more than 75 per cent of UK tender had been used to assist in the ingestion of Class A drugs. Leonard jogged over from the refrigerators and dumped some sandwiches on the counter. 'These too,' he said. 'And a big packet of Golden Virginia.' He looked at the thermometer. 'I'm not putting that up my bum without lube,' he said, laughing. The man behind the counter flashed the woman a wide-eyed look.

Benjamin had to peel another note from the roll to pay. Leonard was over at the coffee counter, squeezing his hand into his tight jeans pocket and sliding out a handful of coins. He huffed.

'I spose you want one do you?' he said.

Benjamin shrugged his shoulders as the woman put Leonard's muddy coffee down on the side. Steam rising from the Styrofoam cup.

'I'm okay. I can't drink it out of them anyway,' Benjamin said.

'Out of what?'

'That cup. I don't like the material the cup is made from. I don't like the texture. I bit one once and it made me feel strange.'

Leonard raised an eyebrow. The woman behind the counter put a biscuit next to Leonard's coffee and slid one over to Benjamin.

'Come on,' Leonard said, walking to the door.

On the way out, there was a panel on the wall by the toilet with five buttons on it. Each of the buttons had a face displaying various levels of satisfaction— ranging from very happy to very sad. Balancing the Golden Virginia, sandwiches and coffee across his hands and forearm, Leonard pressed the indifferent face in the middle.

'I think that's to rate the cleanliness of the bathroom facilities,' Benjamin said.

Leonard looked confused.

'I thought it was to tell them my current mood,' Leonard said.

The car started first time. In the back, Gary's tail thumped the tatty seats as it flicked from side to side, and Leonard fired a finger at the biscuit in Benjamin's hand.

'You going to eat that?' he said.

Benjamin had already read the label and it was stacked full of MSG and terrible fats.

'You have it,' he said.

Leonard unwrapped the biscuit and ate it. He shook the packet over his mouth to get the crumbs.

'Very efficient pit stop that,' he said. 'Fuel for the engines!' He slapped the dash, then his own belly.

Through his jeans, Benjamin checked his roll of cash. It felt depleted, even through the denim. He thought about suggesting they pay half each for the petrol, but couldn't think of a way to say it. Leonard looked intently at the sandwiches. He read the labels by holding the packaging close to his face, then tore them open. He jammed half of one into the packet for the other. Handed Benjamin the half.

'I got you a ham sandwich,' Leonard said.

Benjamin looked at the bright white bread—ham hanging out the side.

'I'm a vegetarian,' he said.

Leonard gave Benjamin's arm an investigative squeeze. 'I should have known. You look like a vegetarian.' Leonard took a large bite out of one of his sandwiches. As he moved the bread away from his face, a delicate strand of saliva connected the sandwich to his stubble.

'Just take the ham out,' he said, chewing.

'But then it will just be bread.'

'They're not my life choices, mate.'

Seventeen

Benjamin held Leonard's coffee with both hands while Leonard swung the car around erratically, skidding it into the corners and accelerating flat out as often as he could.

'The car is feeling underpowered today,' he said as it struggled up a hill. 'It must be the added weight of you and the dog.'

Leonard lit another cigarette, causing Benjamin to lean his head out of the window for fresh oxygen. He wondered if he should be doing that anyway, because: virus, but decided that the damage where Leonard was concerned was already done.

'How much do you weigh?' Leonard said.

'About 55 kilos,' Benjamin said.

'Give it to me in old money.'

'About 8 stone?'

Leonard looked Benjamin up and down. 'We'll eat something when we get to the caravan,' he said, flooring it out of a junction and along a tree-lined back road.

For a while, they snaked along the cliff tops, past rows of empty bungalows that were falling off the edge of the land and into the ocean, walls tumbling down into the sea. Benjamin imagined the bricks gathering under the waves, their neat manmade edges worn down by water.

The houses thinned out, the car bouncing along narrowing tracks between wide, open fields. Leonard stuck his fingers up at some cows.

'Why did you do that?'

'Cows are twats,' he said.

Gary squeezed his head through from the back so he could reach the open window beside Benjamin. As his tongue flapped about in the breeze, Benjamin looked at Gary's teeth, yellowing at the gums. Their condition made him anxious because of the relationship between teeth and heart health in humans. He made a mental note to follow it up.

The car struggled up another hill, filling the cockpit with the plastic smell of clutch. At the top, Leonard pulled into a layby with a gate. Benjamin pretended he couldn't smell the car's components burning. Gary sneezed.

'Like I say,' Leonard said, sniffing the air, 'it's a performance vehicle so it's optimised—power-to-weight-wise—for a single occupant. Not designed for you two lumps, anyway.'

Leonard jumped out of the car and walked up to the gate. It had chains around it and a sign that said: 'DEADLY EBOLA ZONE,' written in what looked like permanent marker on an old piece of skirting board.

'I thought the journey might be further with all that petrol we put in,' Benjamin said.

'I always fill up. It's more economical that way. And if we need to make a break for it we're not geographically limited. We could make it most of the way to Wales on a tank in this thing.'

Benjamin looked at the Ebola sign and wondered what 'a break for it' might entail.

'I've never been to Wales,' he said.

'We won't need to go to Wales,' Leonard said. 'But we almost could. If we needed to.'

Benjamin nodded.

'Do you think people believe your sign?' he said, pointing at it. 'Because that was in Africa, wasn't it?'

Leonard considered the comment.

'There were a few cases here. Anyway, it's just fear, Benjamin. Untamed fear through buzzwords.' He looked thoughtful. 'Maybe I should update it though?' 'ORIENTAL BAT FLU.'

'That seems racist.'

'Just a statement of fact. It is of the Orient. *Vis-à-vis*: oriental.'

Leonard took a key from his jeans pocket and put it into one lock, then spun the combination on another. He dragged the chain off and put his thumbs up at Benjamin.

The car bumped across the grass towards a stack of hay bales piled up in front of a tall hedgerow. Behind the hay bales they stopped next to a caravan covered in green and grey mould.

'I couldn't see this from the road,' Benjamin said.

'That's how I devised it,' Leonard said. 'Like *Grand Designs* for sneaky bastards.'

Benjamin opened the door for Gary to jump out. The dog immediately ran over to the hedgerow behind the caravan and cocked his leg to wee. Relieved, he walked along the rest of its length with his face pressed into the leaves.

'What's he doing?' Leonard said.

'He likes doing that on hedges,' Benjamin said. 'He likes to push his face into them.'

Benjamin turned back to the caravan. 'Is this your holiday home then?' he said, pointing.

'Yep. The Roadmaster VI,' Leonard said.

'So, it's not just where you live?'

'Not really. To be honest, it's easier to sleep in the car most of the time.'

Leonard put a key in the door, turning it slowly like he had crucial knowledge of the lock's inner workings.

'I don't think I can come in,' Benjamin shouted, imagining the spores that would be floating around, filling every cubic centimetre of the caravan's interior. Benjamin assumed Gary had concerns too, given that he was hovering with him, sniffing the air.

'We shouldn't go in there, I don't think,' Benjamin said to the dog, opening one of the tins of food and shaking the chunklets into a plastic takeaway tub from the car. Gary licked the Chum then lifted his head, distracted by Leonard who was lumping objects around inside. Leonard shouted out.

'You know he has no idea what you're saying?' he said.

Benjamin felt the blood rushing into the tiny vessels in his cheeks. He looked at Gary. He didn't think that was true. Maybe the dog didn't understand the words he was saying, but he definitely understood the feeling.

'You do understand, don't you?' he whispered, picking up the tray of reformed meat pieces in gravy and presenting them to the dog.

'Have some,' he said.

Gary looked at Benjamin, briefly, then jogged off. Benjamin walked over to the car and pressed his finger into a patch of rust without thinking. It made a tiny hole in the bodywork. Leonard popped his head out. 'What are you doing?' he said.

Benjamin stopped poking the car.

'You better not be fingering the rust.'

Benjamin looked at the orange dust on his index.

'Why don't you get a new car?' he said.

'I don't want one. It's a depreciating asset. Plus, I like that one.'

'Doesn't this car fail its MOT?'

'MOTs are for lemmings, like TV licences, speed limits and income tax. Besides, if I got a new one that would rust before long. Everything rusts this close to the sea.'

Leonard looked up at the sky. 'To be fair,' he said, thinking out loud, 'rust *is* just another metaphor for the gradual but inevitable decline.'

Benjamin shrugged his shoulders. The idea depressed him.

'Anyway, why can't you come in here?' Leonard said.

'It'll set my asthma off,' Benjamin said.

'What will?'

'Being in there.'

'It's in here, or out there, unfortunately.'

Benjamin didn't want to rush to make a decision. That's how people ended up with hepatitis and legionnaires and babies they didn't have the maturity to successfully care for. He needed to assess the data first.

'I'll think about it for a minute more,' he said, tearing the packaging off the thermometer and putting it in his mouth. Based on the sounds coming from the caravan, Benjamin tried to figure out what Leonard was up to. He heard the metallic dink of a pan being put on a hob, gas igniting, the popping sound of over-hot oil. He heard Leonard say something about 'passing up the opportunity to eyeball your own soul in the wilderness' and assumed it was a reference to his other suggestion of camping out and eating muddy carp. Benjamin took the thermometer out of his mouth and it read 37.1, which he knew to be normal.

'Good,' he said.

Leonard appeared at the door brandishing a pink spatula in one hand and a beer can in the other. He had a pinny on—it had the clearly defined abdominals of a bodybuilder printed on the front.

'Give me that,' he said, nodding at the thermometer.

Leonard wiped it on his t-shirt and put it in his mouth.

'You hungry?' he said mumbling around it, 'I'm cooking eggs.'

'A bit,' Benjamin said, hoping the eggs had those faint pink logos on them, that assured they weren't salmonella ridden. He thought about the residual faecal matter on eggshells that sometimes held on to downy feathers that his nan always made a point of washing off.

'The Egg Lord is in action!' Leonard said.

Leonard ducked back inside and started banging around again. One by one, the caravan windows popped open. Leonard stuck his head out.

'37!' he said, waving the thermometer. 'Absolutely fucking prime.' He threw it over his shoulder into the caravan, clapped his hands together, then picked up two bowls.

'I don't have any bread, so we'll have to eat them as is,' he said. 'Direct from the porcelain.'

Gary ran inside. Benjamin looked at his arm to see a mosquito humping his bicep. He slapped it off. Now that Zika, West Nile, Chikungunya, dengue, and malaria were on the table, going inside didn't seem so bad.

'I might just use the toilet,' he said.

Leonard was working at a hob in the semi-dark, concentrating hard on transitioning an egg from its shell into a frying pan.

'Yeah course. Just mind you don't dip your unit because I think some of the chemicals have made their way back up the waste system.'

'Dip my unit?' Benjamin said.

'Yeah. Be careful your John doesn't touch the water.'

Leonard pointed to a slim door across from where he was cooking that looked like a cupboard.

'In there,' he said, waving the spatula again, flicking bits of hot oil around. Benjamin walked over to the hob and tried to see the eggs' shells. They were all at the bottom of a bin further inside the kitchen.

'In there,' Leonard said. 'Bog's in there.'

The caravan wobbled as Benjamin made his way to the toilet and squeezed past a pile of dirty laundry that stopped the door from closing properly behind him. The toilet water was coated by a colourful film that shimmered like an oil spill on water and there was ivy growing in through the caravan wall. While Benjamin weed, Gary stood next to him, head unnecessarily close to the stream. Benjamin re-emerged to find Leonard coercing the eggs out of the pan with the pink spatula.

'I'm a fried egg specialist,' he said.

Benjamin took out the hand sanitiser he bought at the garage and squirted copious amounts onto his palms. Leonard handed him a fork and then ate his own egg in three untidy mouthfuls.

'Feel free to pepper,' Leonard said, turning a mill over his food like a TV chef. 'I'm going to use the facilities.'

Benjamin looked at the plate. He didn't want to get the shits or die so he checked for see-through bits, then ate some of the white. He slid the rest onto the floor for Gary. The yolk slapped the vinyl and burst. The dog was still licking the blobs from his muzzle when Leonard came back.

'Good?' Leonard said.

Benjamin nodded *yes*. He walked over to the sink to distract Leonard while Gary finished cleaning the floor. Leonard barely seemed to notice.

'Good eggs are all about confidence,' he stated, unprompted.

Benjamin didn't reply because what Leonard was saying didn't really make sense.

'Is this where I wash up?' he said.

'Usually,' Leonard said.

Benjamin rinsed his plate with cold water and put it on the drying rack. He picked up the pink spatula Leonard had used for the eggs.

'This doesn't look like a normal spatula,' he said.

'It's not—it's one of those scoops for cat shit.'

'Why has it got eggs on it?' Benjamin said, piecing the horrible puzzle together, realising that the cat scoop had been involved in the preparation of his food.

'It's got a good angle.'

Benjamin dry heaved. He spat what tiny remnants of egg he could find around the inside of his mouth into the sink.

'What are you doing?' Leonard said, as Benjamin put his head under the tap. He started rinsing and gargling. Spitting at the plughole.

'Steady on,' Leonard said. 'It never saw active duty.' He stuck his tongue out and moved the implement along the counter simulating a scooping. My ex took the cat with her; she just left the scoop.'

Benjamin stopped spitting.

'I'd also probably say it's safer than that water that's in your mouth. I always boil it before I allow any to enter my body because it's just been sat in a huge tank with no lid on it underneath the caravan. I found rats using it like a jacuzzi once.'

Benjamin continued spitting until there was virtually no saliva left in his mouth.

'I'm only joking,' Leonard said, laughing. 'The water is very sanitary.' He went over to Benjamin. 'Promise mate, it's clean.'

Eighteen

Leonard took a handful of clothes and sheets of paper—bills and official-looking documents, mostly with red print on them—off a reclining chair rammed in next to the bed.

'Take a seat mate,' he said, dumping the tat. When Benjamin hesitated, Gary jumped up in his place and curled his body with his nose under his back leg.

'Make yourself at home,' Leonard said to the dog. 'Weird croissant.'

'I can just stand,' Benjamin said.

Leonard tried to get his hands under Gary to lever him off. 'Chairs are for humans.'

'No, don't,' Benjamin said. 'He likes sitting up.'

Leonard shrugged.

'You have to show them who's boss. Put them in their place.'

'Why?'

'You just have to. It's an equilibrium thing.'

Benjamin looked confused.

'Sit on this then,' Leonard said, turning a bucket over and putting it next to the chair.

Benjamin looked around the room, at the cluttered surfaces covered in fishing paraphernalia and takeaway food tubs. He wiped his mouth with the inside of his T-shirt. He knew that if there had been a cat living there it wouldn't be long before he had some kind of a reaction.

'How long ago was there a cat here?' he said.

'Oh, it lived at the house I shared with my ex-wife. So never.'

Benjamin looked around.

'What do you think then? Quite the bolthole isn't it?' Leonard said.

'It's quite untidy,' Benjamin said.

'Wow. Be honest.'

Benjamin shrugged.

'I'm sorry if I don't spend all day arranging my possessions,' Leonard said.

Benjamin shrugged again. He thought about what it might be like to asphyxiate and die in a mouldy caravan.

'You'd prefer it if I lived in a show home, would you?'

Benjamin could see he'd offended Leonard but didn't know what to say to fix it. Things like that didn't always come naturally to him. Leonard stood up.

'I'd rather not fire too many of these glittering days of existence into oblivion by tidying and fussing around after my objects, that's all,' he said.

Leonard walked over to the fridge like he'd made a point. Gary lifted his head and watched Leonard come back with two beers.

'You want one?' he said.

'No thanks. I don't really drink beer.'

'Why don't you drink beer?'

'My nan put some special wine in a tiramisu once and I didn't like how it made me feel.'

Leonard cracked open the can and drank what looked to be half of its contents. Benjamin thought midday was quite early to be drinking beers, but he didn't say so.

'Beer is very refreshing,' Leonard said, holding up the can, looking at it intently. 'And also, it's all I have to drink. Not including the water in the tank. You can carry on drinking that if you want.'

When Leonard wasn't looking, Benjamin did a little spit into the collar of his T-shirt that left a wet patch above his heart.

'Some beers are good for your health,' Leonard said.

'I don't think that's true,' Benjamin said quietly.

'I don't mean, like, Fosters is good for you. I mean *a* beer, in general. I'm not talking about the physical being anyway. It's important to preserve the husk, I obviously know that—' Leonard pointed to various parts of his own slim-limbed body '—but some things are more important. Beers can help you transcend the planes.' He looked around like that had explained it.

Leonard looked at Benjamin directly again, his bright blue eyes unblinking, and neither of them spoke for a while. Benjamin thought about the people he'd seen in the newspaper at the garage, flying back to the UK, and hoped they would be monitored before they were allowed to circulate freely. He looked out of the small, curtained window, at the winter sun, and imagined them seeing the same bright-white silhouette from where they were quarantined. In a bunkbed-filled hangar or an emptied-out Travel Lodge next to a dual carriageway. He thought of his nan, too. He wondered if she was scared of what was happening to her like he knew he would be, or if she even felt things like that now. He couldn't imagine not being scared all the time. Didn't know if it required a kind of numb detachment, or if the absence of fear was something better. Whether you could understand what was happening to your body and still be free of worry.

He thought of all of them. The people on the plane, his nan, Leonard, Camille, everyone at once, pivoting around an identical point in the sky. All of them, in that small way, almost the same. Leonard lifted his head in Gary's direction.

'I sometimes feel a bit like how he looks,' he said. 'A beer definitely helps with that. With the old blue moods.'

Benjamin looked up at Leonard and watched him scratching his stubble.

'It's a fairly robust defence against wanting to swim out to sea until I sink,' he said. 'Which I'd do I reckon.' He took another sip. 'Drift out until I'm swallowed up by the ocean mistress.'

Leonard looked skywards, imagining how that would feel maybe, or whether he really would.

'Potentially, I'd throw myself into a canal if I was somewhere more metropolitan and lacked the necessary beers,' he said.

Benjamin looked straight at him.

'I've filled the quota for wallowing, I know,' Leonard said, opening another can and sliding it across the table.

'Thanks,' Benjamin said, leaving it where it was.

Leonard drank.

'Sometimes I sleep in really late,' Benjamin said.

'Any reason?'

'It just think it feels easier, sometimes. To sleep.'

Leonard smiled.

'I know what you mean. I always think it would be great if they invented a piece of technology—wires to your head, input device like a Game Boy—that can manipulate your consciousness. And you can tell it how long you want your brain switched off for. Or maybe how much time you want to fast-forward through. So that you could avoid being intellectually available for things you don't want to have to deal with. Like court cases, drawn-out divorces, vomiting bugs. That sort of thing.'

It was funny to hear Leonard say that because Benjamin had imagined something similar. A way to switch off his awareness and still progress through unpleasant events or futures. Some days, if he didn't have work, Benjamin stayed in bed until lunchtime. 'I'd use it quite often,' he said.

He wondered if Leonard felt like that because he was lonely. Because he didn't have anyone to make him feel better about things. Benjamin had been feeling that way a lot more since his nan had been in hospital.

'Do you like my portrait?' Leonard said, interrupting the

thought, pointing to a gilt-framed painting of a family hanging on the wall.

'Is that your family?' Benjamin said.

Leonard laughed.

'Oh no. I just found it in a charity shop and liked the composition. The dad looks like an absolute bastard, doesn't he? I bet he makes the children play instruments they hate and forces them to eat asparagus.'

The family looked wealthy. And the dad *did* look like a bastard. Benjamin didn't think making your children eat vegetables made you a bastard, though. Because they're one of the most beneficial food groups. The father in the painting had his face angled upwards, which gave the impression that he was looking down on Leonard's living space.

'I like to imagine they were the victims of some kind of financial ruin,' Leonard said.

Benjamin leant closer. It was clear from the brushstrokes that this was a real painting. There was an overweight labrador by their feet. Benjamin hoped that if they'd suffered financial ruin the dog at least was okay—that he was still alive. The dated clothing made him think probably he wasn't.

Camille had views on dead pets. She said she had a cat with alopecia once. She said that, when it died, she didn't have to be sad because she felt lucky for all the time they'd had together; that the cat was a gift and that wherever it had gone it was nowhere bad. She also said she was fully subscribed to the concept of reincarnation and a cat of that power and divinity would almost certainly be a person in the next life. A famous one, most probably, or someone on the telly like Chris Tarrant or Amanda Holden. Benjamin looked at Gary and knew he was a gift. The trouble was that, in his mind, he couldn't help feeling that the 'nowhere bad' Camille talked about was more likely to be nowhere at all. He wished Camille was there to reassure him.

Benjamin went back to the bucket Leonard had given him

and sat down. Leonard slumped in his armchair. He pressed his weight back until a footrest emerged from underneath on mechanical legs. He opened another beer.

'So you ever had a dog before then?' Leonard said.

'No,' Benjamin said. 'How about you?'

'Nah. I don't like the idea of having petrified shits all over the garden.'

Leonard looked around like he was searching for something else to talk about. He leant over and used his index finger to inspect the dog's leg, touching a soft patch of skin that covered the bone of his ankle and the powerful ligament attached behind it like a sail.

'That's a cool bit that is,' Leonard said. 'Like a paper lantern.'

While Leonard rolled a cigarette on the flattest bit of his thigh, Benjamin looked at the smudged tattoos of flames and a mermaid on his forearm, at the black lines turned blue, dispersing outwards under the surface of his skin. Tattoos made Benjamin feel strange. Permanent marks on soft flesh. Irreversible degradation of a body. He wondered if they'd been done by a professional.

'What do they mean?' he said, pointing at Leonard's arm.

'What do you mean, what do they mean?'

'Your tattoos.'

'That's very personal.'

'Oh, sorry,' Benjamin said.

'No, it's fine. You just have to make sure you don't ask the wrong person. You know, like someone who's been in prison. Don't ask them.'

Benjamin wondered if Leonard had ever been incarcerated. Leonard moved his hand over the skin on his forearms. He looked at his tattoos like he hadn't seen them in a long time, then thrust his forearm up and out in front of him. He pointed at the mermaid.

'I got this the night I met Sally,' he said.

'The one you asked about in the club?'

'Yeah, that's her. The exact reason eludes me. But I suppose mermaids are women, sort of. And Sally is a woman. Wherever she is.'

Benjamin assumed that Sally was Leonard's girlfriend or wife. He imagined waking up with a mythical creature indelibly recreated on the pale flesh of his forearm and felt sick. 'It's nice,' he said.

'She had a kind of follow-me-into-the-abyss black magic that I found very erotic,' Leonard said. 'But she had too many fixed aspects in the end. She wasn't adaptable enough to my fast-evolving and constantly-refining personality attributes. I underwent a personal transformation—like water changing to ice—during our relationship.'

Benjamin nodded like he knew what Leonard was talking about, even though he didn't, exactly. He tightened the laces in his trainers while Leonard stared into the distance at nothing in particular.

'It was basically mutual though,' he said. 'Her leaving.' Leonard scratched at a bit of mud on his jeans. 'The other tattoos are almost all meaningless to be honest,' he said.

After that they both sat watching Gary sleep. It wasn't long before Benjamin's eyelids started to feel heavy again. He rested his head against the wall, squinting through the blur of his eyelashes.

'You look like you could do with a nap,' Leonard said.

Benjamin nodded.

'Now that we're here laying low, there's not much to do. Fuck all actually. Treat yourself to some kip,' Leonard said. 'We can talk strategy when you wake up.'

Even with the tub digging into his backside, it wasn't long before Benjamin nodded off. Not a deep sleep, but a broken and anxious one. He surfaced from time to time and checked on Gary. At some point he woke up and Leonard was gone. He felt a sudden panic, but only until he saw Gary still sleeping in the chair. There was a chill piling in through the open door. Benjamin went to close it and saw Leonard looking straight at him from outside, holding his phone to the side of his head.

'Feeling any better?' he said, as he came back in.

Benjamin nodded and yawned. Leonard slid the phone into a cupboard, then moved some items around in the kitchen, busying himself. He perched on the corner of the bed like he was thinking about something important.

'I know,' he said suddenly, walking over to the fridge. He took a lunchbox from the freezer compartment and opened it up. 'I'll show you my sparrow.'

Leonard held out the tub. Inside it, there was a frozen bird. 'I found this outside. A few years ago,' he said.

Benjamin leant away from the plastic vessel and its contents.

'What is it?' he said.

'It's a sparrow.'

'It's dead,' Benjamin said.

'I know. That's why I have it. Look at his wings.'

Benjamin leant forward but not too close.

'It's not going to bite you,' Leonard said, moving the container closer. 'Have a look. I can't have it out too long though. I don't want him thawing out.'

The bird's body had been suspended in time, its shadow-black feathers coated in swirls of frost. Benjamin imagined its frozen organs, the minute organic structures that Leonard had preserved in his freezer, and it made him feel sad. The bird wasn't alive, but it wasn't completely gone, either. It was hard to imagine what could have changed to account for the difference when its body was so perfectly intact. Leonard pushed the lid closed on the tub and slid it back inside the freezer drawer. He walked to the doorway and lit a cigarette, then stared into the distance.

'They did an experiment once where scientists weighed

people before and after they died,' Benjamin said. 'To see if the life in you has a weight.'

'Weird,' Leonard said.

Benjamin thought about the life in Gary, as he watched him scratching and tunnelling at the blankets on the armchair, piling them under himself. Leonard took a long draw on his cigarette, then blew the smoke out of the door. He turned back and tapped the ash into a mug on the table.

'Never actually seen a dog make its bed better by doing that,' he said.

Benjamin's nap must have been longer than he thought. Outside, it was already starting to get dark. He sat silently while Leonard rifled through a drawer full of batteries and unopened envelopes. He found a torch and disappeared behind the Roadmaster. A few minutes later, a generator fired up and the lights came on.

'I'm going to have a couple more beers on the roof,' Leonard said. 'So I'll just sleep in the armchair. You take the bed.'

After he went out, his disembodied voice shouted back, 'if he's sleeping in here tonight make sure he's careful on the rug.' After a pause: 'It's basically priceless.'

NINETEEN

Benjamin kept his clothes on because he didn't know how recently the sheets had been cleaned. He lay on the covers like he was doing an impression of a pencil—straight out with his hands by his sides—and listened to the sound of Leonard's shoes squeaking on the ladder as he climbed onto the roof. Gary jumped onto the bed and stretched out next to him, squeezing his nose in under Benjamin's side. He was warm like a hot water bottle. Benjamin liked feeling the steady rhythm of his breathing and the weight of him there, pressing on his thigh. For a moment, he let himself believe that Gary was his, that he'd bought him in the normal way, or got him at an animal rescue centre. That he'd trained him not to wee on the carpet and to come back when he called his name. That he was fully insured against illness by a recognised organisation like Norwich Union, and that he had one of those tracking implants with Benjamin's contact details in his neck skin. It made him feel good. Less like it was just him trying to figure everything out all the time. That while his nan was in hospital he wasn't completely alone.

Above them, whenever Leonard shifted his weight or moved around, it looked like the roof was bowing in the middle. As his eyes adjusted, Benjamin could see dark patches all over the ceiling that looked like mould. He closed his eyes and wondered if the roof was designed to support the weight of a man, then swung his legs around and stood up. Gary lifted his head as Benjamin removed his inhaler from the ziplock sandwich bag and took two puffs.

'You stay here,' he said, watching Gary's eyes open and close until he drifted into sleep again.

Outside, Benjamin used the stepladder to reach the height of the roof and peered over the top. Leonard was lying on his back and looking up at the sky with a cigarette in his mouth. He had another beer open beside him.

'Is it safe up there?' Benjamin said.

Leonard lolled his head towards Benjamin and opened an eye. 'Is anywhere truly safe?' he said.

'Yeah,' Benjamin said. 'Police stations and banks are safe.'

Benjamin stepped across onto the roof.

'Hasn't anyone ever told you those give you cancer?' Benjamin said, as Leonard took a drag on his roll-up.

Leonard held up the pouch. 'Course they have. Look at these horrific images.'

Even though it was difficult to make out the detail in the dark, Benjamin still didn't look.

'I couldn't sleep,' he said.

Leonard leant over and held out his beer. 'That's understandable. We're at the centre of a complex moral scenario. Your nap earlier probably refreshed you.'

Benjamin stared at the can.

'I've only just opened it,' Leonard said. 'It's got a clean top—very sanitary, look.'

Benjamin shook his head. Leonard leant down to an unopened can by his side and cracked it open.

'Come on,' he said. 'Have some.'

Benjamin took a sip of the beer and Leonard's face lit up.

'That's better,' he said, laughing. 'Now sit down.'

Benjamin looked around at the roof, at the spots of moss and darker, more ominous patches. Leonard threw him a jumper to sit on and Benjamin managed to crouch down without his hands touching. He looked out towards the rigs, standing upright on a smoky horizon.

'How long have you lived here?' Benjamin said.

'All my life.'

'You must like it.'

'Not sure I like it,' Leonard said, flicking his cigarette butt out into the open air. 'Places like this just have a funny kind of gravity, don't they?'

Benjamin sat staring out. The moon lit up a neat navy-blue horizon in front of them.

'I did think about moving once,' Leonard said. 'When Sally and I parted ways and all that. I lost it a bit to be honest—ended up waving a medieval broadsword around on the high street. All very ugly.' Leonard looked across at Benjamin to see his reaction. He reached into his pocket and took out a brown leather wallet that looked like he'd had it half his life. He showed Benjamin a photobooth picture of a woman behind a clear plastic window. 'I keep meaning to get rid of this, obviously,' he said. 'But that's her. If you're interested.'

Leonard held the wallet unsteadily in front of Benjamin for a second or two. The woman had a nice smile. The kind you know is genuine. 'When she left, the plan was to become a professional driver. I maybe didn't manage the transition that well.'

'You wanted to deliver Chinese?'

'I wanted to be a *professional driver*. Not many stuntman jobs going around here. To tell you the truth, I basically just hate working. It's boring and meaningless.' He took a sip of beer. 'Hence my nomadic lifestyle,' he said, gesturing towards the car and caravan, the wallet hanging open in his hand.

'I don't mind working,' Benjamin said.

'That's because you're of the herd, mate. You crave instruction. I have enough insight to see that it's all essentially pointless and unfulfilling. No offence.'

Benjamin drank another tiny sip of the beer.

'What about you?' Leonard said.

'I finished sixth form last year. Not sure yet. I work at the supermarket.'

Benjamin watched a shooting star slide across his peripherals, scoring a bright white line in the night sky. Leonard didn't see it.

'An educated man then,' Leonard said. He bowed his head slowly, in approval, then took a long drag on his cigarette. He blew the smoke out sideways and rooted around in the wallet again. He took out a few more photos.

'Here I am,' he said, handing over a black-and-white snap of himself shaking hands with another snooker player, both of them with full, flowing hair to their shoulders. Leonard had pale skin and his hair looked clean. Almost unrecognisable.

'I saw some photos of you on the walls,' Benjamin said. 'At the club.'

'I was a professional,' Leonard said, sliding the wallet back into his jeans pocket. 'Won some pretty big championships, actually.'

'I don't have any hobbies,' Benjamin said.

'I only started playing because my old man got to watch the snooker sometimes while he was locked up. I'd never done very much to impress him. But he seemed impressed by snooker players. He died before I was a pro or anything, so he wouldn't have seen my games. But I always imagined him there when I played.'

Leonard fell silent and the wind picked up. The moon was bright enough to light up the field around them, catching in the water droplets that clung to the grass.

'I played at the Crucible,' Leonard said.

'I don't know what that is.'

'Just a big venue in Sheffield. The biggest really.'

Leonard blew air out like he'd had a long day. Or a long life. A mile or so out they could see the red and green lights of fishing boats bobbing around offshore. They seemed small and isolated, surrounded by the great grey expanse of water and sky.

'What do you think we should do?' Benjamin said, interrupting the quiet.

'What?'

'About Gary.'

Leonard laughed.

Benjamin avoided eye contact.

'They might let me see him, do you think?'

Leonard inhaled. Shook his head slowly.

'These people aren't going to let you see him on weekends mate. You took their dog.'

'I didn't take him. He's been following me.'

'Not how they're going to see it, I'm afraid.'

Benjamin suddenly felt the hopelessness creeping in. Thinking about the slim dog lying in the caravan below, someone taking him away, made it feel like the air was less nourishing. Like he needed more and more of it just to stay conscious. He knew they were meant to be together, or Gary wouldn't have followed him home. Wouldn't have stayed with him without a lead this whole time. In the silence, Benjamin could hear the ocean, heavy and deep. He thought about what Leonard had said, about a place having gravity, and, for a second, he wondered if he could feel its pull.

'Why are you helping me, Leonard?' Benjamin said. But Leonard's eyes were closed. He was asleep.

Benjamin climbed down and went back inside. Gary lifted his head as Benjamin lay down next to him in the darkness. Before he nodded off, he heard Leonard in the doorway, brushing his teeth. He spat down into the grass when he was done, then took off his boots and zipped himself into a sleeping bag. Benjamin imagined someone striking Leonard's head. His brain bumping around in his skull.

'When they were beating you up, Leonard,' he said, 'were you scared?'

'Little bit,' Leonard said, then he paused, letting the thought sit. 'Did you know that honey badgers don't feel fear?' he said.

Benjamin didn't reply. He rolled over and looked at the spot on the floor where Leonard was lying in the darkness, then at where he could hear Gary breathing.

'That's freedom,' Leonard said eventually. 'Complete freedom.'

Twenty

When Benjamin woke up, there was a breeze coming in through the open door again. Gary was curled up by his feet, half-covered in blanket. Benjamin's neck was itching, and his lungs felt tight, which he assumed was because of the mould. He took two puffs of the inhaler and walked to the doorway.

Leonard was on the very edge of the cliff, looking out to sea. He was doing slow-motion martial arts without a shirt on. Benjamin walked towards him. He stopped a few feet to his right with Gary close by his side.

'I'm just doing my breathing exercises,' Leonard said without looking at him, the wind blowing his hair around, torso covered in goose pimples.

'Is that some sort of martial art?' Benjamin said.

'No. Martial arts are for wankers. I just make it up.'

'I was going to say. I saw you in that fight,' Benjamin said.

Leonard flicked his burning cigarette at Benjamin's feet. Benjamin and Gary recoiled as one.

'Look, it's very difficult to fight multiple opponents,' he said, rapidly punching the air. 'I got jumped in that snooker club.'

Benjamin kept quiet.

'Anyway, I do this for mindfulness purposes, but also because too many people deny the physical aspect.' Leonard pointed at Gary who was sticking close to Benjamin but weeing on mole hills. 'We're just like him. Only we've shed our fur and moved indoors.' He lifted his leg off the ground and kicked at the air. 'We must acknowledge our need to move.'

From where they were standing, Benjamin could see the beach running along the bottom of the cliff. At the top, there were empty fields, filled with grass that had been left to grow unchecked. The cliff sloped down towards town until it levelled out and joined the front itself. The top of a rollercoaster was looming over the arcades and chip shops, rows of multi-coloured lightbulbs running along its metal body. Some of them flickered in the haze. Leonard finished by grabbing an invisible opponent and throwing a headbutt. The bruises on his face were muted in the daylight, but they still looked very painful. The wind from the ocean blew up and over the hill, pressing the blades of grass down in the same uniform direction. Beyond the front, towards home, Benjamin could just about make out the dead whale, shrunk by distance. The sea was lapping up around it and there were people there. Several small boats were waiting in the shallow water nearby. It looked like they were going to try to drag it back out to sea.

'How do you think it died?' Benjamin said.

Leonard squinted.

'The whale?' he said.

'Yeah.'

'It was probably driven off course by high-pitched underwater sounds from heavy machinery on the rigs,' he said. 'Or for emotional reasons.' He cocked his head to the side and raised his hands to turn the statement into a question. 'Maybe its wife swam off with a more proficient provider of krill.' He laughed briefly, then turned serious. 'Or she was a more proficient provider of krill and he had outdated feelings about gender that caused him significant inner conflict. Destructive insecurities, that type of thing.'

Benjamin gave it some thought.

'But maybe it just gave up,' Leonard said. 'Sometimes it's

too much of a struggle, isn't it? Even for whales. It's probably full of plastic bags, too, the poor bugger.'

'What are they doing to it?'

'If you don't do something with them the gases build up and they explode,' Leonard said.

Benjamin doubted that.

'Honestly. They practically detonate. Bits get fired hundreds of metres into the air. It's terrible for tourism. Chunks of whale carcass landing on little kids. All that stuff.'

When Leonard stopped speaking, a gust of wind made Gary dash forwards as if it was chasing him. He jumped and nipped like it was a game, running one way before changing direction whenever he felt the breeze.

'He's not right,' Leonard said, shaking his head.

After a few bursts, Gary ran further away, stretching his legs. He came back to Benjamin and stood with his tongue dangling.

'Why don't you have a run?' Leonard said to the dog, motioning with his arm. 'You've got a whole field here.'

Gary stayed where he was. He looked between Leonard and Benjamin, then—when a heavier wave came crashing down on the beach—at the sea.

'I've had an excellent idea,' Leonard said, picking up his T-shirt and walking back towards the caravan barefoot. He dragged at a sheet of blue tarpaulin that was covering something over. Whatever it was, it was obscured by weeds, so he started pulling handfuls of those up, too. As the plastic sheet came away, Benjamin saw an old motorbike leaning there, rusted. The stringy undergrowth was growing through and there was bird mess all over the seat.

'Bloody birds have shat on it,' Leonard said, pushing his hair behind his ear and crouching down to assess the damage. 'Can you believe it?'

He pulled the bike out by the handlebars, dragging it with

all his weight, leaning backwards until it came free. He brushed the seat clean with his forearm.

'If we can get this started, we can get him running full tilt,' Leonard said, excited. 'Work out a rough max speed.'

Leonard used the T-shirt in his hand to wipe dirt from the speedo then folded out the kick starter and jumped on it with all his strength. The bike didn't start. His hair fell into his eyes.

He leant the bike from side to side. 'It sometimes helps to slosh the petrol around. To reinvigorate it,' he said.

After a few more kicks the engine spluttered and Leonard beamed. He pushed his hair out of his eyes then slapped the tank and nodded. When he tried again the bike sounded closer to life. He jumped—his face reddening, a bead of sweat sliding down his forehead—and opened up the throttle to catch it. Black smoke came piling out of the exhaust. The sweet smell of petrol and two-stroke. Gary stayed well back, eyeballing the bike as it popped away, Leonard holding it upright.

'Can you ride?' Leonard said, revving erratically and grinning.

'I've never tried,' Benjamin said, taking in the run-down motorcycle.

'Today's the day then.'

Leonard swung his leg over the seat and pulled away. 'I'll do a safety check,' he shouted back. 'After that you can have a go.'

Benjamin shook his head. Motorbikes didn't interest him in the slightest, particularly ones as poorly maintained as this. There was no telling what could go wrong—he could be left lying in the middle of the field with the bone sticking out of his leg and bits of hedgerow skewering his organs.

'I'll be fine,' he said, but Leonard didn't hear. He was crunching through the gears and bouncing across the pasture. Gary sat by Benjamin's feet watching the motorbike as it moved along the far side of the field, then along the higher edge of the hill. Leonard was grinning, his hair blowing around the sides of his face. After a couple of laps he came back.

'Your go,' he said, leaning the bike on its stand.

Benjamin looked down at his own feet. 'I'm fine,' he said. 'I don't like that sort of thing.'

'What? Being alive sorts of things?'

'No, dangerous sorts of things.'

Leonard's shoulder sank for a second like he was genuinely disappointed.

'Wait there,' he said, running to the caravan, disappearing inside. Benjamin heard him going through cupboards again. A few seconds later he came running back out with a white motorcycle helmet that was missing its visor. He held it up, inspecting it at range.

'Here it is,' he said. 'A premium helmet! You'll be indestructible in this.'

Leonard handed Benjamin the helmet like it was something very valuable. It was covered in knocks and marks and the orange foam lining was crumbling away.

'Put it on and I'll do it up,' Leonard said.

Benjamin moved the helmet closer to his head. He looked inside at the perished rubber seals.

'It's fully certified for its safety this one mate—all the proper stickers.'

There were green circles of mould on the leather lining. Leonard pointed at a golden sticker on the back.

'This one means it's signed off for racing,' he said. 'One of the most premium lids money can buy. Or it was, when I found it.'

Leonard stepped forward and lifted the helmet, but Benjamin recoiled. Leonard nodded at Gary.

'Honestly mate, you won't regret it. You'll be able to inhabit his world.'

Gary ran over. He was breathing hard and looking happy. As

improbable as it seemed to Benjamin, it genuinely looked like the dog was smiling.

Benjamin shifted his weight around, bouncing from one foot to the other in the way he always did when he was nervous.

'Maybe I could try,' he said.

Leonard did up the strap under Benjamin's chin, looping the fabric through two metal rings. His hands smelt oily and mechanical. The helmet flopped about on Benjamin's head.

'It's a perfect fit!' Leonard said.

He talked Benjamin through the controls. 'It's so simple,' he said. 'Twist the right handlebar to go, pull the right lever for the front brake and push the foot brake on the right side for the back. Gears are on the left.'

It didn't sound simple. Gary held back while they talked, watching the two of them intently as Leonard explained. 'Explained' felt generous. It was more like Leonard was saying left and right over and over again. Benjamin climbed on.

'There's no clutch so even a simpleton could ride it,' Leonard said, revving the engine again. 'Just stand on that to put it in gear.' He pointed at a metal bit near the footrest. 'Then twist the throttle when you're ready.'

Benjamin was sweating so much his hands felt wet. He rubbed them on his legs, watching Leonard click the bike into first.

'Give it some revs,' Leonard said, manipulating Benjamin's hand so the bike crept forwards. It didn't really need any revs to roll in first. Benjamin kept his feet down for balance and Leonard manually rolled him along to make him go. As Benjamin started moving off across the grass, Gary made a muted barking sound. He took a few steps forwards, then started running.

'That's it,' Leonard shouted as Benjamin pulled away: 'now second gear and open it up!'

But Benjamin carried on at the same speed, in the same gear. He was about 20 metres away when Gary lengthened his stride to keep up, to stay close to him. Benjamin laughed when he saw the dog following with his tongue hanging out.

'He's like a nature documentary,' Leonard shouted.

And he was right. When he was running, Gary looked like a different animal. Not shrinking like he did in the cold, but unfolding, becoming the thing he was supposed to be. His lean body and slim legs all conspiring to move him forwards, as though running fast was the most natural thing in the world for him. As though all this time he'd been still and quiet, he'd just been waiting to go.

Benjamin's eyes flicked between the grass in front of him and the dog beside. Seeing Gary run made him start to relax. He twisted the throttle a fraction more and crunched up a gear, changing the pitch of the engine, feeling the spongy suspension soaking up the bumps in the field. With each stride, Gary's body stretched out then contracted, bringing his four legs under his stomach to a point of almost touching.

Benjamin cut a diagonal line across the short green grass of the field. About halfway, Gary accelerated and pulled away from him, running a huge loop, leaning into the corners with his eyelids pulled back and his tongue hanging from his mouth. The bright sun reflected off the fur on his ribs. And even over the rumble of the engine, Benjamin swore he could hear the sound of Gary's paws drumming the earth, feel each rapid step in the fullest part of his chest.

Twenty-one

Benjamin rode around the field in wide, slow circles until Gary stopped to defecate.

'I'll get you a bag,' Leonard yelled, walking in the direction of the caravan. 'He's really pumping one out. Like Mr. Whippy.'

Leonard came back with a carrier bag and Benjamin took it, still wrestling to get the bike on its stand. When he started organising the carrier bag around his hand, Leonard burst out laughing.

'I was only joking,' he said. 'It's just a shit in a field.' He pointed at the caravan. 'I did an inventory while you were sleeping. I'm probably going to need that bag for supplies, anyway.'

'I thought you had food inside?' Benjamin said, sure he'd seen some in the cupboards.

Leonard shrugged. 'We're definitely all out.'

Gary was pacing to cool down. His ears lying flat on his head, fleshy pink bits facing out like he'd opened his vents. Leonard pointed at them.

'That's excellent,' he said. 'Sports Mode.'

'Are you sure you need to go shopping today?' Benjamin said. 'Don't you think we should stay here?'

'We can either go and get something in town, or I can use my air rifle to shoot a rabbit?' Leonard said. He looked at Benjamin from the corner of his eye. 'Killing a rabbit is definitely something I could do for us.'

Benjamin looked around at the cloudless sky.

'Did you know the technical term for skinning a rabbit is 'unzipping?' Leonard said. 'Very vivid, isn't it?' He repeated the word slowly. 'UN-ZI-PPING. I also did a pigeon once. On a survival training weekend. I had to put my thumb down its neck hole.'

Benjamin gagged. 'The supermarket makes sense,' he said, repulsed by the image but also upset by the realisation he was supposed to be at work. He shot Leonard a panicked look.

'I'm supposed to be at work today,' he said. He flapped his hands about.

'At the supermarket?'

'Yeah, back tills. They'll be short.'

Camille would normally have been doing her round soon, depositing the cash into large plastic envelopes, heels slipping from the backs of her worn black flats. He pictured her distractedly pressing a biro into the soft, white flesh on her hand to write down which tills she'd collected from. She'd probably have to cover him later if he wasn't there.

'I should tell Camille,' Benjamin said.

'Tell her what?' Leonard said.

'That I won't be in.'

'What if she asks questions?'

'She won't. I trust her. I can tell her I'm looking after a dog. She likes animals.'

'I'm not sure that's a good idea,' Leonard said.

Benjamin began scripting the conversation in his head.

'I just won't tell her what dog it is.'

Leonard screwed his face up.

'I think I should do it,' he said. 'Save you lying.'

Benjamin hesitated.

'I'll just say I'm your uncle and you've got the shits.'

Benjamin assumed his face had contorted because Leonard revised the offer.

'I'll tell her you have a high temperature and a loss of taste sensation,' he said, holding out his phone and winking.

Benjamin didn't want to lie to Camille. Camille said that lying could indicate a blocked throat chakra. She said that if this was the case, a person's ability to speak their own personal truth and express their fundamental human creativity could be hindered. Benjamin didn't know what his own personal truth was, but he wanted to be able to speak it if he ever needed to. He also didn't like the idea of being directly dishonest to her.

He punched in the number.

While the phone rang, Leonard cleared his throat. He put the phone on speaker so Benjamin could hear and waited until Camille picked up.

'Hi, I'm looking for Camille?' Leonard said.

'Speaking,' she said.

'Hi Camille, this is Leonard.'

'Hello, Leonard.'

'I'm Benjamin's uncle.'

'Ah lovely, such a wonderful boy.'

'Thank you so much for saying that, Camille. We're all very proud of him.' Leonard did a comedy eyeroll.

Benjamin couldn't take his eyes off Leonard as he spoke—the ease of his fabrication, the comfort of his performance, was shocking.

'He's not mentioned an uncle before,' Camille said.

'No, no. Well. I've been away for some time.'

'How lovely. Have you been travelling?'

'In a way, Camille, yes. In a way. So, about Benjamin?'

'Oh yes. Benjamin.'

'Unfortunately, he's not going to make it in for his shift today. He's sick.'

Camille emitted the universal tut and yawn of sympathy. 'I knew something didn't feel right,' she said. 'In a funny way, I could sense it.'

Leonard raised his eyebrow at Benjamin. Camille continued.

'I looked at his name on the rota and it was like this—disturbance. What's ailing him?' she said.

Leonard stuttered. 'He's got the shi. . . the shingles.'

'Oh dear,' Camille said. 'That is bad.'

Leonard gave a solemn nod, an echo of his dedication to the performance.

'Do you need any remedies?' Camille said. 'I could drop some off? Or some fish oil.'

Leonard moved the phone away from his face so she couldn't hear him laughing. He obstructed the sound with his hand until he'd composed himself enough to bring it close again.

'Camille,' he said. 'That is such a kind, kind offer—but I think we'll be fine.' He looked around. 'I'm actually a medical professional, myself,' he said.

Even Leonard looked surprised by this new riff on the backstory.

'Oh fantastic,' she said. 'What a lucky nephew.'

Leonard raised his eyebrows.

'So lucky,' he said. 'So so lucky.'

Camille didn't say anything to that. Leonard cut in again.

'Anyway, Camille. It's been a pleasure, but I must go. Patients . . . to see.'

'Goodbye,' Camille said.

When Leonard hung up, Benjamin half-expected him to bow. He followed him to the caravan and waited while he retrieved some bags for life from inside.

'That was brilliant,' Leonard said. 'Very exhilarating.'

Gary had fallen asleep on the rug. Every few seconds his legs all moved in unison like he was running.

'He's dreaming about running,' Benjamin said.

Leonard turned to look at the dog. He laughed. 'Aren't we all,' he said.

He waved the bags in the air. 'I was thinking about that

shopping trip I mentioned,' he said, walking to the door. 'I think the best thing to do is for you to wait here. I'll take the dog with me so you can relax.'

Benjamin didn't like that idea.

'I want him to stay with me,' he said.

'Okay,' Leonard said. 'But I've heard his owners are Japanese Yakuza or something.'

Benjamin thought about it.

'In Norfolk?'

'Yeah, or similar. Maybe they're Russian Mafia. Anyway, ethnicity aside, it would be good for him to hang his head out of the window of a moving vehicle. Dogs love that.'

Benjamin was sure. 'I'm keeping him,' he said.

Leonard stood thinking for a bit. He made a pained face.

'Okay,' he said. 'If that's what you want. I'll go lone wolf. Just make sure the Prawn Lord doesn't get up to no good.'

Benjamin nodded. He liked the idea of staying with Gary and definitely not killing a rabbit. Leonard looked at the grass around his feet.

'Have you got any more of that wedge, by the way?' he said.
'Wedge?'

Leonard rubbed his fingers together. 'Money, mate,' he said.

Benjamin reached into his inside pocket and took out the roll of notes. He looked at the money for a second, then gave Leonard a twenty.

'Might be safer if I have £40, I reckon?' Leonard said, looking at his shoes.

'Will you get him something too?' Benjamin said, talking about Gary. 'He didn't really like the tins I got him.'

'Yeah, well—he's economical, isn't he. What's he eaten since you've had him?'

'He's eaten a bowl of porridge. Some spring rolls. The Chinese food you gave him. And some ants.'

Benjamin remembered the ants darting across the back

porch of the caravan. About their lives ending in the acid in Gary's stomach. He swam a little, at the idea of their small and compact existences coming to an end with the wet press of a dog's tongue. It was all very bleak, the idea a little too big to fit.

'A diet like that—he's living like a king by the sounds of it, but I'll see what I can do.' Leonard tapped the side of his nose.

Benjamin sat on the step as Leonard bumped back across the field in his car. Gary had woken up and appeared in the doorway, his head hovering over Benjamin's shoulder. He slipped past, then walked over to the hedgerow to urinate in the spot where he'd previously rubbed his face along the heavily-scented leaves. Benjamin watched as the dog sniffed bits of grass that seemed significant, remembering the way Gary had watched him go inside the hospital like he was worried about being away from him. He imagined the hospital hallways again, his nan in her room, body so slight the bed looked empty from her neck down. His skin felt strange. He thought about the parts of him he wanted to wash, then about the exact moment the whale on the beach had swum too far inland to ever make it back out again.

'Let's go for a walk,' he said, standing up.

Once they'd left Leonard's land, Benjamin and Gary skirted a farmer's field cut up by heavy black channels. They walked between tall yellow crops, Gary jogging a few feet in front while Benjamin held his hands above his head in case the farmer had used hazardous chemicals or pesticides to make the produce grow. As they walked uphill, Benjamin looked out at the unbroken horizon, at the waves rolling in and breaking.

After a while they came to a road. The verges were overgrown and it was covered in potholes like it had been forgotten about a long time ago. It led to the bungalows they'd driven past in the car—the ones all balanced on the cliff edge, sliding inch by inch into the ocean. The houses were surrounded by metal fences with warning signs, overgrown front gardens with sun-bleached pots full of weeds and dry mud. Sad museums to the people who used to live there.

Benjamin walked past a letterbox that lay rusting on the floor. He crouched down to read the address but could only see some of the name.

David T—, it said.

He was imagining a man called David planting bright flowers in the pots, mud pressed deep into the cracks of his fingers, when he looked up to see Gary slip through a gap in the fence and into the open front door of the bungalow nearest.

'Gary,' he said, panicking. 'Gary!'

Benjamin ran to the fence. From there he could see through the window—he could see blue skies and ocean where the entire back wall had fallen into the sea.

'Gary,' he shouted again.

Benjamin said the dog's name over and over but he didn't come back. He ran around the side of the house to get a better view, trying to stay back from the edge, remembering, vaguely, a nature documentary about a bridge in Scotland that was an optical illusion for dogs, one that inexplicably made them feel like it was safe to leap over to their deaths.

'Gary,' he shouted, his mind quickly rendering the worst-case scenario.

He worried about Gary's depth perception, that it might be faulty, that he'd walk off the edge and into the ocean. He stood fixed to the spot, scratching his left arm until the flesh was raised and pink. He shook his hands by his sides for a bit, then squeezed through the gate.

'Gary,' he said, placing his feet down gently, heel to toe across the lawn in a half-squat.

As he got closer to the house—to the edge—his body felt like it was pulsing. He felt the height of the cliff in his stomach, leaning on the wall beside the door to steady himself. It didn't help. He put his hands on the floor for balance. Things felt like they slowed a little then. Somewhere in the distance he could hear a tractor in one of the fields, a few gulls screaming as they swung around in the air.

Benjamin pushed the door open and leant around the corner. He saw Gary there, sitting on the front-room floor looking out. The dog turned to him. Behind him the open hole of the bungalow was like the frame of a painting, the vast dark-blue ocean pressing in.

'Please come back,' Benjamin said. 'We'll fall into the sea.'

Gary didn't move. He sat still on the rug, his ribcage swelling with each gentle breath, while Benjamin crept forwards, keeping his weight low, until he could stretch out his arm and touch the hairs on Gary's back. The dog wagged his tail like he hadn't seen Benjamin in a long time. Benjamin put his flat hand on the dog's ribs and Gary relaxed his legs until Benjamin could feel the weight of him. His fear drifted and its edges dulled. He took another look out of the back wall, at the water, then at the objects around them, left when the tenants decided to cut their losses.

'Let's go,' he said, inching backwards as Gary trotted towards the door.

As they walked, Benjamin stayed away from the cliff edge. Gary shadowed him, drifting ahead as they followed the natural slope downwards and onto the beach. Walking along the sand, Benjamin thought about the bungalows and the people who lived in them before the battered cliffs had slipped. He thought about the plant pots and damaged garden furniture. The broken window frames, the last few bricks, all tumbling down into the water, the only physical evidence of entire lives, maybe. The he wondered where he'd be when it happened, if Gary would be with him then.

Twenty-two

At the caravan, Leonard was sitting in a deck chair on the roof with four empties beside him. There were two carrier bags full of sandwiches by the steps. Most of them had yellow 'reduced' stickers on.

'They don't look very fresh,' Benjamin said.

'Rude,' Leonard said. 'Anyway, they aren't. But they are edible. I got some other stuff, too. Culinary options, if you will.'

Leonard climbed down and upended another plastic bag onto a fold-out table he'd erected. He had a tub of egg mayo sandwich filler, a selection of pastries, some steaks and raw meat (that Benjamin couldn't eat), and several tuna sandwiches.

Benjamin definitely didn't want tuna because it has very high levels of mercury and mercury is extremely poisonous. It made him think about the Chinese emperor who chose to be buried at the centre of a mercury river because he believed (ironically) that it held the power to grant eternal life. He didn't tell Leonard the fact, or that he didn't want the tuna, because people don't usually like to have their errors highlighted.

'This feels quite continental actually,' Leonard said. 'Like tapas.' He pointed at the dog. 'I got these for him.' He dangled a bag of dried sprats. Leonard stuck his head in. 'Cawww. They're the good ones.'

Gary caught the scent in the air and lifted his nose up high. He jogged over to Leonard and sat down in front of him. Leonard threw him a fish. He caught it with a snapping sound, crunching its tiny, sun-baked bones.

'Did you spend all that money on this?' Benjamin said.

'No, I got loads of change. What's with the attitude anyway? I hunted and gathered for us. I thought you'd be pleased.'

Leonard sounded angry. Benjamin looked at the man in front of him, the one he barely knew, and felt the isolation of the field, the distance from town. He wanted more than anything to be able to talk to his nan. He wanted to sit down in the kitchen and tell her about Gary, so she could say something that would make him feel better, make him feel less like the world was one huge spinning concern. It was a while since she'd been able to do that. Leonard threw Gary another fish and he missed it, then hoovered it up from the grass by his feet. Benjamin wished Gary was closer. Wanted to reach out and touch his fur.

'Did you go anywhere else?' Benjamin said.

Leonard swayed on the spot.

'When?'

'When you were out?'

Leonard squinted.

'I feel very targeted,' he said, climbing up the ladder. 'I told you. Just the supermarket.'

Leonard stayed on the roof and continued to drink beers as the sun fell away.

'You should put him inside,' Leonard shouted, laughing.

'Why?'

'They hunt in the half-light—he'll probably go all funny. Like a werewolf.'

Benjamin didn't reply. He just looked at Gary. He couldn't imagine him killing anything bigger than an insect, which he'd already witnessed. He hoped he wouldn't.

Leonard shimmied down the ladder, keeping as many parts of his body in contact with the metal as he could. He slid down the last bit with his face on the window.

'I need more beer,' he said, disappearing inside. He came

back out with a bottle of *sake* like the ones in the back of the car and held it up. 'Special occasions and all that,' he muttered, taking a swig, dribbling some down his chin and wetting his T-shirt.

'Do you ever imagine what he'd be saying,' he said, squinting. 'If he had a voice in his head?'

'Not really,' Benjamin said.

'I sometimes do. Like: "I'm so fast. Look at my fast legs." That sort of thing. "These are the fastest legs on any dog," he would say. I think he would say that.'

Leonard took another huge swig of the *sake*. He seemed to be moving and speaking very quickly.

'I also wonder if you could teach a gorilla to lift weights,' he said. 'Like imagine how strong a gorilla would be. It would break all of the human records for weightlifting immediately. Even a weak one.'

Leonard looked around with a blank expression on his face, like he was looking beyond everything in sight, trying to spot something very far away but failing.

'Are you okay?' Benjamin said.

'Absolutely fine.'

For a second, a look of concern appeared on Leonard's face. He held his hand up to his cheek and rubbed the bruises unnecessarily hard. He winced like a child.

'Let's cook some of this food,' he said, opting for an Australian-sounding accent. 'Let's have a barbie.'

Leonard dragged a heavily-soiled barbecue out from under the folding table, then through the door at an angle, bashing it into things. He pulled hard to get the widest part through the gap, then checked its sturdiness with his hands, wobbling it, legs slightly wonky, in front of Benjamin. He dragged a bag of charcoal and a broken-up pallet from under the caravan, then hit the pallet repeatedly with an axe until the bits were small enough to fit in the grill.

'It's nice to cook outside,' Leonard said.

As he built the fire, Gary stood and watched, pushing his nose up towards the grill, smelling the air and picking up the scent of burnt-on meat.

'I'm going to use petrol,' Leonard said—to himself more than Benjamin. 'It's not always recommended.'

Leonard was distracted as he produced a petrol can from behind one of the caravan's wheels. Benjamin backed off and Gary followed him, standing behind his legs.

'The main thing is that we keep this receptacle well away from the fire,' Leonard said, pouring petrol over the coal and the wood. He screwed the cap on again and threw the container fifteen or twenty feet away behind the hay bales.

'That should be fine,' he said.

It was getting dark and the clouds were closing in. When Leonard dropped a match onto the barbecue, for a split second, the flame illuminated everything around them. It burst out sideways and upwards, a warm orange orb that flashed hot against Leonard's face and made him fall back onto his hands. Gary shrunk behind Benjamin, tail between his legs. When the flame had retreated, he pushed his head between Benjamin's knees and watched Leonard with more focus than before.

'Fuck,' said Leonard, looking into the heart of the fire. 'I like fire.'

As he said it, it started drizzling. Benjamin listened to the sound of rain hitting hot wood and hissing. Leonard poured the rest of his beer on the coals, the steam lifting in a haze.

'Fairly typical of my life, that is,' he said, laughing, nodding up at the clouds. 'Let's go inside.'

As the grill in the caravan heated up, it made a faint metallic pinging noise. Leonard opened one of the meat packets and threw on two lamb chops, then pushed them under the heat. Benjamin sat with his hand on Gary's head while the meat cooked, and Leonard stood without talking. When the chops were done, Leonard slid them onto the same plates they'd eaten the eggs from. He put pitta and taramasalata dip on the side and drank more *sake*. He was too drunk to see Benjamin feed Gary the chop.

By the time they'd finished eating Leonard was so drunk he was leaning on things to stand up. He went to the window and peered through the shutters, separating them with his long fingers. It was tipping it down, large blobs hitting the caravan's plastic roof. Leonard closed the curtains.

'Look at this dog,' he said, 'loping around. A loping specialist.' He sniggered at his own joke. 'I like this dog,' he slurred, lunging next to Gary and using his fingers to simulate dog ears on his head. 'He's a prime specimen. Like the two of us.'

Benjamin nodded.

'We are prime, Benjamin. Mighty fuckers of the corporeal form.' Leonard leant down and breathed in a long, unsteady breath with his nose pressed into the dog's head and ear.

'In medieval times people would have revered a union such as this. As that we have.' He waved between himself and the dog. 'We'd have romped about chinning booze and eating hares.' Leonard used his fingers to gently move Gary's gums away from his teeth. 'Behold these ivory blades,' he said.

Leonard sat back in his chair, squinting at the dog. Then he leant forward and put his hand on Gary's face. 'He's got pretty eyes,' he said, 'like Cleopatra.'

He stayed there for a moment, gazing at Gary, then pushed him weakly away. 'Go on you sop,' he said. 'Go and see him.'

Leonard walked over to the wall and flicked the light switch, then stood peering out into the blue-black of the field.

'We should keep these off,' he said. 'To save power.'

Gary jumped on the bed and Benjamin didn't stop him. He sat down and put his hand on the thick muscle of his back leg. The sound of rain hitting the roof seemed to get louder and louder. They sat there quietly, Benjamin with a metallic taste in his mouth, a fear he couldn't name exactly, and Leonard, finishing off a second bottle of *sake* before throwing the empty out of the door.

Leonard laughed, slumping onto the floor. 'Don't get your germs on him or he'll die,' he said to Gary. Then he said 'ivory blades' again, less coherently, and fell asleep on the ground.

Benjamin tipped a handful of sprats onto the floor and Gary picked them up in two or three bites. After the dog had finished chewing, Benjamin reached out and touched the side of his face. It felt soft like moleskin trousers. He got a blanket and put it over Leonard, thinking about how easily—how convincingly—he'd been able to lie to Camille. Then he sat by the window, staring out across the field. Afraid to stay the night, too scared to walk out into it.

Twenty-three

When Benjamin woke, Leonard was scrambling around on the floor. He'd crammed his feet into his shoes without tying the laces and was pulling on a shirt.

'We need to leave immediately,' he said.

Benjamin sat bolt upright on the bed and Gary jumped down.

'Why? What's happening?'

'We just need to leave,' Leonard said, forcing a smile. 'You're already wearing your shoes, so that's good.'

Benjamin swung his legs off the bed, battling the fat feeling of stress. Of unhappy escalation.

'Please tell me what's happening, Leonard.'

Leonard ran both hands through his hair. 'I fucked up,' he said. Then he thumped the side of his own head. 'I did something but now I've changed my mind.'

Leonard threw random items into a bag.

'What did you do, Leonard?' Benjamin said.

Leonard stopped and looked around the room. It wasn't clear what he was looking for.

'I told some people we're here,' he said.

Benjamin stood up. He scratched the inside of his arm, reddening the skin, and paced up and down the caravan. Gary followed. Benjamin's throat felt like it was closing up and his chest was tight. He shook his hands, fingers splayed, like he always did when things seemed to be spiralling out of control. He took out his inhaler.

'What time is it?' Leonard said.

Benjamin looked at his watch. 'Five minutes to nine.'

Leonard ran over to the windows and did his best to shut the blinds, fussing over the slats. Benjamin shook the inhaler and took it, holding the sweet medicine in his lungs while he counted to ten for maximum absorption.

'Is someone coming, Leonard?' Benjamin said.

'Hopefully not.'

Benjamin waited for Leonard to look at him.

'Who's coming, Leonard?' he said.

It was then they both heard it. The sound of an engine in the distance, moving closer. Leonard used his fingers to separate the blinds and peered out. He spun around to look at Benjamin, his eyes darting around like an animal trying to survive, then dived under the bed and pulled out an air rifle.

'I fucked up, Benjamin,' he said. 'I'm sorry.'

Benjamin ran to the window. He tried to look out without being seen.

'Who's here, Leonard?' he said.

Leonard hesitated.

'It's the people who own Gary,' he said.

Then he ran out of the door with the gun in his hand, slamming it shut behind him before Benjamin could follow.

Benjamin heard the door being locked from the outside, then watched from the window as a Range Rover bounced across the field at high speed. Gary wagged his tail, excited by the activity. When the vehicle skidded to a stop, Leonard laughed hysterically and waved his arms. He leant the air rifle up against the caravan as two men climbed out.

'You'll never believe it!' Leonard shouted. 'I've actually got the wrong dog!'

The men walked towards Leonard. The passenger looked to be about sixty and walked with a very slight limp.

'Good to see you Alf!' Leonard said, speaking to him.

Alf had an unusual body. He was barrel-gutted, paunch spilling over his belt, and he had slender, shapeless limbs. The other man was almost Alf's opposite. He was much younger, probably in his thirties, and strong-looking. Not like a bodybuilder though: more like someone who did a manual job. Or a boxer. Long sinewy limbs with veins in his forearms like cables. There was something predatory in the way his shoulders rounded over forwards, too. In the angle of his neck and precise eyes. He was holding Gary's red lead, the one Benjamin had found Gary dragging when they met. The one he'd left in the caravan.

'I've actually got the wrong dog,' Leonard said again, trying to laugh.

Alf smiled. 'You've what, Leonard?'

Leonard repeated himself, less confidently, looking at the ground as he said it.

'It's the wrong dog, Alf. I got it wrong.'

Alf didn't respond to what Leonard was telling him.

'I'm not sure, Leonard,' Alf said, grabbing the red lead from the other man.

Leonard was quiet. Alf noticed the marks and bruises on his face.

'Is everything all right, Leonard? he said, changing the subject. 'You look like you've been in the wars.' Alf turned to the younger man. 'He looks like he's been in the wars, doesn't he?'

Leonard raised a hand to the bruises on his face and the younger man watched.

'This is my friend Vasile,' Alf said. 'He helps me over on the farm. He's from Romania, aren't you, Vasile?'

Vasile nodded.

'I like Vasile. He has sound values and an old-fashioned work ethic. Don't you Vasile?'

Vasile looked slightly confused.

Inside the caravan, Benjamin was looking frantically around for a way to get out. The windows weren't big enough to climb out of, which seemed like a fire risk. He crammed his things into his bag and pulled Gary close. His body tingled, as if his every atom was vibrating at once. Alf walked forwards.

'Not like these weak millennial cretins,' he said. He covered his mouth with a hand and whispered. 'The only real challenge, you know, in the workplace,' he said, 'is that his English is quite shit.'

Alf turned back to Vasile and spoke loudly, like a certain kind of person on holiday, in a continental bakery.

'But we're working through it with language tapes and such? Aren't we Vasile? For constant improvements?'

Leonard gestured at a smile and stared at Vasile's ears. They were bumpy and swollen along the top edge, the fold of the skin pressed down on itself. Benjamin thought about the reasons someone might have cauliflower ears. All of them required a familiarity with impacts to the head that generally wasn't a good sign. Benjamin could see that Leonard was sweating a lot.

'Yes,' Vasile said. 'Improvement.'

When he smiled it seemed unnatural. Creepy. Alf clapped like a seal.

'The reason I'm telling you about the language barrier,' Alf said, 'is that if I instruct him to go in there and get that dog, there's no telling how he might interpret it.' Alf shook his head. 'He had a very troubled youth. It could end up being nasty.'

Leonard stood staring at Vasile in the same way someone might observe a big cat dismantling an antelope.

'What I'm trying to say, Leonard, is that violence is one language he does *not* struggle with.' Alf let his eyes linger on the air rifle, then laughed.

'What's that for, anyway?'

Leonard looked at the gun like it wasn't his—like he'd forgotten it was there.

'I was just taking precautions,' he said. 'Given that I previously believed I was in possession of one of your very valuable racing dogs. But obviously I'm not, so—'

Leonard took a few steps towards the air rifle. 'I'd make us a cup of tea, but I don't have any bags,' he said.

Vasile moved to cut him off. He picked up the gun and broke the barrel to look inside. 'Uninhabited,' he said.

Alf tilted his head, then nodded, like the explanation was good enough.

Inside, Benjamin heard a bird on the roof and zoned out. His brain took a split-second of rest, which was long enough for Vasile to see him before he thought to dip back behind the cover of the curtain. Vasile got Alf's attention and lifted his chin in Benjamin's direction.

'There,' he said, pointing. 'Dog.'

'I see you've got a friend inside, Leonard,' Alf said.

At the window, Gary was standing up, his wet nose smearing the glass. Benjamin tried to pull him down out of sight, but it was too late.

'It's funny, Leonard,' Alf said. 'That dog in there—the one that just jumped up at the window—he looks *very* much like one of my dogs.'

Vasile nodded. 'Dog,' he said, again.

Leonard's face was white. 'You can see how I got mixed up, can't you?'

Inside the caravan, Benjamin crouched out of view. He stayed low and moved over to the back window. Alf saw him trying to lift Gary onto the worktop.

'Shall we get him, then?' he said. 'I've no idea what he thinks he's going to achieve with all those fucking gymnastics, but I'm worried he's going to damage the animal.'

When Leonard didn't respond, Alf looked at Vasile, which he took as an indicator to move towards the caravan. Leonard reached for the gun, then lunged at the men, feigning an attack. Neither of them flinched.

'Open the door Leonard. Or I'll have to get Vasile to kick it in.'

Leonard stopped where he was with his arms dangling by his sides. There were bags under his eyes. He looked very hungover.

'Open the fucking door,' Alf said again.

Leonard did what he was told. From the other end of the caravan, Benjamin watched the empty space by the front door until Vasile filled it, stooping. He bent his neck to keep his head from hitting the roof. Behind him, Alf was leaning round, trying to get a look at Benjamin and Gary. At some point, he caught a glimpse of himself in a wonky mirror on the wall and paused, staring, while everyone waited for him to finish. He turned to Benjamin.

'Hello mate,' he said, speaking like Benjamin was a child. 'We're here to collect my dog.'

Benjamin couldn't move his mouth to reply. His tongue felt dry.

'Get here, dog,' Alf said, clicking his fingers.

Gary lowered his head, curving his body around Benjamin, leaning on him.

'Come on, lad. Get that dog over here or I'll have to ask Vasile to do it. As I expressed previously—I don't know if you could hear me—he could end up doing absolutely anything. Like something physical. A strike or such.'

Benjamin tilted, unconsciously, and put his hand on Gary's back.

Alf rolled his eyes. 'Okay fine,' he said, turning back to the door. 'Leonard! Come in here and make yourself useful.'

Leonard appeared.

'You're going to keep your friend out of the way, for his own protection,' Alf said. 'While we rightfully reclaim the property. Also known as the dog. Does that sound reasonable?'

Leonard pushed his hair back. He scratched his stubble, half-turned away with a pained look on his face, then walked forwards with his head low and his shoulders slumped. When he got to Benjamin, he wrapped his arms around him, linking his hands behind Benjamin's back for a better hold. He said 'sorry,' very quietly. He smelt of cigarettes and body odour. At first the two of them barely moved, but Benjamin pulled away more and more vigorously until they both fell over. Benjamin scrambled to get to his feet, Leonard grabbing at his ankles, and Gary shrank away. They knocked over a dead pot plant.

'He belongs to them,' Leonard said, his face sweaty and red. 'Just let him go.'

Benjamin twisted around to look at Leonard, to see his face, to tell him he hated him. But Leonard had his eyes squeezed shut, trying not to look. Gary had just started to bark when Vasile looped a rope around his neck and dragged him towards the door.

'He's just a dog, mate,' Leonard said, holding on tight to Benjamin's torso. 'He's worth a lot of money.'

Leonard managed to hold on to Benjamin while they took Gary out. When Benjamin finally scrambled to his feet, Leonard threw himself in front of the door, while Vasile led the dog to the boot.

Benjamin was crying now. He swung at Leonard, but Leonard dodged the punch. It enabled Benjamin to break free from his grip and surge down the steps. He ran at Vasile, without a clue what he'd do when he got there. Vasile decided for him. He moved only fractionally, side-stepping, but dropped Benjamin with a perfectly timed jab to the nose. Benjamin tried to stand but his legs were unsteady. When Vasile hit him again, he fell a second time. The blood dripped onto his T-shirt.

Benjamin rolled over and looked at the sky. It seemed incredibly bright. Leonard put Benjamin's head on his knees and held him there.

'Fuck's sake,' Leonard said, inspecting Benjamin's face. 'There was no need for that.' He pointed at Vasile. 'Fucking blunt instrument, he is.'

Vasile didn't pay any attention. He was lifting Gary into the boot of the Range Rover, and the dog was struggling, extending his limbs in awkward directions and wriggling to be released. Vasile squeezed him harder.

'Don't be so melodramatic,' Alf said. 'It was just a little punch. What was Vasile supposed to do?'

Vasile shut the boot and Alf waved at the dog through the glass in the rear window.

'Where's his collar gone?' Alf said, looking genuinely put out.

Leonard nodded at Benjamin. 'I've no idea,' he said, 'maybe he took it off?'

'What do people think? That these things are free? Christ. That thing was full-grain Italian leather.'

Vasile wiped his hand on a rag from the back seat of the car. He stood staring at his knuckles as if he were in a trance.

'He's not going to give me any trouble after this, is he?' Alf said, motioning at Benjamin.

'I don't think he's all there, to be honest,' Leonard said, cradling Benjamin's head.

'That's something, at least,' Alf said. 'I'd tell you to send my best to Sally, but I know for a fact she left you, so. Anyway, thanks again for phoning Leonard, you've done a very honourable thing here.'

Leonard hesitated. He started to speak, stopping more than once.

'What about the—the reward?'

Alf put his hand to his ear.

'What was that, Leonard?'

Leonard said it again, quietly. 'What about the money?'

'You're going to have to speak up.' He turned to Vasile. 'Can you hear him, Vasile?' Vasile shook his head.

'The money,' Leonard said, almost shouting.

'Ah right. That. So the thing is Leonard, I feel like, given your history, it would be irresponsible of me to give you this money. It would probably just *facilitate* a relapse. Wouldn't it? Don't you think? And also, there is the not-so-insignificant matter of the lost appendage. The collar.'

Leonard turned to look at the man. 'I've got people to pay. I have to pay them,' he said, gesturing at his face.

Alf smiled.

'Okay Leonard, I'll tell you what, I'm a reasonable man. Minus deductions, let's call it a hundred quid and I won't tell the police it took the pair of you three days to call me. And I won't tell any of the numerous shit pieces around town that you owe money to exactly where your degenerate little dwelling is? Sound fair?'

Leonard squinted. His head slumped to one side and his shoulders loosened. He watched Alf throw five twenties on the floor in front of him.

Alf banged on the car window which made Gary shrink, leaning away, averting his eyes. 'I honestly don't know why people get so worked up over these things,' he said. 'There's basically nothing going on up there,' he said, pointing at Gary's domed head. 'Don't get me wrong, he's a good dog. I don't hold it against him, because he runs like the clappers—never seen anything like it in all my life—but that *is* what he is. Just a dog. Just a fucking running dog,' he said, walking around the car and climbing in.

Then they started the engine and they took Gary away.

Twenty-four

Air rushed into Benjamin's lungs. He sat bolt upright and touched his face with the tips of his fingers. The blood was still wet. Snippets of what had happened came back to him. He was feeling the panic that Gary was gone all over again when Leonard came running out of the caravan with another beer in his hand. He'd shaken it up in his rush, bubbles rolling up and out of the top. He stood in front of Benjamin, stuttering and pale.

'I didn't mean for it to go like this,' he said. 'Things have been tight Benjamin. I didn't know you really. You nicked their dog.'

Benjamin rubbed his head. It hurt. 'I didn't nick him,' he said.

Leonard fixed his eyes on Benjamin. It looked like they were red and wet but it was hard to tell with the bruises.

Leonard exhaled long and hard. 'I know, I know,' he said quietly. 'But you know that's not really how it works. I asked him about the options. Like, if you could buy him, or have him when he retires or something.'

Benjamin squinted, trying desperately to stop himself from getting upset. When he looked up, Leonard shook his head.

'I could help get you another one? Anything you want,' he said. Leonard's eyes lit up. 'How about a staffie? You don't want a weedy skinny dog, anyway, do you? Get one with a bit of something about it.'

Benjamin got to his feet. He looked Leonard straight in the

eyes, then made a wobbly line for him and tried to punch him in the face.

'Go, easy lad,' Leonard said, dodging the shot. 'I'll help you find another dog mate. Steady on.'

Benjamin threw another punch but Leonard slipped it, grabbing hold. Some of the blood from Benjamin's face was on Leonard's T-shirt.

'He's not just a dog,' Benjamin said, his voice breaking, Leonard holding him tight.

'Come on lad. We tried. You—you tried. Sometimes there's nothing you can do though. Larger cosmic mechanisms.'

Benjamin pulled himself away.

'What does that mean? Larger cosmic mechanisms? Is that why your wife left you?'

Leonard grimaced.

'Life isn't always black and white you know,' he said, mumbling. 'You just do what you think is right.' He shrugged. 'Sometimes you do what's easiest.'

Leonard walked away and sat on a tyre by the barbecue. He leant over and started pulling up blades of grass—letting them go in the breeze.

'Were you going to try to leave me at the hospital so you could take him then? When we went to see my nan?'

Leonard looked out to sea and pulled one of the blades apart between his fingers. 'I'd have been doing you a favour really,' he said. 'You might not have cared so much if I'd taken him then.' Leonard turned his whole torso away from Benjamin and wiped his eyes with a sleeve.

'You're an awful person,' Benjamin said, matter of factly.

Leonard shook his head like a dog shaking off snow.

'It's a shock to you, isn't it? That I'm a piece of shit. Well, I've had a fair while to get used to it,' he said, standing up.

Leonard went inside and Benjamin sat looking around the field. He watched the clouds making slow progress from left to right and thought about Gary being shut in a cage, his bony sides bumping into the mesh. A kind of autopilot moved him to his feet and to the caravan.

'Why did those men in the snooker club beat you up? Was it really because they were trying to get Gary?'

Leonard looked at his boots.

'Why, Leonard?' Benjamin shouted again, his raised voice a kind of release.

'I owed them money,' he said weakly.

Leonard's betrayal swirled around in the pit of Benjamin's stomach. Leonard was foreign blood rubbed in cuts, he was the piss-flecked tiles under a urinal. He was dirty tissues and hospital oxygen. Everything blurred. Benjamin thought of Gary with those men and felt unsteady on his feet. He needed air. To stand outside again, away from the cramped caravan. He stumbled back out. There was blood running down his top lip that left a metallic taste in his mouth. He wiped it away with his arm, something building inside him.

Benjamin leant in the open window of Leonard's car. The keys were dangling in the ignition so he took them out, fiddling with a rubber playboy keyring on his way to where Leonard had parked the motorbike. The helmet was balanced on a breeze block under the tarpaulin. Benjamin put it on, fastening the strap around his neck. He could hear Leonard making a lot of noise inside. He was huffing and knocking into things. A radio turned on, playing 'Run to the Hills' by Iron Maiden. Benjamin climbed onto the bike and rocked it off its stand. His limbs were shaking and his mouth was dry. He looked back at the caravan one last time as the song reached its fitting chorus, RUN TO THE HILLS, then he stamped down hard on the kick-starter.

Sweet black smoke came tumbling out of the exhaust, the rumbling engine vibrating the handlebars and Benjamin's body. Leonard started shouting. He came crashing outside as

Benjamin bounced across the field towards the gate, jerkily changing up through the gears.

'Stop you idiot!' He shouted as Benjamin rode away.

But it was too late. Benjamin couldn't hear him. He wasn't thinking any more, just trying to move away from something painful. From failure and damage and the feeling of letting someone go. Of not doing enough to stop it.

Twenty-five

Benjamin skidded out of the gate and onto the road, the early-morning chill already working its way in. It was making his thoughts difficult to organise, pulling him further into his body.

His neck ached from the punches and his lip was sore. He wanted to probe the spot where it hurt but his hands were dirty, so he poked at the bumps with his tongue instead. He blinked a few tears out and felt the chill from the wind in the wet stripes running down his cheeks.

After a couple of miles, he pulled into a lay-by that overlooked the sea. He put his hands on the warm plastic panels above the motor, opening and closing them to get the blood moving. While he listened to the bike's engine popping, he pictured Gary. He saw the slender, wobbling shape of him in the window as the car drove away and was taken over by the loss of the dog so completely that he felt the energy in his body leave, like a wave retreating. He squeezed his eyes shut and let the memories wash over him.

He was on the decking again, sitting across from his nan in a plastic chair. She had her hair up, held in place by a tie-dye headband. As he served their lunch onto plates she frowned, reaching down to rub her legs. She was thinking about something, but he didn't know what. It was an expression he didn't recognise on her. Of worry. Her breaths seemed harder to come by than normal.

'Are your legs all right?' he said.

She looked down towards the beach. 'Just a bit sore,' she said.

She waved out and around them, changing the subject. 'When we moved here, I didn't know how I felt about it. I thought I might feel a bit cut off. Like we were on the outside. At the end of things.'

Benjamin nodded.

'But after a while, I realised I liked it.' She pointed at the sea. 'I realised we're not at the end of anything. Just the start of something else.'

Benjamin looked at her. He knew what she'd been afraid of because he felt it too, sometimes. The sensation of being disconnected, of being a long way away.

'Benjamin. I need to ask you to do something,' she said. She tried to fix his gaze, but he wouldn't let her, busying himself with the plates.

'Ben,' she said, waiting. 'If they try to take me back, I don't want you to let them.' He turned to face her. 'I'm tired,' she said. 'Promise me you won't let them take me?'

Benjamin fidgeted, scratching at his forearm.

'But if you don't go to hospital, you won't get better,' he said, looking at her, at the failing components of her body. When she caught his eye, he worried she knew what he was thinking.

'I know things aren't great,' she said. 'I just can't face all those machines again. All those people I don't know. I'd like to be here. With you.'

Benjamin was quiet. When he didn't say anything, she started eating.

'This is nice,' she said, picking up a tomato.

Benjamin shrugged like it wasn't much.

'I like eating *al fresco*,' she said. 'It reminds me of Italy. Not that I've ever been.'

He looked at her.

'It means eating outside, though. *Al fresco*.'

He nodded. She smiled again.
'Promise me Benjamin?' she said.
'Okay,' he said quietly.
'I love you,' she said.
He smiled.

When Benjamin opened his eyes, it was raining. He walked to a bench that faced out towards the water and climbed up onto it. He put his hands over his mouth and shouted. After a while, he stopped trying to stifle it, and let the sounds emerge. In the quiet that followed, he watched the raindrops hitting the ocean and the ripples moving out. A seagull flew past. He followed its path through wet and squinting eyes as it glided along the beach towards a point in the distance he knew wasn't far from the caravan. Although he couldn't see it from where he was, he thought about it. About the tired decking outside. The broken door. Water soaking the doormat and spreading out under the carpet, eventually going mouldy.

Then he thought about his nan as she was now, the machines whirring quietly around her. In a peculiar way, he thought he could feel the distance between the two of them in the cells of his body.

He remembered what Mike had said, about telling her things that were important—the promise he'd made to go back—and he realised where it was he needed to go.

Twenty-six

Blobs of rain slapped the concrete of the hospital car park as Benjamin climbed off the bike and pushed it onto its stand. There was a box of disposable face masks by the door, which made him feel validated and disturbed in equal measure. He put one on and walked inside the large sliding doors of the entrance to a new table that he hadn't seen before. It was blocking access to the hospital, with an employee manning it. The employee was talking to a middle-aged couple. He slid the point of his index down a clipboard then shook his head and the man in front of him sobbed. The man's bulky frame jerked up and down as the woman with him became more animated. It was difficult to be sure with the mask, but it seemed like she was angry. When the couple moved away, the man glanced across and saw Benjamin standing behind a pot plant, waiting for the lift.

'Excuse me!' he shouted, stepping forward. He turned back and forth between his desk and Benjamin, like his left foot was attached to the floor, clearly conflicted about abandoning his post. The lift arrived and Benjamin stepped in.

'You can't just go up there!' The man shouted. He picked up a walkie-talkie, but it was too late. As the doors slid closed, Benjamin heard him shouting from his little table.

The door to the ward was locked so Benjamin ducked inside a toilet to think. When the light switched on automatically, he looked at his face in the mirror for the first time, leaning in close to inspect the damage. The blood was still working its way out of his upper lip. He pressed a hand towel to his cheek and wiped it, revealing the yellowed flesh where the bruises were going to be. While the reddy-brown water spun away into the plughole, he listened to the fan and the distant sound of hospital beeps.

He looked at his face again. Something about it was different. Not just the marks and the blood, but the architecture of it— the sum of its parts—seemed subtly changed. He lingered a moment, trying to work it out, until he heard footsteps further along the corridor. He used his elbow to lever the door open, peering out. A nurse appeared. She drifted along without looking up, staring at her phone. When she opened the ward door and went through, Benjamin lunged across and stopped it with his hand. He stayed close to the wall as he made his way to his nan's room.

Her board had been rubbed clean and there was a new name written in green marker. 'June Easter,' it said. Someone had drawn a patterned egg below.

Benjamin read the name a few more times, trying to resist the sensation of panic that was squeezing its way in. Coming here, he'd felt as though he'd been holding his breath, swimming up towards air. Now that he'd made it, he couldn't break the surface.

He heard the main door swing open and a doctor appeared. She was walking an uncertain line as she read over her notes. She took off her glasses and polished them on her scrubs, then rubbed her temples. She didn't see Benjamin push his way into his nan's old room.

The cubicle smelt like cigarettes and antibacterial cleaner. Over by the window, a woman in her seventies was slouching with a cigarette. She was propping her elbow up in front of her stomach with an open hand, using it to keep the cigarette properly located. When she saw Benjamin, she whipped it behind her back and squinted at his face.

'Thank Christ,' she said, relieved. 'I thought you were security.'

Benjamin's eyes followed a tube that was running to her body from what looked like a metal hat stand.

'Who are you?' she said.

'I'm Benjamin Glass.'

She pointed at his mask.

'You can take that off if you like,' she said. 'I can't hear a thing people say when they're wearing those.'

Benjamin shifted his weight. The lady coughed.

'The other day they handed me a receptacle,' she said. 'But I didn't have a clue what they wanted so I ended up urinating in a pot they wanted me to spit in.' She laughed. 'It was like specimen roulette.'

Benjamin looked at her. 'I can't take it off,' he said, shaking his head.

The woman took a step or two forwards, pulling the tube taut. Benjamin worried she'd die if it popped off.

'Have it your way,' she said. 'But don't blame me when I fill your little pot up wrong.'

Benjamin looked around.

'I don't work here,' he said. 'I'm just looking for my nan.'

'Oh, right,' the woman said.

She looked in a cupboard, adding a touch of theatre by exaggerating her movements. 'She's definitely not here,' she said. She offered her hand and it wobbled in the air between them. 'My name's June.'

'I'm sorry,' Benjamin said, trying to sound apologetic. 'I don't normally shake hands.'

June looked at him more seriously. She balanced her cigarette on the edge of a glass ashtray, then turned to reach for a small bottle of sanitiser. Benjamin noticed the back of her gown hanging open behind her and looked at the ceiling as she pumped out a blob of alchohol gel onto her palm.

'There you go,' she said, shooting out her hand again. 'I've disinfected myself.'

Benjamin carried on looking at the ceiling. June raised an eyebrow.

'Is there something up there?' she said.

Benjamin could feel his face flushing red.

'I'm just looking away,' he said. 'Because your gown is unfastened.'

The woman looked down at what she was wearing, the fabric ties all flailing undone.

'Ohh. Yes, it is. It always does that,' she said. 'I keep telling them. But to be honest, my rump's seen better days anyway. A little exposure is the least of my worries.' June laughed at her own joke. 'I'd happily return my cell to your nan,' she said. 'If that's any consolation.'

'Do you know where she is?' Benjamin said.

June shook her head.

'I don't, I'm afraid. I only came here yesterday. I've been lugged about all over the place, but I think this ward is for people without 'symptoms.''

Benjamin looked around. He could feel his body tingling, his skin warming up with panic.

'What about anyone who's not clear?' he said.

'They're all on the ward I used to be on, I think. Trinity Ward.'

June placed her hand on her chest and cleared her throat. 'I obviously shouldn't be doing this,' she said, picking up the cigarette and holding it out. 'They told me if I smoke with the oxygen on I'll explode. So I turned it off at the wall.' June looked around. 'Sometimes that feels like a reasonable response, though. Exploding.' She laughed again and wheezed. Benjamin remembered Leonard talking about the whale, the build-up of gases spreading its matter out across the beach. He tried to smile.

'I might have to speak to someone about where she is,' he said.

'I don't think you can just walk in, love. They're not allowing visitors any more.'

June took a lighter from her draw.

'Mind?' she said.

'I have asthma,' Benjamin said.

June smiled, taking him in.

'You're a bit like my granddaughter, you are,' she said, laying the packet down, balancing her lighter on top. 'A bit of a worrier. Are you single?'

Benjamin was thrown. The question floated around between them.

'Single?'

'Yeah. You know, romantically unattached? She told me the term is DTF now.'

Benjamin shrugged and June looked around, weighing it up. She laughed.

'I think it means 'Down To Flirt.'

Benjamin didn't respond. He felt awkward.

'I used to be a top flirter,' June said. 'A saucy bit of kit.'

She laughed again, then turned serious. '*Do* you have anyone at home? To look after you while your nan's in here?'

'Not really,' Benjamin said.

June tilted her head.

'There must be someone?'

Benjamin thought about it. He remembered Camille sliding the newspaper onto the scales of his till. The grainy picture of the whale, laying there in a faded halo of its own blood, her connection to the animals of the earth. The way she always put him at ease.

'My supervisor at work is a really nice lady,' he said.

Without the paper, Benjamin would have walked straight home after work. He'd have watched TV until sleep closed his lids and he'd never have found Gary. That made him feel sadder, the loss deeper. The slim chance of their being together more precious to lose.

June gestured at the touchscreen to the side of her bed on an extendable arm.

'Do you want to phone her?' she said. 'I've got close to unlimited credit because you can't use these things for BetFred or PaddyPower. My daughter keeps topping it up.'

'I'm okay,' Benjamin said, looking around.

June shrugged. 'Suit yourself,' she said.

Benjamin saw the row of stones he'd lined up on the windowsill were still there.

'My nan's stones are still here,' he said, gesturing.

'I wondered where those were from,' June said. 'They're nice. I like the one with the cloud on it.'

Benjamin looked at the stones.

'Do you mind if I take them?' he said.

June shook her head like she'd been asked a very important question. 'Course I don't.'

Benjamin walked over to the windowsill, passing June. Along with the smell of cigarettes, she had a slightly floral odour. He picked the stones up and began putting them into the various pockets of his jacket, so they wouldn't damage each other.

'Put them in this,' June said, emptying most of the cigarettes from a packet directly into her drawer. Benjamin avoided looking at the grotesque imagery on the side and dropped the remaining stones in.

'I'll leave you this one,' he said, holding up the one with the wispy white flash that June had liked. The one that looked like a cumulonimbus.

'It looks too bare otherwise,' Benjamin said.

June smiled. They were standing there in silence when the door swung open and the doctor backed her way in, dragging a little machine. June did a face. She stubbed the mostly dead cigarette out in the ashtray and turned on the oxygen. She was bundling her paraphernalia into the cupboard when the doctor turned around.

'Hi there,' she said, surprised, looking at Benjamin. 'Who's this young man, June?'

June spoke like Benjamin was an old friend.

'This is Benjamin Glass,' she said. 'He's looking for his nan.'

The doctor hesitated.

'Do you know Benjamin then?' she said.

'Do we ever really know anyone? June replied. 'I thought I knew my ex-husband until I found him in the conservatory with his trousers down. Elizabeth from bowls fully astride.'

The doctor spoke to Benjamin.

'You know you absolutely shouldn't be in here?' she said. 'Because of the highly contagious respiratory virus?'

Benjamin looked at the floor. He felt very hot. Itchy, too.

'Sort of,' he said. 'I saw something on telly. I turned it over.' After a pause. 'I really need to talk to my nan.'

The doctor was thrown. She stood taking it in. 'I'm going to have to take you down to reception,' she said. 'Is that okay?'

Benjamin nodded. The doctor looked at June.

'I'll be back up,' she said.

June nodded and waved. She looked very directly at Benjamin.

'I hope you find your nan,' she said. 'It seems like the two of you are very close. Love like that is very valuable. My husband taught me that when I realised he was full of shit and our marriage was a sham.'

As they were leaving the room, the doctor turned back to June.

'I told you what happens when you smoke with oxygen, didn't I?'

June laughed. 'June wallpaper,' she said.

Out in the hallway, Benjamin followed the doctor to a telephone where she punched in a number and stared at the wall. She had smudged biro notes on her forearm and bags under her eyes. She was swaying from what seemed like fatigue. Camille said that healthcare workers had very pure hearts, and that those pure hearts had been exploited by a succession of self-serving government representatives who owed their positions and power to generational nepotism. Benjamin didn't know much about politics.

'I just need to see if I can find out where she is,' she said, slipping off a shoe to stretch out her foot, exposing a hole in her sock. Someone answered.

'I've found a young man,' the doctor said. 'He's looking for his nan.'

After some back and forth, she looked at Benjamin and mouthed: 'What's her full name?'

'Theresa Glass,' Benjamin said.

In the atrium, a man in a black tunic with stripes on it was waiting to speak to them. A pager in the doctor's pocket went off for the third time since they'd left June's room.

'Benjamin, meet Seth,' the doctor said. 'Seth, meet Benjamin.'

Seth waved.

'Seth's going to help you find your nan,' the doctor said.

'I am smiling,' Seth said fairly abruptly. 'In case you're wondering. Under my mask. I'm smiling. Appropriately though, not inanely.'

The doctor's eyes bounced between the two of them. Benjamin stared. 'I'll leave you to it,' the doctor said, not waiting for an answer, moving off at pace along the hallway.

Seth gave Benjamin a wide-eyed look.

'You're lucky you got handed over to me. There are other people who would be pushing to have you arrested for breaking into a ward.'

'I didn't break in,' Benjamin said.

'Yeah, yeah. All good. All good. I'm mega chill about it anyway. I take a lot of vitamins, which afford me a certain level of protection.'

Benjamin didn't feel mega chill.

'My nan's name is Theresa Glass,' Benjamin said. 'I really need to see her.'

'Oh for sure, for sure. And you can! Let's look her up.'

Seth worked a tablet, slow-typing with a stylus. He paused before speaking again.

'She *is* on Trinity Ward,' he said. 'Super-unfortunately.'

Benjamin looked at him like that didn't mean anything.

'It's where we're keeping any patients that might be positive . . . for the virus,' he said.

'Positive for the virus?' Benjamin said.

'Yeah, but it's just a precaution. Because she's been on a ward with several people who've had symptoms.'

Benjamin felt a sickness in his stomach, an overwhelming nausea that drew the blood from his face and hands and made his limbs tingle. He looked around.

'So, if she has it, will it be because she was here?' he said.

Seth looked up.

'I mean, *if* she has it, it would be *likely* that she'd got it here, yeah.'

Benjamin wanted to hold his breath, to refuse the oxygen. The tall white walls of the hospital were closing in.

'Shouldn't everything be clean?' he said.

Seth scratched the side of his head. 'It's really difficult to keep everything clean in a hospital,' he said. 'Lots of people are very sick at the moment.'

Benjamin was sweating.

'We could arrange a video call? Seth said. 'We just received a load of new iPads.' Seth prodded the screen. 'They don't have Angry Birds, unfortunately.'

Benjamin shook his head. A video call didn't make any sense. Someone would have to hold the tablet up and aim it at her and she wouldn't say anything because she was asleep. He shook his head more vigorously than he meant to. A bright-red patch of blood bloomed on his surgical mask.

'Wow. Are you injured?' Seth said, stepping forwards. 'I could take you down to A&E for someone to have a look?' he said.

Benjamin felt very overwhelmed.

'I need to tell her things,' he said.

'And you will!' Seth said. 'Let's use the tech! Honestly, it's so slick. You can tell her on there.'

Benjamin looked around for directions to Trinity Ward. He was feeling more and more like the entire hospital had raw chicken breasts smeared all over it. Or vomit. Or chicken vomit.

'You're giving me running-away vibes if I'm honest,' Seth said.

Benjamin squinted at a sign on one of the walls. It said Trinity Ward on it.

'Honestly mate, even if you Usain Bolt, you won't get in up there. It's completely locked down.'

Benjamin felt like he was swimming in clothes, sinking, taking in mouthfuls of water.

'But I've come back,' he said. 'To tell her things. Important things.'

To tell her she was a lighthouse on a rock, and that the light made him feel safe. That how he felt was more permanent than fragile bodies, that it existed outside of time. That he loved her and he always had, and would, even though he'd probably never said it directly.

He'd almost decided to run for the ward when he saw Mike at the hospital coffee shop, pushing a patient in a wheelchair. When Mike saw him, he let go like he wanted to run over, but he hesitated. He looked at Seth. The man in the chair craned around to see what had halted their progress. There was a look on Mike's face that terrified Benjamin. That made him want to run again. Benjamin experienced the overwhelming desire to be outside, in the clean air, away from sickness. Away from words that could never be taken back once they were spoken. The man from the front desk appeared at the end of a corridor, followed by two security guards.

'That's him!' he said, pointing. 'The vector of disease!'

Twenty-seven

Benjamin stumbled away, back out into the rain, not really sure who he was speaking to.

'It's all right,' he said, over and over again, knowing under everything that that's exactly what it wasn't.

He looked up at the hospital as he ran and thought he saw the tiny luminous glow of a cigarette in one of the windows higher up. He remembered the conversation he'd had with June about Camille, and a time on the back till when a man called him a bastard because the barcode on a gammon joint was twisted and wouldn't scan. He remembered the way he felt when Camille got there, like the volume had been turned down.

He wanted to speak to her, thought maybe it would help, so he ran over to a payphone by the taxi rank, watching the door in case they followed him out. He dialled the number for the back office and listened to it ring. When Camille answered, all Benjamin could do was cry.

He ran to the bike. For a moment, he watched the raindrops taking it in turns to slide down the metal tank of the motorcycle, then he took off at full speed towards town.

Twenty-eight

Benjamin stood inside the automatic doors of the supermarket, dripping on the tiles, while an employee called Elliot mopped around his feet without talking to him. Elliot put a wet floor sign down and looked at Benjamin like he'd caused him physical pain.

'Is Camille in?' Benjamin said.

Elliot lingered. His top lip twitched.

'I don't know,' he said. 'Ask at cigarettes.'

Benjamin drifted along the aisles, past rows of neatly-stacked produce. As he skirted the deli, he glimpsed chunks of uncut ham that reminded him of the whale. He sucked in a lungful of cold air from the milk fridge and looked around.

Something about the supermarket felt different. Like there was some subtle change to its dimensions that Benjamin couldn't put his finger on. He squinted, adjusting the angles, but it didn't help. It was as if the colours were muted, the sounds all occurring at the end of a very long tunnel. The air felt colder too. More stale than he remembered. Something about it felt small and meaningless. Without Gary, without his nan, he wondered whether everything might be.

When he reached the front, Benjamin stood at the counter and waited for a lady called Jill to look up. She didn't, so he coughed to get her attention.

'Is Camille in?' he said.

Her eyes lifted from a magazine. The kind that prints

unflattering images of female celebrities, climbing out of taxis.

'She is. Would you like me to get her?' she said.

Benjamin nodded. The woman swivelled in her chair and leant over a small microphone on a stalk. When she pressed the button to talk, her lips bumped the foam covering and made a sound that echoed through the aisles.

'Camille to front kiosk,' she said. 'Camille to front kiosk.'

She went back to her magazine. A few seconds later Benjamin heard Camille's voice through a walkie-talkie positioned below the cigarettes.

'On my way, Jill,' she said.

While Benjamin watched for Camille, Jill spoke to him without looking up from her magazine.

'You've missed a few shifts recently by the sounds of it,' she said, squinting at a blurry picture. 'You should be careful. There are people with their eyes on that Saturday afternoon back-till shift of yours.' She looked up and leant in conspiratorially, nodded towards Elliot who was now piling tins of condensed milk and watching. 'Not me though, I don't need the money. I started an OnlyFans account.' Jill eyed Benjamin for understanding. When she realised that he clearly didn't know what she was talking about, she pushed her hair up in the way that people do to show they're being glamourous.

'JillOnTheTills if you're interested,' she said, looking him up and down. 'I might be a bit mature for you,' she shrugged. 'But you never know.'

Camille appeared at the end of the aisle, scribbling something down in a notepad. When she saw Benjamin, she leant on the shelf beside her with her hand over her mouth. She shuttled down and hugged him.

'I knew I was going to see you today,' she said, putting a clammy palm across his forehead. She held up a crystal that was dangling around her neck. 'All of the signs were there,' she said.

Camille looked him over.

'Are you feeling any better?'

Benjamin shrugged. 'I'm really sorry I missed my shift,' he said.

Camille smiled and leant in.

'We're just flogging melons,' she whispered. 'None of it really matters.' Then she squinted as her eyes darted between the tiny flecks of blood inside his nostrils.

'Have you been bleeding, Benjamin?' she said.

Benjamin avoided eye contact. He could see the wobble of Elliot and Jill by the till through the tears that were squeezing their way out. Camille walked him out of earshot with a serious look on her face.

'Tell me,' she said. 'What's happened?'

Benjamin stopped to breathe. He felt terrible, for so many things, all at once. Like letting them take his nan, like losing Gary. It made him feel sick that he couldn't explain it to them either. That they might never understand the detail of what had happened. That they trusted him and he'd let them down.

'They won't let me see her,' Benjamin said.

'Who won't? Who won't they let you see?'

It was hard to get the words out.

'My nan,' he said.

Camille put her arm around Benjamin's narrow shoulders and squeezed him in. Then she moved away again to see the cuts and marks on his face.

'They said I had to talk to her on an iPad.'

'But why are you bleeding?' she said.

Benjamin shook his head.

'That's something else.'

'What?' Camille said.

Benjamin wiped his wet face with the back of his hand.

'I found a dog,' he said. 'And I think he was mine. But they took him.'

It was strange to hear it out loud like that. Calling Gary his. But Benjamin knew that Gary was his dog. And he was Gary's person.

'He was mine and they took him,' he said a little louder.

'Let's go and talk in the cash office,' Camille said.

In the office, they sat on a rug that Camille brought in when she was promoted to Store Supervisor. She had to roll it up and put it in a cupboard for area manager visits, but said it gave her a sense of tranquillity in the workplace that was worth the rigmarole of having to conceal it from Andy Nelson (the area manager). She said Andy Nelson was a jobsworth anyway. Benjamin ran his fingers along the stitches, looking at the embroidery—a moon and star with human faces. His stomach rumbled.

'Are you hungry?' Camille said.

Benjamin didn't want to eat. He wiped his face with the inside of his T-shirt and Camille took out her phone. She started playing rainforest music.

'You wait here and try to feel the music as deeply as you can—it'll help if you lie on the rug—and I'll get you something to nibble.'

Camille dimmed the lights. Benjamin lay down and closed his eyes, but sunshine was slipping through the blinds. At first, it made him think about the plastic seat by his nan's bed in hospital that got hot on summer days, burning the back of his legs. Then about Gary in the caravan, laying his face in sun-warmed spots. He saw a version of himself that hadn't let them take him yet. He rubbed his feet together and tried to stop the feelings swallowing him up. He put his hand in his pocket to find Leonard's keys and squeezed them until his hand hurt.

Camille came back with a purple packet. Benjamin sat up.

'What are they?' he said.

'They're little digestive biscuits in the shape of animals,' she said. 'They've got chocolate on top.'

Benjamin looked at the nutritional information. Normally he'd tell her he avoided anything with the red boxes on the front, preferring green, but allowing amber if it happened to be reduced. He was used to explaining why he didn't do lots of the things other people enjoyed doing. Like drinking alchohol and smoking. Or eating food that was high in saturated fat and sugar. Or raising his heartrate too vigorously. Exposing himself to contaminants. But as he opened his mouth to speak, it felt as though he was just going through the motions of caring. And he didn't. Not really. He tore open the bag.

'Thanks,' he said, piling three or four into his mouth. He chewed.

'She shouldn't be in there,' he said.

'In the hospital?'

'Yeah.'

'Of course she should. She's poorly.'

Benjamin took more biscuits.

'She's on a ward for people who might have that virus,' he said.

Camille put her hand to her chest. She turned the rainforest music down.

'I'm so sorry Benjamin.'

He ate another animal biscuit. Camille looked him straight in the eyes.

'No one wants to be in hospital,' she said.

'I know,' Benjamin said, thinking of the night she'd gone in. Of sitting at the table with the heating off for almost a day, trying to figure out what he should do. Cleaning every surface in the caravan in case it was corrupted, panicking he'd already been exposed and it was degrading his heart, clogging it or fatiguing it, or turning the tissue necrotic.

'I was scared,' he said.

'Of what?'

'Of what was wrong with her.'

'That's okay, Benjamin.'

He shook his head.

'Now she's probably got something worse.'

Camille was quiet.

'I let them take her when I shouldn't have done,' Benjamin said, 'and now I've let them take Gary.'

Camille pointed at the cuts on his face.

'It doesn't look like you *let* them take Gary,' she said.

'It's the same though. I should have stopped them, and I didn't.'

'Have they closed the wards properly now then?' Camille said.

All of the muscles in Benjamin's body seemed to slacken at once. He felt like he might fall over. He nodded, yes.

'Oh love,' Camille said.

Sometimes when Camille wanted to show deep understanding she closed her eyes and nodded. She was doing that now.

'Tell me about the dog,' she said.

Benjamin took some time, thinking about everything that had happened.

'I went to see the whale on the beach,' he said. 'Because you said I should see how it made me feel.'

Camille nodded to encourage him.

'He was there, licking it. Licking its blubber.' Benjamin shuddered at the thought. 'Then he followed me home.'

'The dog?'

'Yeah.'

'I ordered us takeaway. He ate a spring roll.'

Benjamin remembered the way the pastry had lodged itself in Gary's whiskers, then how the dog looked at him and yawned when he cleaned his pissy legs with a rag. He missed the quiet proximity of that. Camille handed him a tissue.

'He urinated on his own leg on the decking,' Benjamin said.

Camille smiled in a sad way. 'I could feel something powerful pulling you there,' she said. 'I thought it was the whale. But I can see now, it was the dog.'

Benjamin looked up. Talking about Gary made him feel closer to him.

'The man who delivered the takeaway said he'd help me. He just wanted the reward though,' he said.

'The reward?'

'Yeah. There was a reward. He's a racing dog.'

Benjamin reached into his pocket and took out the newspaper clipping. His hand wobbled as he handed it to Camille.

'This is him,' he said.

'Oh dear,' she said, looking at the picture. 'This is a lot to take in.' She placed her hand over the image of Gary. 'You have a very similar essence,' she said.

While Camille read the article about Gary's disappearance, Benjamin thought again about the missed shift and Leonard lying on the phone. Camille tutted as she read.

'Tell me about this delivery driver then,' she said. 'The one who claimed to be your uncle.'

Camille had a way of doing that, of bringing up what was on your mind. Benjamin looked up and Camille was smiling.

'Oh Benjamin,' she said. 'It's okay. I assumed it was what you required of me. To trust. The words we speak rarely have much to do with what we end up actually *saying.*'

'I'm so sorry,' Benjamin said.

'You don't need to be. Was I wrong?'

'About what?'

'Was there a reason?'

Benjamin nodded.

'I needed to stay with him,' he said.

Camille tilted her head, reassuring him.

'There you go then. I was right. You're a good person Benjamin. There's nothing more than that.'

Camille looked around the cash office. She turned the rainforest songs up and closed her eyes, taking in a lungful of air through her nose.

'I'd read tarot cards for you, but we don't have time,' she said. 'I'll burn something instead. For focus. So we can think.'

Camille lit the incense and closed her eyes, swaying gently. Benjamin watched the wisps of smoke lifting.

'I'll tell you what I think,' Camille said eventually. 'I think that you mustn't give up on that dog.'

'But I've already let him go,' Benjamin said, feeling hopeless. Feeling as though Gary was a million miles away. A fading image. Camille stood up.

'You just need to get him back,' she said.

Benjamin squeezed his eyes tight shut, to stop himself getting upset.

'I don't know where he is.'

'But you said it yourself. He's yours.'

'The police won't think that,' Benjamin said.

'Well. There are complex questions of morality at play that have nothing to do with law enforcement. For example, I was thinking the other day, about pets. We definitely don't own them. So, it's very much up to the individual to make sure the animal is at peace with the partnership. But also, what if Gary is actually a reincarnated relative? Imagine what that would throw up? How it would muddy the water?' Now I've seen him I actually think it's very viable that he's your grandfather.'

Sometimes Camille's thoughts were like fireworks going off. Benjamin stuck with the first.

'I don't know where he is,' he said.

Camille looked at him. 'I think you do.'

Benjamin shook his head and Camille grinned.

'Do you know where he is?' Benjamin said.

Camille closed her eyes and breathed out.

'I do,' she said.

'How?'

Camille held her phone out. 'I can feel certain vibrations. But also, I Googled it.'

Benjamin looked at the little screen. It was a racing schedule for the dog track.

'He's running in the 18:45,' Camille said, beaming.

Camille looked at Benjamin's clothes. 'There's a tub full of returned items there. Have a sort through and change your garb if you want,' she said. 'Those ones are quite dirty. I finish at six. We'll head over then.'

Benjamin hadn't had time to look at his clothes. He was covered in mud and there were red marks on his jeans that he assumed was blood—that he hoped desperately was his.

A voice crackled through the walkie-talkie. 'Camille to front till for an age check,' Jill said.

'I'm on my break,' Camille replied.

There was a short pause before Jill came back on again. 'For what it's worth,' she said, 'I think this is a Code 4. Or a Code 6. I can't remember. Whichever one is the one we say when there's a shoplifter.'

'Jesus Christ,' Camille said, hustling herself towards the door. 'I'm on my way, Jill.'

By the time Camille returned, Benjamin was wearing a white dress shirt and a track jumper like a sprinter might wear. On his lower half he had a pair of combat trousers. He pressed the poppers shut on the leg pockets.

'I've been reflecting on our situation,' Camille said.

Benjamin liked that she said 'our situation,' even though he knew it was his and she was just being nice.

'I have a really big garden, don't I? He can live with me until we figure out exactly what we're going to do. You can stay in the spare room while your nan's in hospital and see him every day.'

Benjamin had seen Camille's house. She was a good person, and if absolutely forced he would probably go round instead of hurting her feelings, but he knew with 100 per cent certainty that their domestic styles did not line up.

'You'd love the spare room: it's got fairy lights and rugs on the wall,' Camille said. 'It's also where I keep the bulk of my healing crystals and spiritual figurines.'

Benjamin looked at Camille.

'I have to look after the caravan,' he said.

'We could do that together. Swing by, do a refresh every couple of days.'

Benjamin looked at Camille, his gaze unwavering.

'Do you actually think we can get him back?' he said. 'Really?'

'I know we can,' she said.

Camille dragged some clothes out of the returns bin.

'I need something to obscure my uniform,' she said. 'I don't want to waltz in there in company get-up.' She threw out a parka with a fake fur collar. 'How did you get here by the way?'

'On a small motorbike.'

Camille spun round.

'That seems very unlike you. Do you have a licence?'

Benjamin was holding a pair of sunglasses up in front of his face. He looked at Camille through the dark lenses.

'It's Leonard's,' he said. 'I borrowed it without asking.'

'Fair enough,' Camille said.

Benjamin followed Camille around the empty store while she cashed up, licking her finger to peel the notes as she counted the stacks. He'd already warned her about cocaine residue, so he assumed she liked to do it. He lifted the divider from the conveyor belt of the back till, feeling strangely reassured as he watched it turn on its infinite loop.

'I just realised,' he said. 'I only have one safety helmet.'

Camille waved him away.

'I've got my pushbike helmet,' she said.

'That won't be sufficient.'

Camille stopped counting.

'There are occasions when it's worth the risk,' Camille said.

Benjamin hadn't thought of it that way before. As though bravery were a currency and some items were expensive.

'I don't think I'm very brave,' Benjamin said.

'Bravery is a skill.' Camille said. 'You just need to practise. Let me set the alarm and I'll meet you outside.'

The car park was mostly empty. In the far corner, under some trees, there were three or four saloons with the windows steamed up. Camille shook her head.

'I've never really seen the appeal myself,' she said.

Benjamin didn't know what she meant.

'Vehicular eroticism,' she confirmed. 'I had an ex that drove lorries who was really into it, but it seems very unhygienic.'

Benjamin pointed at the bike. 'I haven't ridden it with two people on it before,' he said, considering the added difficulty of another person flopping about on the back. The stress triggered a bout of terminal thinking.

'What if I wobble over and one of us gets impaled on something?' he said.

Camille clipped her bicycle helmet on and smiled.

'Impaled on what?' she said.

'A fence?' Benjamin said. 'Or damaged road signage?'

Camille climbed on and started the bike without looking.

'We won't get impaled,' she said. 'Get on.'

Everything was happening very quickly. Benjamin hadn't been able to hash out the logistics.

'How will we get him back to yours?' he said. 'Once we've got him? Because he definitely won't stay still on the back.'

Camille tapped the side of her nose.

'I've got a plan,' she said. 'But we need to leave now or we'll miss the race. I don't know how long he'll be there.'

'Can you ride?' Benjamin said.

'You're about to find out!'

Benjamin took a deep breath. He climbed on and Camille kicked the stand up and manoeuvred the bike until they were aimed at the exit. She seemed very competent, revving the engine. Before they pulled away, she tapped Benjamin's leg, shouting over the noise.

'Did you manage to figure out what the whale made you feel?' she said.

'Not yet,' Benjamin said, 'no.'

Twenty-nine

Mike picked up the phone at the nurse's desk and punched in the number on the computer screen in front of him. He wrapped the cable around his finger while it rang through to the empty caravan.

The walls absorbed most of the sound. It didn't stop a seagull from jumping off the roof and into the open air, startled, before drifting over the caravans and back out over the sand.

Thirty

The motorcycle's headlight surged, bathing the concrete in yellow light as Camille pulled away. Benjamin leant on her back as she picked her way through a labyrinth of terrace houses then rode along the subtle curve of the front. They whipped along the line of a metal defence designed to stop cars from falling on sunbathers and Benjamin watched the blur of the uprights sliding by. He spaced out, imagining a car careening off and lumping on top of him. When Camille accelerated, he nearly fell off the back.

'Make sure you hold on tight,' she shouted, 'we're nearly there.'

Benjamin squeezed Camille's fleshy middle and thought about what she'd said, about bravery, about it being worth the risk. Camille was brave. He knew that as he watched the short hairs on the back of her neck flapping about below her inadequate bicycle helmet. He tucked in closer to shelter from the wind as she propelled them forward, the tiny engine wailing into the salt-heavy air.

Thirty-one

Camille bumped down through the gears and swung in under a pink neon sign in the shape of a dog. She skirted the puddles to a space near the ticket desk, then jumped off and rubbed her ears enthusiastically.

'They feel like they're going to fall off,' she said. 'It's tremendously cold.'

Benjamin felt bad his helmet gave better protection from windchill than Camille's. A chunk of yellow foam fell out when he took it off which made him feel slightly better. The shit condition made him think about Leonard. He put his hand in his pocket for the keys and felt angry again. He wanted to throw them into the ocean, imagined them sinking through murky water and rolling around in the wash.

'When we get inside,' Camille said, 'we need to make sure that we act *casual*. So we don't arouse suspicion.'

'How will we do that?' Benjamin said.

'There are lots of ways, but mostly, just act like other people,' she said. 'Like someone who would be here normally.'

Benjamin looked at the ground and nodded like he knew what she meant.

'Who would be here normally?' he said, for clarity.

Camille looked up, thinking about it. The rain had stopped but the sky was still swollen and grey.

'The collective term is "punters", I think,' she said. 'The main thing is to look like we're here recreationally. We can pretend to sip alcoholic drinks in the bar while we look for him.'

'Is that what punters do?' Benjamin said.

Camille nodded.

'It's one of the things.'

Camille made her way over to the ticket booth and joined the queue. There was a speaker above the window playing something from the eighties. She swayed in time to the music. After a minute or so, she covered her mouth and yawned.

She leant towards Benjamin. 'That was fake,' she said, grinning.

Benjamin raised an eyebrow.

'What was?'

'My yawn. Could you tell?'

'Not at all,' Benjamin said.

Camille seemed buoyant. She nudged his shoulder with hers.

'I was being nonchalant,' she said. 'Like I come here all the time.'

Camille stepped forward to buy the tickets. The woman in the booth had a bored face, like her features were very heavy and she struggled to animate them. Benjamin bobbed his head to the music from the tinny speaker like Camille had done, but he felt self-conscious and stopped. He'd never really been comfortable doing that. He felt looked-at when he danced in public. After moving, though, the stillness felt strange. Like he didn't know what to do with his body.

'Two tickets to the dog racing please,' Camille said.

The woman sniggered. 'The dog racing?'

Camille looked at her serenely. She slid a twenty-pound note across the counter under her index and middle finger.

'Yes please,' she said.

There was a moment where nobody did anything. Everyone just looking at one another. Then Camille moved very slowly through the turnstile towards the entrance and Benjamin followed. The woman watched them go.

'Walking slowly is another way of appearing casual,' she said over her shoulder.

At the door, Camille pulled a notepad out of her coat pocket and wrote down the cost of the tickets.

'I'll pay you back,' Benjamin said.

'Don't be silly. That's just so I remember what I've spent, so I can donate the same amount of money to a greyhound charity after.' She used both of her hands to frame the building. 'I'm not one-hundred per cent sure all this is all bad,' she said. 'But my gut feeling is that whenever money is involved, people compromise their values.'

Benjamin looked up at the neon dog sign, the single bulb twisting along an unbroken line. He thought about what money does, of what it makes you do. The bulb flickered.

'That makes sense,' he said.

Camille activated the sensor that opened the door. As it unveiled the people inside, Benjamin peered through the widening gap.

'It's very busy in there,' he said.

Camille nodded. 'It is,' she said.

'I'm just concerned about pathogens,' Benjamin said.

Camille took Benjamin's hand in hers.

'I know,' she said.

They walked in under a surge of heat from above the door. Camille made for a bar called 'The Dog's Bowl' and ordered two diet cokes. She sat down near a lady with turquoise eye make-up just as the lady took a large bite of her burger and jetted warm sauce onto her blouse.

'It feels a lot like I'm in one of my programmes,' Camille said. 'One of my crime thrillers!' She eyed the room.

'What we're doing here is commonly called "casing the joint",' she said. She took a sip of coke, wetting the fine dark hairs along the top of her lip, then lined the spine of her notebook up with the edge of the table.

'"Case" just means we look at it closely,' she said. 'Observe the comings and goings.'

Benjamin did a head-dip to show he understood.

'Will you take more notes then?' he said, gesturing at the pad.

Camille weighed it up.

'I could,' she said. 'If I need to record any details or anything. But we'll probably just play it by ear.' She smiled. 'These could easily be Bacardi and cokes you know,' she said, holding her glass up, using it to partially conceal her face like she was sharing a secret. 'We're fitting right in.'

Benjamin looked around the room. He scanned the names of the dogs about to race on a flatscreen mounted on the wall. Born Slippy, Trevor's Revenge and Lady GoGo all made an appearance, but no Gary. It prompted a subtle flap of Benjamin's hands. Camille noticed.

'His race doesn't start for a bit love. Let's try opening ourselves up to his presence. See if we can't locate him via alternative means?'

'Alternative means?'

'Spiritual channels.'

Benjamin didn't know much about those.

'The things that connect us aren't always visible,' Camille said. 'It's still about looking, just not with our eyes.' She moved her hand in a circular motion over her chest. '*Looking*,' she said with intensity. 'Just not with our eyes.'

Benjamin wasn't entirely sure what she meant. He also didn't know if this would help find Gary. He didn't want to upset Camille so he tried to concentrate anyway. It was hard because there was a race starting and the noise of the people was intrusive. As their collective volume swelled, he couldn't help thinking about the air they were sharing.

'I don't think I can,' he said.

Camille squinted and pressed her lips together like she was very determined.

'Sometimes you have to close your eyes,' she said.

Benjamin did, briefly, but the voices were starting to overwhelm him. He looked around. He tried to calm down by reading the words on a bright red advert for a white-collar boxing night. It didn't work because he ended up thinking about repeated trauma to the head.

'I can't sense anything,' he said, eventually.

Camille shrugged like that was very normal. Benjamin thought about Leonard again, what Camille had said about people compromising their values. He took a sip of his coke and felt the bubbles on his tongue, turned the metal loop on the car keys around the cheap rubber fob in his pocket. Something pierced his anger. He saw, fleetingly, that tangled up in the complicated and general sadness he was experiencing—had been experiencing for a while—there was a new and specific one. Two in fact. One was obviously for Gary, but the other was for Leonard. For what Leonard had managed to become.

'It probably just means there are physical structures blocking the signals,' Camille said. 'You know, walls and the like. Between you and Gary. Sometimes spiritual connection is a bit like Wi-Fi.'

She tried to demonstrate by moving her hands around in the air.

'It's a shame I hadn't connected with him previously,' she said, shaking her head, 'I'd have been able to do this much easier.'

Benjamin tried to use his face to express understanding and non-directional disappointment, but it was difficult to maintain. He could feel Gary's absence in his body, in the shallow breaths he was taking, the ache in his chest. It made him want to lie on the floor. Camille sensed it because she held him up at the elbow.

'You're sagging,' she said, reaching forwards to pull the material on Benjamin's shoulders upwards. She exposed the purple packet of animal biscuits in her coat pocket.

'I have more of these if you want? For the sugar.'

Benjamin didn't. He didn't feel hungry at all. He was watching the woman with the ketchup spill again, dabbing at it with a cloth while her husband hawked the room, more interested in whether anyone had noticed than whether she was feeling okay about it. It added to his sadness. Camille looked around, then rose from her chair.

'He's here,' she announced, pointing to a screen opposite, suspended from the ceiling. It showed track-side footage of a group of dogs being led out, with a list of names beside them. Camille gave Benjamin the thumbs-up and he felt an overwhelming surge of excitement.

'We're going to get him back,' she said, looking Benjamin straight in the eyes.

'Promise?' Benjamin said.

'I promise,' Camille said.

Camille made for the long, glass window overlooking the track, signalling for Benjamin to follow, but he stayed where he was. The volume of bodies was stressing him out. Their features seemed grotesque and exaggerated, huge mouths and wide eyes all filled with some basic enjoyment he didn't understand. Camille locked eyes with him. She used her hand and face to demonstrate a sequence of mindful breaths. When she gestured at the track like she might be able to see Gary directly, Benjamin stood up and tucked in his stool.

He got there in time to see the dogs in the traps, lunging forward and bumping into the gates.

'It can't be very good for their self-esteem, can it?' Camille said, leaning in.

'What's that?' Benjamin said.

'You know. Losing. For the ones that lose all the time. I can't imagine they feel very good about themselves.'

'Probably not,' Benjamin said.

Camille thought about it.

'I might set something up,' she said, earnestly. 'A home for dogs that tried their best, but weren't quite up to scratch.'

'How would you know they tried their best?' Benjamin said.

'Animals always try their best. But even if they didn't, I don't think effort is the only quality deserving of love.'

The woman on the tannoy cut through. Something about 'phenomenal form' and a 'late entry.' Camille looked at her wristwatch then twisted her arm to show Benjamin. Both of them looked out at the brightly-lit oval of track.

'It's time,' she said.

The lure came shuttling around the inside of the track and the gates lifted. A second later, the dogs exploded onto the sand, kicking it up in arcs behind them. Their mouths were uniformly open, tongues flapping between their teeth.

The dog in front was Gary.

It wasn't even a race. On the first straight he surged ahead and never slowed down, leaning into the long corner of the track, moving so fast his body was a blur. As the fake hare spun around and the gap opened up, the other dogs seemed to lose heart, knowing in their bodies they'd never be able to beat him. Camille put her hand on Benjamin's shoulder.

'That's him isn't it?' she said.

Benjamin pressed his hand to the glass.

'That's him,' he said.

Gary looked incredible. His strides had a perfect rhythm, feet so perfectly in balance that it looked like he was floating. Spectators were on their feet. They were crowding the window to see Gary cross the line. Benjamin couldn't take his eyes off him. When the race finished, one or two of the dogs trotted about but Gary just stood with his tongue hanging from his mouth, breathing hard, waiting to be collected.

Benjamin slammed his hand into the window, wobbling the glass. Camille took hold of his wrist.

'Stop it,' she said. 'We're being *casual*, remember?'

It almost looked as if Gary was going to turn in their direction, so Benjamin struck the glass again. People were looking. One lady backed away, sheer terror on her face, like this was the moment she'd been dreading her entire life.

'That's dramatic,' Camille said to the lady. 'He just gets very into his racing, that's all. Very involved.' Camille took a step forward, trying to reassure people by talking quietly and holding her hands up, palms forward.

When she turned back, Benjamin was already running.

He crashed through a door that said 'Trainers Only' and followed the sound of barking. His footsteps echoed as he ran along the corridors and the noise of the crowds began to fade. For a few moments, it felt easy. Like he could just keep running until he found Gary. Like a momentum would carry them all the way to the caravan, and further than that, too. Away from all of it. He stopped at a fork in the tunnel and heard a man's voice from a doorway just behind. That feeling fell away.

'You lost?' The man said.

Benjamin turned. Reality interrupting like earplugs being pulled out in the middle of a song.

The man stood holding a cup of tea, hot wisps steaming his glasses. Benjamin avoided his gaze. He looked at the shiny floor and the scuffed walls. The time between seconds seemed to stretch unnaturally and everything slowed. Everything except his heart, which hammered.

'Are you lost?' the man said again.

Benjamin felt Gary slipping away. He looked at the large window to his left, the bright-white barrier around the track outside and all of the faces in the stands, blurring together to form a living mass.

'I just needed a wee,' he said.

The man looked confused. He pointed back in the direction Benjamin had come from. 'The toilets are upstairs,' he said.

Benjamin's gaze followed the skirting board to a door at the opposite end of the corridor.

'No,' the man said, watching Benjamin's eyes. 'Back the way you came.'

Neither of them moved. The man tried to smile but the confusion pulled his face out of shape.

'Thanks,' Benjamin said.

The man raised his mug in a lazy toast. There were a few awkward seconds while he waited for Benjamin to leave, interrupted by Camille who came bombing around the corner. Her cheeks were red and she was breathing hard.

'Step back,' she shouted, rooting around in her bag. 'I've got pepper spray!'

The man looked at Benjamin, confused, a request for further explanation that didn't require words.

'I was just looking for a toilet,' Benjamin told Camille.

She pivoted.

'No law against that!' she said.

The man looked between the two of them. 'I didn't say there was!' he said.

Benjamin nodded. Camille was flustered. The man weighed things up.

'Do you know her?' he said.

Camille scoffed.

Benjamin wasn't used to seeing Camille like this. Even when a man tried to rob the supermarket with a plastic gun, Camille hadn't got angry. She just used what Elliot called her yoga-instructor voice while he marched around stuffing DVDs into the front of his coat. The man arched his eyebrow. Camille's hands were shaking.

'I don't really understand what's happening here,' he said. 'But if we all head back out now, there's no harm done.'

No one said anything for a bit.

'But there is, isn't there?' Camille said. She moved forwards to read a name badge on his chest.

'There is what?' he said.

'Harm done! Look around *Brian*.' She added some tone to his name now that she knew it. 'How do you know these animals are fulfilled? Have you even had anyone ask?'

Brian exhaled. His small eyes flicked between Benjamin and Camille.

'Are you two activists then or—?'

Camille thought about it. She pointed at Benjamin. 'He's not,' she said. 'I don't even know him.'

Brian did a face that suggested he didn't believe that at all.

'Are you Greenpeace or something?'

'Oh *Brian*,' Camille said, widening her eyes so that more white was visible than usual. 'That's a little naïve.'

Benjamin thought Brian was being quite reasonable given the situation. He wondered whether calling him naïve was a step too far.

'If you have concerns about the safety of the dogs, you should sign up for one of our tours,' he said.

That stumped Camille.

'Tours?' she said.

'Yeah. We run monthly tours so that people can see how much we care about the welfare of the dogs. We get all sorts coming. From charities to local journalists to famous celebrities. We had Paul Gascoigne once.'

Benjamin didn't know who that was.

'He played for England,' Brian said.

When Brian turned back to Camille, she was spacing out,

staring at the people in white coats as they led another group of dogs to the starting cages, shepherding their slim bodies along the path.

'We don't have time for this,' Camille said, talking to herself more than anyone else.

'You what?' Brian said.

Camille paced, getting herself worked up. Her eyes settled on an emergency exit that led to the track.

'We don't have time for this Brian!' she bellowed.

Even Benjamin didn't know where Camille's performance was headed. He was still trying to work it out as she leant her weight onto the green push bar of the emergency exit and fell out onto the track.

She'd made it to the middle of the oval before Brian even reached the door. He smacked his shoulder into the doorframe, holding it as he chased.

'I've hurt my pigging shoulder!' he shouted after her.

Camille ran until she was visibly fatigued, which wasn't far, then she lay down on the sand. She swept with her arms and legs like she was making a snow angel.

'Sorry Brian,' she shouted. 'I am sorry.'

Benjamin watched while Brian attempted to pull Camille to her feet. Whenever he tried to scoop her up by her armpits, red-faced and breathing heavily, she slumped back down, dead-weight. Her hair had fallen inelegantly over her face. It lifted as she panted.

Camille carried on sweeping the sand with her arms. She shouted, 'think of their self-esteem!' while Brian caught his breath. He was taking a rest by putting his hands on his knees when Camille made another break for it. She made it ten or fifteen feet by the time he caught up with her again.

The people in the stands didn't know what to make of it. A few of them cheered whenever Camille got away. Some threw their plastic cups at Brian to give her a better chance.

When Brian finally got a decent grip, linking his hands together around her, Camille dragged her heels and kicked her legs until one of her shoes came off.

'Wait, wait!' she shouted, looking genuinely distressed. 'My work pump.'

It threw Brian for long enough that he stopped dragging her and she was able to lock eyes with Benjamin. She did the deep-sea diver's sign for *okay*.

'Don't worry about me,' she shouted.

Benjamin wasn't exactly sure what she meant. He lingered, but the indecision felt wrong. Camille wrapped her arms around Brian so it looked like they were embracing, pinning him to the spot.

'Shit,' Benjamin said.

Then he went belting down the corridor.

Thirty-two

Benjamin followed the sound of barking until he found the kennels. It smelt clean and animal at the same time, like a veterinary surgery. At the back of the room, there was a row of small cubicles for the dogs. A few of them poked their noses through and sniffed the air as Benjamin worked his way along, looking for Gary. When he got to the last enclosure, a black dog watched him with interested eyes. Benjamin heard voices from the hallway.

'Absolute fruit loop!' someone said, laughing.

Benjamin panicked. He pulled a dirty blanket over his head and crammed himself into an empty kennel, looking out from the narrow slot in the front until a man with patchy facial hair came into view. He shook his head as he walked into the room.

'Absolute fruit,' he said again, simulating a flurry of punches. 'If it'd been me, I'd probably have socked her. Or I'd have deployed some jiu jitsu shit or whatever because it's like, equal opportunities.'

More people came in, chatting and laughing. They were leading the dogs from the race just run. Benjamin only had a slim view of the room.

'Did you know The Mighty Gary was missing until this morning?' a man said. 'Apparently Vasile got him back.'

'I heard that,' a woman said, sounding impressed, like the thought was getting her all jazzed up.

'He's an ominous guy.'

'Yeah. Ominously sexy,' she said.

A few of the others laughed.

'It's just a shame for the dog he didn't stay missing, if you ask me,' the man said. 'Wherever he was, it was probably better than being with Alf.'

No one replied. The man turned to the door and saw Vasile standing there with a lead looped around Gary's neck. It explained the awkward silence.

'I didn't see you,' the woman said, blushing. 'We were just joking.'

Vasile walked away. He didn't wait for Gary to cotton on that they were moving and yanked him by his collar. The dog was craning to look into the room like he had a reason to be in there.

'That was really embarrassing,' the woman said.

Someone piped up.

'You will go around objectifying sociopaths.'

Benjamin waited while they put the dogs away in silence. When they were gone, he crouched out of the kennel and stood up, muscles tight from hunching, and started running. He burst out through the fire exit just as the black Range Rover was wheel-spinning onto the main road, pulling out into a small gap in traffic.

He wanted to follow, but the bike was too far away. The 4x4 was already turning a corner, its brake lights shrinking into the distance. He felt like he'd been punctured, a cheap inflatable with the air all piling out.

Over by the kiosk, the woman was leaning against the wall with a cigarette between her fingers, scrolling through something on her phone. Its bright light illuminated her face. Benjamin looked around, thinking about what Camille had said—that bravery was practised. A few feet to his right, there were four industrial bins overflowing with waste, empty boxes stacked up beside them. He hoped they didn't have anything disgusting in them like raw egg albumen, or fish intestines, and picked one up. He turned it over so it look sealed, then he carried it to where the woman from the kiosk was leaning. He stood in front of her until she looked up at him.

'What are you? Some sort of mime act?' she said, going back to her phone. Benjamin didn't move. 'You want a ticket or something?' she said.

'I work for Alf,' Benjamin declared. 'I have to take this to him.'

The woman pulled her eyes away from her phone to look at him directly. Her gaze made him uncomfortable, like that was a serious thing to have to do.

'You work for Alf?' she said.

Benjamin hesitated.

'Yes. Sort of. It's part-time.'

The woman did a thinking face.

'You bought a ticket earlier though, didn't you?'

Benjamin didn't know what the correct answer was. He nodded.

'You know trainers and staff don't have to buy tickets?' she said.

Benjamin shrugged.

'He wants me to take this to his house,' he said. 'Do you know his address?'

'Don't *you* know his address?' she said.

'He did say,' Benjamin said. 'But I forgot.'

The woman looked upwards like her memories were a star map she needed to navigate.

'It's inland a way. Go to the roundabout by the supermarkets. Take the exit towards the city. When you can see a windmill from the road, you turn off. Then you follow that for a few miles—you'll know it when you see it. There's two great stone lions either side of the driveway. A bit melodramatic if you ask me.'

They both stood for a time without saying anything.

'Hopefully he's out and you can dump it on the steps,' she said.

'Thanks,' Benjamin said.

Then he walked across the car park and tried to make it look like he wasn't carrying an empty box.

Thirty-three

Benjamin set off riding slow and close to the kerb. At the windmill he turned right and followed the road like the woman had said. It was lined by banks of uncut grass and leafless hedges that leant inwards over the road to a point of almost touching. The vibrations through the bars made his hands feel numb.

At the top of a hill, the hedges disappeared, and the fields opened up—big slabs of darkness that made Benjamin feel a long way from things. He tried not to look as they whipped by, beginning to doubt the directions, until the white lions appeared in the distance. They were lit up by spotlights on the outside of a large house. Benjamin pulled over in a lay-by and killed the engine, breath drifting up like smoke signals. He headed towards an old barn for cover. The door was rotten and hanging from its hinges, and one of the walls looked like it was crumbling in on itself. Without the sound of the engine the silence pressed in on him. He kicked the bike onto its stand, then rolled his shoulders to loosen them up, waiting for his eyes to adjust. He was glad he did. The barn was full of rusty metal and farming equipment that looked like it had been strategically placed to give people tetanus. He stepped inside and looked up, saw the stars through splits and breaks in the sheet-metal roof. There was a pile of curtains on the floor, so Benjamin threw one over the bike to camouflage it. He made a mental note to avoid touching his face, in case someone had used the curtains to help a cow give birth and wiped placenta on them. It was impossible to know with farms when that might have happened.

After a few minutes, Benjamin heard a car start up. The Range Rover came rolling back out from behind the house. He obscured himself from view but felt the light of the headlights wash over him as it drove back past on the road. The glare stopped him seeing who was inside.

Once the silence returned, Benjamin watched the farmhouse. The crops in the field beside him leant over in a cool breeze and the odd cloud drifted by, silhouetted in the moonlight.

It wasn't long before Benjamin's eyelids started to feel heavy. He picked a section of concrete that looked free of debris and sat cross-legged by the door. It made the meat of his legs and bum feel cold. He fought sleep, blinks extending until his eyes were closed for longer than they were open. Drifting in and out, he kept picturing Alf in front of the caravan. Hearing the words he'd said: 'Just a dog. Just a fucking running dog.'

Barking shocked Benjamin into alertness. The dogs were setting each other off from somewhere behind the farm, their sounds carrying across the open land. Benjamin tried to work out if he could hear Gary, but it was impossible. He watched the house for movement, staring at the lit windows upstairs, waiting for the dogs to quieten down until the air was still again. He put his hands in his pockets to warm them and found Gary's collar there. It felt like he was close to him now. He had to be.

Benjamin didn't need his inhaler, but he took it out anyway. When he pressed the cylinder down, and breathed it in, the taste was reassuring. The lights in the house flicked off. Benjamin stood up and walked across the road.

At the edge of the lawn, Benjamin broke into a run, staying low as he skirted the blackest edge of the drive. He ducked down behind a wall and took in a lungful of crisp air, then peered over the top. He could feel himself swaying, like his body was trying to keep itself centred in a wobbling universe.

An outside light triggered. It cast gloomy shadows across the concrete, pinning Benjamin in the glare. The dogs barked again and he ran, following the gravel drive around back where it widened into a courtyard. There was a low brick building on the other side. More lights flooded the open ground. Benjamin ran towards the building and pushed his way through a grated metal door.

He stood catching his breath, desperate for the darkness to return. When it did, his night vision was gone. He heard movement somewhere inside, but it took a few seconds for the dark animal shapes to appear in the shadows of the cages. He went to one and leant on the mesh. There were several dogs inside. Two came up and sniffed the air, wagging their tails. Benjamin's eyes moved over each of them, but Gary wasn't there.

He walked to the next kennel. It was further from the main door so less of the light was making it inside. He picked up a torch from a worktop and shone it in.

The beam reflected off the eyes of a single dog like a pair of pale moons. It grumbled and dipped its head as Benjamin aimed the beam a few feet to its right and saw the patterns in its fur. White, brown and tan like a tiger. It was Gary. He was lying in the back corner on a bath towel, licking his paws. Happiness flooded through Benjamin. It filled him. Heavy tears fell onto his coat.

'It's me, it's Benjamin!' he said.

Gary ran to the fence. His tail flicked from side to side and he yawned, stretching his front legs out, lowering his chin until it almost touched the floor. He'd just pushed his nose through the mesh when Benjamin saw the large padlock on the door. He poked his finger through the squares to scratch Gary's muzzle and Gary licked it. As he wagged his tail his whole back half was swinging left and right.

'I've come to get you. If you want.' Benjamin whispered.

Gary ran over to his towel and picked it up. He dropped it on the floor in front of Benjamin with his mouth wide open. Benjamin looked around at the concrete and metal. At the solid structure of the kennel between him and the dog and the large padlock securing it. Gary whined.

'We just need to work out how to open this,' Benjamin said, pulling on the lock. He balanced the torch so he could see what he was doing, then hunted around for something he could use to break it. There was a screwdriver on the floor. He concentrated on trying to force the lock, leaning his weight into it, and didn't notice the floodlight switching on outside. The screwdriver bent in his hands as he heard the hinges of the outer kennel door swinging shut behind him.

It registered late, like a memory.

He turned to see the shape of a man at the door. It was Vasile, bright light surrounding him, face flat and expressionless. There was a scraping sound as he slid the bolt across, then a silence broken only by the click of another padlock. Vasile floated backwards into the courtyard and out of view.

Benjamin ran to the door and grabbed the bars with both hands. He pulled, but nothing happened. It made his chest feel tight, like a heavy weight was pushing down on his heart and reducing the space in his lungs for air. He went back to Gary's kennel and leant on the door. Gary licked his hand again and his tongue felt rough. Benjamin didn't usually do it, but he took two more puffs of the inhaler, even though it was technically an overdose.

Benjamin walked around looking at the walls and floors. He examined the ceilings and the corners, leant in close to where the panels connected and tested them with his weight. Everything felt sturdy and fixed. He looked at the only door again, then dragged a food tub over to where Gary was standing motionless inside, staring at him. Benjamin sat down on the tub and leant his head on the mesh. He could see his breath in the air and feel the cold on the back of his neck. He rubbed his arms to stay warm, but it wasn't long before his whole body was shaking. He couldn't keep his teeth together in his mouth. Gary was shivering too. At the end of the corridor there was a pile of towels on the floor. Benjamin picked a couple up, squeezed one of them through for Gary.

'Lie on that,' he said.

Gary licked his lips. He watched as Benjamin sat back down and wrapped the towel around his legs.

For a while, Benjamin tried to think of a way out. The problem was, even if he could free himself, Gary would still be locked inside. And he wouldn't leave Gary. Not for anything. He squinted at shadows, watching his cool breath rising and thought about the caravan. If something happened to him, dust would settle on everything, and the corners of the rooms would get mouldy, black spots creeping up the walls and onto the ceiling. He thought about all the hours his nan had spent combing the tassels on the rugs and polishing the surfaces—caring for the items she'd collected. He worried that if those things were gone there'd be less of her, somehow. He imagined the caravan sliding into the sea like the bungalows up on the cliffs and wondered what would be left of them both, knowing that the answer might be nothing at all.

The sound of gravel shifting under tyres interrupted his thoughts. After a few minutes he heard a voice, the sound of feet on the stones, and laughter. Alf limped up to the door with Vasile a few feet behind him. When he leant in, it was like he was looking at a wild animal. All teeth—a dirty great grin—swaying and holding onto the door to steady himself. He seemed intoxicated.

'Leonard told me,' Alf said. 'That you weren't going to cause me any problems.'

Benjamin didn't answer. Alf turned to Vasile.

'I said I'd seen him sneaking about with some woman, didn't I Vasile?'

Vasile nodded. Benjamin looked Alf in the eyes.

'This is all really irritating, you know,' Alf said. 'Not to mention ridiculous. Did you think you'd just walk out with him or something? Swan about town, like Rudd Weatherwax and Lassie? Was that the picture?'

Alf waited a beat for Benjamin to answer, but he stayed quiet.

'That was Lassie's owner and trainer. If you're wondering. Rudd Weatherwax.'

Benjamin nodded his head. Alf carried on.

'I think you're thick,' Alf said, his cheeks filling with blood. 'Young people all seem to believe the world is revolving around them. Putting all their stupid video-logs up online like somebody gives a shit.' Alf moved one hand around the other like planets orbiting. 'Is that what you think? It's all just—revolving—around you?'

Benjamin shook his head, no. He felt like it was the opposite. He was insignificant matter, not dense enough to be held by gravity, falling away from the things that he needed most.

'I think you do think that,' Alf said, walking towards him. 'But you should know, I'm a member of the Council. And a mason. People in the community respect me. You'll probably go to borstal when they find out you were trying to steal a dog from a retiree.'

When Benjamin still didn't say anything. Alf laughed.

'Do you know what thalassophobia is?' he said.

Benjamin did because he had an extensive knowledge of phobias, but he didn't tell Alf.

'It's a fear of the vast emptiness of the sea, amongst other things,' Alf said. 'A fear of waves. A fear of being away from land. It's the vast emptiness bit I like.' Alf leant in and out, changing the aperture of his big bloodshot eyes to focus.

'You're a very long way from land, Benjamin. Is my point.' Alf squinted. 'Why do you give so much of a shit about that particular dog anyway?' he said.

He pointed at Gary, twisting his finger in the air as if he was screwing it into Benjamin's chest.

'You know what he's worth or something?'

Benjamin shook his head no. He knew that he was worth a lot, but it had nothing to do with money. He looked at Gary. He didn't know *why* he was special, particularly. Just that he was. He shrugged, which annoyed Alf.

'For someone about to be arrested you'd think you'd have an idea,' Alf said. He turned to Vasile for validation, but Vasile wasn't really listening. He was carefully peeling the wrapper off a bar of chocolate.

'I have the munchies, Vasile,' Alf said. 'Give me some of that.'

Vasile looked longingly at the bar, then broke half off. Alf put some in his mouth and swayed.

'Want some?' he said to Benjamin, showing him his brown teeth, talking and chewing at the same time.

Benjamin shook his head. 'No thank you,' he said.

Alf smirked.

'Maybe I'll give some to the dog then,' he said. 'He'll like that. A lovely bit of chocolate.'

Benjamin looked up. 'Chocolate is poisonous for dogs,' he said.

Alf mocked surprise.

'All these years and I didn't know that,' he said. He threw the rest of the bar into the kennel with Gary. Gary ate it. 'I'm sure he'll survive,' Alf said, laughing.

Benjamin watched and worried as Gary chewed the bar, working it round, caramel sticking to the roof of his mouth. Alf got a kick out of it.

'I could help look after him,' Benjamin said.

Alf burst out laughing.

'Yeah! We could all be best friends and go to Center Parcs. Leonard could come, too.'

That made Benjamin feel stupid. He could feel himself blushing and looked at the ground. His teeth were chattering again. He clenched his jaw to try to stop Alf seeing but he'd already noticed.

'Cold in there, is it?' he said.

Benjamin shook his head; *no,* and Alf pressed his face up close to the grate. In the moonlight he looked pale and sweaty.

'If you're not cold, you won't mind waiting in there until morning, will you?' He laughed. 'I don't want to drag the police over in the middle of the night. I was hoping to keep them out of this completely,' he said. 'Because I have somewhat of an aversion.' Alf looked at Vasile. 'Don't I have an aversion, Vasile?'

Vasile grinned. Alf tapped his fingers like a pianist on the metal of the door.

'Check him for a phone,' he said.

Vasile removed the padlock. He grabbed a handful of the material above Benjamin's shoulder and patted his pockets down. When he looked him in the eyes Benjamin could smell his sour breath.

'No phone,' Vasile said.

'How do you do all your social media whatnot?' Alf said.

'I don't do that,' Benjamin said.

'You are a weird kid,' Alf said.

Vasile took the torch and locked the door behind him.

When they were gone, Benjamin sat back down on the bucket. A few minutes after that the light switched off and the kennel was plunged into darkness. Benjamin's limbs felt heavy with the thought of everything he'd touched since he last washed. He squeezed the last bit of sanitiser out onto his hands and waited for it to dry. Gary was standing as close as physically possible on the other side of the fence. The sound of his breathing, of the other dogs in the kennels dreaming, distracted him a little. Gary pressed his body into the mesh so that his skin and fur was divided up into little squares.

Benjamin laid down on the towel. He squeezed his arm through the gap under the gate and stroked Gary, moving his fingers over the soft hairs on his leg. He flipped open the cigarette packet June had given him and took out one of the stones, smoothing it between his thumb and forefinger until he felt something like sleep, consciousness fading in and out. Then he heard something outside. A dragging noise and the sound of someone whispering, maybe. He lifted his head.

'Benjamin!'

He wished he had the torch.

'Who's there?' he said.

Leonard was pulling himself across the concrete, dragging a pair of bolt croppers and the leather duffel bag Benjamin had left at the caravan.

'Keep it down you nimrod!' he said, lifting himself up onto his elbows to inspect the heavy lock on the door. He reached up slowly and tried to exert all of his force instantaneously. When it didn't work, he relaxed, then tried again—dangling his weight from the lock. It didn't give. Leonard motioned for Benjamin to bring his face closer, waving him in until they were inches apart on either side of the mesh. Leonard used the dim light of his phone to show Benjamin his face. His black eyes looked darker, like make-up, or military camouflage. He pushed his hair behind his ears. The dogs were stirring.

'What are you doing?' Benjamin said, sitting up away from the door. He didn't want to look at Leonard.

'What does it look like? I'm here to extract you. This is a rescue mission.'

Benjamin returned to the tub, his back to Leonard.

'How did you know I was here?' he said.

Leonard gestured at a bag by his feet. 'I didn't, actually. I just came here to repossess some items,' he said. 'Up to the value of what they owe me. Lucky I did, really.'

'That's not true,' Benjamin said.

Leonard laughed.

'No, it isn't. Camille texted me.'

'Camille?'

Leonard used his phone to demonstrate sending someone a text.

'Yeah. We've been texting. It's cool she got chucked out for streaking.'

'She didn't streak. She wasn't naked. How do you even have her number?'

'From that time I called in sick for you. Besides, you didn't tell me she had such an allure.'

'What's an allure?'

'A mystique. Like a French woman.'

'You're being weird,' Benjamin said. He thought about it for a few seconds. 'How do you know what she looks like?'

'She sent me a selfie.'

'No she didn't!'

'No. She didn't,' Leonard said. 'I looked her up online and found a local news piece from the time she got held up in the supermarket. She was doing the requisite Trauma Face for the news people, but it didn't stop her from being visually appealing.'

'How did she know I was here?'

'Oh, that bit was me. She told me to meet you both at the track. By the time I managed to find my spare car keys and get there—at great personal risk might I add, because I have a lifetime ban—you were just leaving. On my motorcycle. I had a feeling this was where you might be headed.'

They were both quiet. Leonard pointed at the lock. 'Chunky old bitch that, isn't it?' he said.

'Yeah,' Benjamin said.

Leonard tapped the padlock with the cutters, weighing it up, then rummaged through the bag.

'Going to need something a bit more heavy-duty for this,' he said. 'I think I saw something appropriate in one of the other sheds.' Leonard laid down flat again. 'Won't be long,' he said, crawling out of view.

In the house, the lights had gone off. Benjamin pulled the towel further up and around himself, then watched the door while he waited for Leonard. The time dragged. He started to wonder whether Leonard had left him there and felt angry all over again. Leonard was probably the worst person he'd ever met. Worse than Alf and Vasile because he was a liar, too. He couldn't stop remembering the things he'd come out with. In the caravan and at the snooker club, out on the cliff top doing his stupid martial arts, all he'd done was lie. Leonard appeared at the door again.

'This pair of bastards should have it off,' he said, waving a pair of bolt croppers around. 'And don't be too pleased to see me.'

Leonard put the jaws around the shackle and squeezed, gritting his teeth. It took much longer than it did in films. For a time, it didn't look like anything was happening, then the lock gave. The bolt croppers slipped off and lumped the door and a metal sound rang out across the yard. It set the dogs off again. Gary stood up and motioned to bark in sympathy, but Benjamin held his mouth closed.

'Shhhh,' he said. 'Please.'

Gary didn't bark. The other dogs were unsettled though, pacing around their kennels. Leonard was laying very still. He had the croppers resting on his chest with his eyes closed. Benjamin watched the house.

After a few seconds, Leonard opened his eyes, one at a time. He sat up and slid the lock open. Benjamin stood as Leonard walked straight over to the other cage of dogs. He was letting them all lick his hands and fingers and fussing them.

'Be quiet, you lunatics,' he said.

Once the dogs had settled down, Leonard walked over to

Gary's kennel and broke the lock. It was smaller and went easier than the one on the outside. Gary backed off and stood in the corner. He looked at Benjamin. Benjamin let the towel fall to the floor.

'What the hell's that?' Leonard said.

'A dog towel,' Benjamin said.

'Not like you. Looks like it's covered in all sorts of shit.'

Benjamin hadn't really thought about it. He looked at the towel laying on the floor and felt the stress he'd been too distracted to register earlier on. Realised it was actually the second dirty covering he'd utilised that day.

'Could even be actual shit,' Leonard said, leaning in to sniff it.

Benjamin looked at his hands. He was thinking about how much he wanted to wash them when Leonard swung the door open and Gary bounded over, jumping up, trying to lick his face.

'Sickeningly loyal, those things,' Leonard said, grinning.

After Benjamin and Gary had had a few seconds, Leonard spoke up.

'Listen, mate,' he said. 'I'm— you know. For everything and stuff. You know?'

Benjamin waited for Leonard to say what he was getting at. Leonard stared at the concrete floor of the kennels.

'Maybe we should go,' he said. 'Talk and that—later.'

Benjamin nodded.

'Where's the hog?' Leonard said.

'What's a hog?'

'The bike. The motorcycle mate.'

'Oh. I parked that in the barn,' Benjamin said.

'That's a thoughtful strategy,' Leonard said.

They walked out of the kennels in short procession with Leonard leading the way. Gary trotted along a few inches from Benjamin's ankles, occasionally brushing his trouser leg.

Benjamin felt vulnerable in the open, expecting the bright lights to switch on or to hear Alf's voice again. As they rounded the corner Leonard pointed towards his car. It was parked at an angle in a lay-by, halfway up a grass verge. Benjamin could see the first signs of morning in the distance.

'I'm there,' Leonard said, grinning.

'How did you manage to get past the light?' Benjamin said.

Leonard reached into his pocket and produced a pair of wire cutters. 'Via espionage. I was a sparky by trade, for a while. You know. After snooker. Before professional driving.'

They were about ten feet onto the front drive when the lights triggered. They both stopped and Leonard spun around.

'That's annoying,' he said, looking up at the house. 'There must have been a decoy wire.'

Benjamin checked for Gary. He was waiting patiently by his feet.

'We should leg it,' Leonard said, breaking into a run, sprinting down the drive as fast as he could with the bag swinging around on his back.

Benjamin and Leonard tripped on clumps of mud. Lights were switching on inside the house and all of the dogs were barking. As they made it to the road the farmhouse door crashed open.

'Stay in there,' Leonard said, nodding at the barn. 'They'll follow me.'

His eyes were soft as he said it. Benjamin thought about arguing but stayed quiet.

'Get that stubbly torpedo out of here,' Leonard said, throwing the duffel bag. 'Your tent's in there. And other essentials. Head for the place I told you. The woods by the sea.'

Benjamin crouched in the shadows, hoping they hadn't seen him. He held Gary around his chest and neck. Not because he needed to stop the dog from leaving, but because it made him feel safer. He put his hand on Gary's back and ran his fingers along his spine. Leonard was trying to start the car but he was struggling. He was bashing the steering wheel, shaking it. The lights of the 4x4 at the farm flicked on and its engine roared into life.

Leonard's car was making a whirring, electrical sound. Just as the Range Rover went bouncing over the corner of Alf's lawn it fired and Leonard put it into gear, revving it like he was a racing driver. The engine sounded broken when he stamped his foot flat, spinning the tyres on the gravel. The car snaked along as it picked up speed. He was only fifty yards down the road when the Range Rover came hammering past the barn, the front end bouncing high over the verge. Benjamin saw a flash of Alf's face and couldn't imagine a hatred more vast and cruel.

Benjamin watched Leonard drive flat out along the road, turfing a dust cloud up in the air with the Range Rover following. He waited for the sound of the cars to fade before he broke cover. He looked around. Only half of his head was out of shadow when he saw Vasile on the drive, watching, motionless. He didn't wait to see him run, just turned and dragged the curtains off the bike. He pushed it outside and started the engine, revving, black smoke tumbling out of the exhaust.

He dragged the bag onto his back and pulled on the helmet. Behind him, he saw Vasile running across the field, covering the ground at a speed that seemed unnatural.

'You have to follow me,' Benjamin shouted to Gary as he pulled away. 'You have to follow me.'

And Gary did.

Thirty-four

Benjamin took turns at random, hoping to shake Vasile, craning his neck to see if he was following. He heard the constant pitch of the engine in his helmet and the sound of his own quick breaths. On the wider bits of road, Gary ran in front, crossing the bike's path with loping strides. He was good at timing it. After each burst he'd slow, dropping back next to Benjamin for a stint with his tongue hanging from his mouth.

The rising winter sun strobed between the hedges and filled Benjamin's eyes with buttery light. When they were far enough away, Benjamin backed off, taking glances at the dog, waiting for Gary to catch his breath. As he watched him stretching out and contracting, his muscles moving him easily and naturally along the potholed road, Benjamin felt like there was a current flowing through him. Something straightforward and chemical. And as he watched Gary, he knew the dog was feeling it too. Vibrating with something so powerful that a moment felt like forever.

Benjamin had been given something back that was lost, something he needed to hold on to with everything he had. He headed for the place Leonard had talked about. The woods by the ocean. A place, he hoped, where no one would find them.

Thirty-five

Benjamin pulled into the car park and cut the engine, rocking the bike onto its stand. His hands were shaking. He waited while Gary ran a loop or two around him with his mouth open and his eyes wide. The dog's ears were lying flat on his head when he walked over to a muddy puddle to drink.

'Sorry,' Benjamin said.

Benjamin was worried he'd made Gary run too far. He took a water bottle from the duffel and poured some into his cupped hand. 'This will be cleaner,' he said.

Gary watched the water trickle through the gaps in Benjamin's fingers, then drank from the puddle again. As he did, Benjamin stared at the dome of his head, at where his brain was located. Benjamin thought about the thing that made the dog alive, made him more than bones and fat and tissue. Then about the inevitable dying of cells over time. When Gary returned, Benjamin could see the dog's heart beating from the subtle movement of his ribs. He crouched and Gary walked to him. When Benjamin put his arms around the dog, he felt Gary's eyelashes brush the skin of his forearm. He leant his face on Gary's back, pushing his fingers into the coarse hairs again and felt his warmth. Holding the dog made Benjamin's shoulders and back and body feel light and loose in a way he'd almost forgotten. He felt a kind of helplessness. Not because of what was happening, but because he realised how much he needed Gary to exist forever. So that whatever happened, wherever Benjamin was, he could think about the dog walking around and smelling things. He could think about him lying in slices of light with the sun warming his fur, internal organs all functioning perfectly, and he would feel okay.

'I never want you to die,' he said.

Benjamin heard a car approaching and panicked. He rushed to the bike and tried to push it into cover, but the mud was thick and slowed him down. He wasn't even halfway there by the time the car was at the entrance to the car park. He watched it stop, engine idling, exhaust smoke rising up in the cold.

There was a family inside. A small girl in the back had her hand flat to the window while her parents argued in the front seats. They were bickering over a map. The girl waved at Gary with a wand, watching him stretch out his legs. It was the kind of wand you dip in Fairy Liquid and water to make bubbles. She opened the window and blew a big one, then lots of little ones, their unstable shapes trembling in the air, colours shifting as they drifted into the woods. One of them made it to Gary. He opened his mouth to bite it, but it popped just in front of his nose. Benjamin thought about the oxygen that was trapped inside the bubbles as the car pulled away and disappeared down the road. He thought about everyone on Earth breathing them out. About all of the contaminated air floating around at the track and the garage, the supermarket and the hospital. He waited for the silence to return.

When everything was still, he angled the bike behind a tree so it couldn't be seen from the road. The stand sunk into the mud and the bike fell over. Gary jumped. He watched with his head dipped as Benjamin tried to lift the bike again, but it wouldn't move, so Benjamin covered it in sticks and branches, concealing its shape with handfuls of leaves. Benjamin felt the damp earth on his hands. When he was finished, he felt it drying on his skin. The trees loomed over them.

'We can always come back,' he said, 'if we need a vehicle again.'

Gary's tail wagged.

There was a metal fence running around the outside of the wood. At regular intervals, signs with red writing threatened trespassers with prosecution. Gary urinated on the mesh and caught up with Benjamin by a break in the boundary, near a stream that flowed into the woods with purple oil swirls on its surface.

Benjamin edged his way down and Gary watched, blinking frequently. The thick mud sucked at Benjamin's boots as he talked himself through the procedure.

'I'm going to work my way down slowly,' he said, transferring his weight around the end of the fence, stretching out a leg and pulling himself towards the other bank. 'I need to be careful,' he said, eyeballing the rusty metal.

He slipped. Before he could stop himself, his trailing leg was in the river. It dragged his trousers across the sharp ends of the fence and grazed the skin on his thigh. He let go and fell into the stream.

'Fucking hell,' he said, looking at his feet, socks soaked through in his boots.

Gary was watching intently. He turned towards the sound of another car driving past on the road as Benjamin scrutinised the rip in his trousers and the bright red blood squeezing its way through the pin-pricks of his graze. He hoped there wasn't river water inside his leg, dabbing at it with his sleeve, wondering if the oily swirls were toxic. He did everything he could not to think about tetanus.

He was staring at the cut, sweating, when he heard the snapping sound of stepped-on twigs. Gary balanced his weight across three paws with his ears pointing upwards and looked around. Benjamin couldn't see anyone. He bent over and picked Gary up, feeling the uneven weight of the dog across his biceps and forearms, and shuttled towards the stream. Gary was just as awkward to carry as he had been in the caravan—all legs and ribs and backbone. He wriggled around, his weight compressing Benjamin's chest, stopping his lungs from fully inflating.

'You're making this difficult,' Benjamin said, trying to rub Gary's back leg, to soothe him. 'We need to get across the water. They could be following us.'

He didn't know how likely that was, but something about Vasile terrified him. He was shark-like. Serene on the surface with a darkness just beneath.

At the sight of the river, Gary fidgeted more persistently. Benjamin adjusted his hands to get a better hold and Gary seemed to relax. He leant into Benjamin's chest, settling enough to be carried, just as Benjamin stumbled forward and dropped him into the stream.

The dog ran so fast he fired water and stones into the air behind him as he surged up the bank. At the top, he shook himself dry.

'I'm sorry,' Benjamin said, dripping river water onto the mud beneath his feet, making it slippery. He sat down on a stump to decompress. Before he could stop him, Gary pressed his tongue against the blood on Benjamin's shin. It felt coarse and warm. Benjamin pushed him away gently. He spat on a tissue from his pocket and wiped it over the blood, swapping his spit for the dog's. He looked at the red streak on the tissue and thought about Victorian operations. Dried blood on handsaws.

Benjamin opened the bag. His nan's tent from the caravan was inside along with an aluminium saucepan, which had been heavily used. There was also:

- three tins of beans;
- Some camping cutlery;
- the bottle of water;
- and several adult magazines.

Benjamin zipped it back up. He had one last look around—not certain why Leonard considered pornography an 'essential'—before walking into the woods with Gary skimming alongside, a low fog blanketing the ground.

Benjamin felt himself moving away from the noise of everything, good and bad, with each quick step that he took.

Thirty-six

Mike parked his Nissan Micra in a visitor's bay at the California Sands Caravan Park. He pulled a hoody on over his tunic, then took a crumpled piece of paper from his pocket with Benjamin's address on it. At the caravan, he walked up the steps and knocked on the door. There was a line of beach stones in the front window that told him he was in the right place, but no one answered. Benjamin's neighbour leant out of his porch door.

'The boy's in bother, isn't he? I knew something untoward was going on.'

Mike took the neighbour in. It looked like he was only dressed from the waist up.

'Have you seen him?' Mike said.

The neighbour took on a conspiratorial tone, leaning closer despite the fact that he was twenty feet away, whispering at speaking volume so he could be heard.

'I saw him a couple of days ago,' he said. 'It all seemed very dubious, so I've been keeping watch. There was a greasy and dishevelled-looking man with him and an Eastern European on their tail.' The neighbour narrowed his eyes, suddenly suspicious. 'Are you CID or something?'

'Not quite,' Mike said. 'I'm here in an official capacity though, don't worry.'

The neighbour seemed pleased. 'That's good,' he said. 'It's time the authorities were involved. Are you social services then, or—?'

Mike shook his head.

'I can't really say. To be honest, it's on a bit of a need-to-know basis.'

'Say no more! I can appreciate the need for discretion.'

The man looked away and Mike shook his head in disbelief.

'I'm going to check around back,' Mike said.

The neighbour nodded. 'I'll keep an eye out this side, for interlopers,' he said.

On the decking behind the caravan, Mike noticed the crack in the door, the dark footprint on the panel. He pushed it open until it bumped into the sofa inside, holding it in place.

'Benjamin,' he called in. 'It's Mike. Are you in there?'

'He's not in there.'

The neighbour was standing behind him in a dressing gown.

'It doesn't seem like he is,' Mike said.

'I would know. I keep the curtains open so I can monitor the lights.'

The neighbour dashed forwards to inspect the door.

'Look at that!' he said. 'He's hardly keeping the place in a good state of repair, is he? That's in all the contracts. A good state of repair. It says it very clearly.'

'I'm not sure that was him,' Mike said, taking his phone out of his pocket.

'Well, whoever did it, it will need to be made right, let me assure you.'

Mike ignored him. He walked down the steps to a bench out of earshot. He turned back to see the neighbour peering around the caravan wall and felt a very genuine concern for Benjamin. He took out his phone and dialled 999. It connected almost immediately.

'Police please,' he said. Then he talked them through everything he knew, right from the beginning.

Thirty-seven

Benjamin and Gary followed a narrow animal track through the woods until it opened up into a clearing. Ribbons of soft light were breaking through the trees, warming the spongy moss that covered the ground. It felt bouncy beneath Benjamin's feet as he looked for somewhere to pitch the tent. When he found a spot flat enough, he lined the poles up on the floor and laid out the groundsheet. The loose corners flapped in the breeze until Gary walked over and stood on top.

'You'll damage it,' Benjamin said, moving him—gently—with his foot. 'If you make holes in it, leeches could get in.'

Gary didn't seem to understand. He continued trying to position himself on the sheet until Benjamin had managed to put the tent up. Benjamin didn't know how long they'd have to stay in it, but he wanted to keep things hygienic. He took off his boots, because he'd been in public toilets and probably trodden in animal droppings, then lined them up by the entrance. He crawled inside with Gary watching.

'You'll need to come in here at some point,' Benjamin said. 'This is where we're going to live.'

Gary didn't move. He watched Benjamin organise their supplies, then line up the stones he'd put in June's cigarette box along the outside edge of the tent. It started spitting, raindrops sliding down the canvas and into the mud. Gary came inside and stood like his paws were glued to the floor, so Benjamin gave him another gentle nudge to get him moving and build his confidence.

Gary walked around, standing on Benjamin's legs and the duffel bag. He left bits of mud on things and sniffed at the walls until he got bored and tried to lie down. He aborted the first couple of tries because the groundsheet made weird noises, and, presumably, because the material felt strange. When he finally settled, Gary yawned, exposing the pink and black ridges on the roof of his mouth. It made Benjamin worry that the dog was dehydrated, so he poured water into the saucepan and put it on the floor. Gary drank some, then stood blinking. Benjamin finished what was in the bottle.

After that they listened to the gentle patter of raindrops on the outside of the tent. It was soothing, the wind working its way through the trees, lifting fallen leaves a few feet into the air before dropping them.

When it stopped, Benjamin unzipped the tent and found his soaking-wet shoes outside. He turned them upside down so the water could dribble out and rummaged around in the duffel where he found some plastic bags to put on over his socks. He pulled the shoes on, then began collecting the driest wood he could find to make a fire and dry them out properly. The damp moss left green marks on his hands, so he wiped them on the thighs of his jeans. When he had enough wood, he used a log to dig out a shallow fire pit away from the tent, so they wouldn't burn to death in the night. He scrunched up pages from Leonard's erotic magazines to get the wood going and dropped a match onto the paper.

Once the fire was established, Gary moved close enough that the heat made him pant. He sat with his mouth wide open, tongue suspended between top and bottom jaw like a water slide. Normally, the idea of inhaling smoke from an open fire would have made Benjamin more uncomfortable. He worried that breathing too deeply would welcome something ominous in, embedding it in the spongy alveoli of his lungs. But Gary wasn't thinking about the depth of his breaths. He was just there existing and feeling good in the warmth. Watching him made Benjamin feel better about things.

The dog licked his front leg, dragging his tongue across the fur, and closed his eyes for long enough that it looked like he might be asleep. Benjamin watched the flames creeping across the logs. He reached into his pocket and took out the clipping Leonard had given him, the one with Gary's photo on it, and read the words again. '*Dog that never loses, lost,*' it said. He looked at the grainy image, then at Gary who was still lying down and panting. He put his palm on Gary's ribs. Then he dropped the page into the fire and watched the flames turn it black.

After that he lost touch of time and his mind wandered. He thought about his nan, trying to picture the familiar features of her face, the pores of her skin, but he worried about the accuracy of his memories. That he was forgetting details and she was fading. He made himself remember the different shades of grey in her eyebrows and the smell of the perfume she wore when she went shopping. He thought about sitting in the kitchen, her spreading thick-cut marmalade on buttery toast, and tried to hear her voice, the feeling of it. The warmth. He thought about her giving him long words to spell from the doorway to help him fall asleep when he was younger.

'I'll cook,' he said to Gary, rousing himself.

Benjamin balanced a tin of beans in the fire and watched as the paper burnt away and turned the metal can black. When the beans were bubbling, he put the tin on the floor to cool down and Gary loped over.

'Those aren't all yours,' Benjamin said, tipping half of them onto a folded-over picture of a topless lady.

Gary ate the beans like they were very special, licking the magazine cover until it started wearing through. Benjamin gave him his share, too. The salt in the beans seemed to make Gary thirsty. He licked the empty bottle that was leant up inside the tent and whined. Benjamin knew human beings can't live without water for more than three or four days, but he wasn't sure about dogs. It was concerning. He dropped some wood onto the fire to keep it going. It hissed and bubbled in the flames.

'Let's go for a walk,' he said. 'We'll find you a stream to drink from.'

Benjamin knew it was a good start for the water to be flowing, in a survival sense, so the two of them headed out of the clearing and away from the oily stream they'd crossed to get into the woods. Benjamin ducked under branches and stepped over ferns with Gary in tow. The dog stared at Benjamin's feet as they slipped around in the bags.

When they found another part of the stream, Benjamin crouched down to assess it. It was barely a trickle, but it looked clearer. He lowered the bottle into the flow and watched the water swirl around the opening. When it was full, he held the bottle up to the sun and watched the particles drifting around inside while Gary walked to the edge and lapped at it directly.

'I'm going to boil it,' Benjamin said, swilling it around, scrutinising the debris. 'I might also filter it with a T-shirt,' he said.

He'd seen people do that before. He'd also seen people extract the moisture from camel shit in a similar way, but he wouldn't have been able do that, even if it had passed through a t-shirt and even if there had been camel shit available. He'd probably end up waiting to die.

The wind whipped through the trees around them. When it settled down, Benjamin heard the sea. It felt unnatural to hear it in the woods. It was as though it were beckoning him.

'I'm channelling my ancestors,' he said. Then he laughed because it felt like something Leonard might say. Now that Benjamin had Gary, his anger towards Leonard didn't feel quite so acute. When he thought about everything that had happened, Leonard seemed small in his mind. Weak and sad. His betrayal diminished him, and in a way, made Benjamin feel sorry for the things Leonard was so damaged by. Things like disappointment, and rejection. Loneliness. He pitied him for having the life that had pushed him to do what he'd done.

The closer Benjamin and Gary got to the ocean, the sandier the undergrowth became. At the edge of the wood, Benjamin found another hole in the fence. He almost forgot to pull his sleeves down to protect himself from tetanus as he crouched through. When he thought about doing that at the caravan park, it made California Sands feel like a long way away, somewhere he'd seen in a film or a dream. The ocean rolled and roared. Its scale was comforting. It was so large and permanent that it made him feel small and unimportant in a way that was freeing.

He looked up and down the flat expanse of beach, but there was no one there. The tide had drawn out to reveal a dark flat, chopped up by skinny channels of water. There were patches of green where seaweed had been left on the land, out of place. It felt funny to think about gravity doing that, of the sun and the moon holding back such enormous weight, moving the water up and down the beach. Gary walked ahead, pressing a steady chain of paw prints into the sand and, for the first time in a while, Benjamin thought about the whale. He looked in its direction, at a tiny point on the horizon where it should have been, but it wasn't there. Just open sky. The absence of something.

He assumed the tugs he'd seen had pulled it into deeper water and let it sink, that it hadn't blown up like Leonard had suggested. He wondered about the condition of its massive body, thought about it shuddering to a stop on the cold, dark sand at the bottom and imagined the weight in it resting there. He could almost feel the chill in its thick meat. It was only a few days since he'd first seen it, but it felt like longer. He experienced the void of time between then and now in a physical way, in his limbs, in the cuts on his face and the dirt on his hands. He squeezed his eyes shut and made himself think about other things. He picked up a stick and waved it.

'Want to play?' he said.

Gary wagged his tail. He unweighted his front feet, rearing up, and opened his mouth. His tongue flopped out and his eyes flicked around while he watched Benjamin wave the stick. Benjamin threw it across the sand. Gary looked like he was going to run but turned back.

'You have to chase it,' Benjamin said, jogging to pick it up. Gary didn't understand so Benjamin showed him again. 'I lob it. And you get it,' he said, pretending to throw the driftwood a few times, making sure Gary's eyes were following. He let go, watching the stick slap the sand. Gary stood where he was.

'It's an obvious thing to do anyway,' Benjamin said. 'I know you're not really like that.'

Gary stood still, save for the shuttering of his eyelids, not shivering or moving off. He stood by Benjamin's legs, existing in a single, satisfied moment. A place without a before or an after. For a second, Benjamin managed to do the same. Not thinking beyond the sand under him or the sky above until that's all there was. Just the two of them standing on the beach, watching the waves from a long way away.

Back at the camp, the fire had gone out. When Benjamin got it going again, he balanced Leonard's saucepan on top of two sturdy logs and filled it with the river water. Steam rose as it heated up. It took a long time to boil, but when it did, Benjamin let it cool, then poured it into the bottle. It looked like very weak tea and had an earthy smell. Benjamin moved his tongue around in his mouth. It snagged on the dry spots.

'I can't drink it,' he said, tipping it back into the pan for Gary.

Benjamin could see the licks of flame in Gary's eyes as he lay by the fire. When the heat reached his organs, the dog moved away and stood in the shadows, panting. The fire burned low and the darkness began to close in, settling into spaces the orange glow couldn't reach.

In the tent, Benjamin pulled the sleeping bag over his legs and listened. The sounds from around them, in the woods, made him feel more awake than he'd been in days. He remembered the way Vasile had moved across the field at the farm. A dark blur, heading towards him. In the quiet, he thought about the difference between being awake and asleep, between being alive and just not *being* at all. He thought about where his nan might be now, in which part of the hospital, and hoped that, wherever she was, she was dreaming. Or wandering through nice memories. Of being young and strong. Benjamin put his jumper on the floor next to him and patted it until Gary came over.

'You should sleep,' he said.

Gary rotated on the spot a few times, then slumped himself down. Benjamin put his hand on the dog, and then his head. With his ear pressed to Gary, he could hear the dog's body working, the gurgling of his organs. He breathed in the smell of mud and fur, felt the coarse hair prickling at his ear.

He wanted to sleep but couldn't. The dog was kicking his legs and shuttering his eyes, chasing something in a dream. When he kicked too hard or clawed at the wall, the dog woke himself up, occasionally angling a glossy eyeball towards Benjamin to see where he was. A few times, Benjamin woke him on purpose, so he didn't feel so alone.

If Gary dreamt, Benjamin hoped it was of things they'd done together. He didn't know if it worked like that. If they saw sequences playing out, or what. Maybe it was feelings, or errant signals, but he hoped that Gary was there in the field, standing by the metal helicopter on that first day they'd found each other, big dark trees swaying around behind them.

At some point, the energy in Benjamin's body seemed to bleed away, sinking into the floor through his hands and legs until he felt so heavy he couldn't move. Until it felt like he was just mass. Until finally, it felt as though he couldn't push things out any more. Memories washed over him. Hundreds of days and moments flooding in like a photograph album spitting out pictures. One settled. It was of her, standing in the doorway of the caravan. She'd been looking out at the rippling waves for most of an afternoon.

'I want to swim,' she said, breaking the silence.

Benjamin smiled. 'Where?' he said.

'There,' she said. 'In the sea.'

He laughed.

'I mean it,' she said.

'Have you even got a costume?'

She lifted the shoulder of her jumper so he could see she was wearing it.

'How will we get there?' he said.

'I was thinking about a limo?'

Benjamin shook his head.

'I don't weigh a lot. You can carry me,' she said. 'Just make sure that if you drop me, it's on my head. I don't want to bruise my model's legs.'

At first, she felt impossibly light, but they still had to stop so Benjamin could adjust his grip. A few times he put her down to give them both a rest.

'Take your shoes off,' she said. 'And roll up your trousers.'

Benjamin felt the cold wet sand swallowing his toes. As they made their way unsteadily down the beach, he looked around for razor shells and hypodermic needles. He put her down. She filled her lungs with ocean air, then took small but certain steps towards the lapping water. She dropped her dressing gown and stood under a flat, grey sky. The bumps of muscle in her shoulders had softened and she was paler, but it reminded Benjamin of the image on the mantel. The one where her hair was hovering sideways in the breeze.

She held her hand out for him, gripping him tight as they moved towards the water. She didn't even flinch as they walked in up to their knees.

'I'll be fine from here,' she said.

Benjamin stopped. He watched her move out far enough that the water took some of her weight. She let it, sinking until her head was the only thing above the surface. The sun was leaning out from behind a cloud. He wanted to shout something but didn't know what. As she swam, slowly, carefully, the drops of water looked like they were sparkling as they fell from the back of her arm.

'Isn't it cold?' Benjamin shouted.

'Yeah. But that's okay,' she said, moving out and away from him, tiny waves sliding towards a crisp horizon.

In the tent, the image of her was shrinking in Benjamin's mind. He pulled Gary in close and shut his eyes, hoping sleep would come, feeling the years of love for her so intensely that it hurt.

Thirty-eight

Gary's barking woke Benjamin. It was a bark he'd not heard before, a troubled one. Gary was already outside of the tent, moving away with his front half low and his teeth showing. Benjamin crawled out. There was a person lumbering through the undergrowth.

He thought about telling Gary to be quiet, but it was already too late because the person was about fifty feet away and heading towards them. Benjamin couldn't make much out through the undergrowth, but it looked like they were wearing a balaclava. He ducked behind a tree and picked up a log. Gary didn't stop barking as the person got closer. It was enough of a distraction that they walked straight past Benjamin—didn't see him hiding until the very last minute—when he swung the log at stomach height. Hard. He felt the connection in an oddly satisfying way, as the person, a man, folded over and held onto his ribs. Benjamin carried on swinging. The man fell backwards and Gary barked louder.

'Fuck! It's me,' the man shouted.

Benjamin hit him once more and snapped the log. The man dropped a plastic bag onto the floor and several cans of beer spilled out. Benjamin swung but the man managed to scoot out of the way.

'Go easy,' he shouted, rolling the balaclava up. 'Benjamin, it's me, Leonard!'

Leonard cowered on the floor, rubbing his side.

'It's me,' he said. 'Christ alive.'

Leonard looked up at Benjamin who still had half the branch held up above his head as if he might hit him again. His hair was in his eyes and his face was red.

'As if I haven't been subjected to enough of that already,' Leonard said, rubbing his ear. 'Did you need to hit me that hard?'

Benjamin shrugged.

'I didn't know it was you,' he said. 'Why are you wearing a balaclava?'

'Because espionage! Because we're on the run. Look!' Leonard said, reaching into his pocket. 'I made one for him! He pointed at Gary and dangled something. 'It's a sock with eyeholes cut out.' Leonard wriggled around in pain.

'I thought you were Vasile. Or Alf.'

'Alf's got a fucking gammy leg!' Leonard said. 'You won't find him hobbling around in the jungle.'

Benjamin threw the piece of wood to the floor and Leonard flinched. He scooted a few feet further away.

'I had to abandon the car in the chase,' Leonard said. After the farm, I lost my whole supply of *sake*.'

Benjamin raised his eyebrows. He didn't really care about that. 'Why are you here?' he said.

Leonard put his palms together like he was praying.

'To help.'

'Yeah, but why?'

Leonard took a deep breath, made a serious face.

'For redemption,' he said.

'I don't believe you,' Benjamin said.

Thirty-nine

Benjamin sat down on the log by the fire and watched the embers flicker. He avoided looking at Leonard, who was picking up his beers, making pained noises each time he bent over. Leonard pulled his comb from his pocket and pushed it across his scalp, but it was clear it hurt to lift his arm.

'Your face looks worse,' Benjamin said.

'It doesn't feel brilliant,' Leonard said.

'Does it hurt?'

Leonard shrugged. He walked around the white pile of ash where the fire had been, to a fallen tree a few feet away.

'There was another altercation when they caught up with me,' he said, lowering himself. 'Mind if I sit down?'

'It would be stupid if you just stood there,' Benjamin said.

Leonard rubbed his hands on his legs and looked around.

'I was just being polite,' he said. 'Normally, if someone is already sitting, they ask you if you want to sit down too.'

'You don't need to sit down,' Benjamin said. 'You're not staying.'

Leonard looked around at the tent and the fire. 'Don't be like that,' he said. 'I thought we were all right. You know, after I saved you.'

Benjamin looked at the broken log. He felt like picking it up again.

'I did say sorry,' Leonard said.

Benjamin turned to him. He could feel his face twisting up.

'When did you say sorry?'

Leonard looked surprised.

'At the farm. As we were evacuating. I said it then.'

Benjamin jabbed at the ashes, disturbing them. Smoke rose as he leant forward and pressed his forehead against Gary's.

'You might not remember the exact wording because it was such a dynamic situation.'

Benjamin ignored him. 'Do you know if Camille is all right?' he said.

'Yeah, she's fine!'

Benjamin glared at Leonard.

'Really fine,' Leonard said, smirking.

'She didn't get in trouble?' Benjamin said.

'No, no, she didn't get in trouble. She went straight home. No worries. I'm fairly sure.'

Gary yawned.

'He's looking good,' Leonard said, motioning towards the dog. 'You're taking good care of him.' Leonard rubbed his thumb and forefinger together, scrunched up his lips and made a kissing noise to beckon Gary over. It was weird and made Benjamin uncomfortable. Gary didn't move.

'He probably doesn't trust you any more because you betrayed him,' Benjamin said.

Gary was standing perfectly still with his head dipped low and his ears slicked back.

'Dogs don't understand betrayal,' Leonard said.

Gary pushed his head through Benjamin's knees and exhaled.

'Why is he standing here then?'

'He's probably constipated or something.'

Benjamin didn't respond. He looked at the dog. He wanted to say that dogs understand all sorts of things. That how could he know to lean on your shin when you felt shit otherwise. Or lick the back of your hand, even if it *is* unhygienic. He didn't say that though, because he didn't care what Leonard thought. He reached across and felt the warmth of the dog's body.

'He knows,' Benjamin said.

Leonard reached inside his pocket and produced a bottle of hand sanitiser.

'I brought you this,' he said, smiling.

Benjamin looked at his hands. They *were* incredibly dirty but he didn't want Leonard's help.

'I don't need it,' he said.

Leonard looked surprised. He gestured at the cut on Benjamin's leg and the mud on his jeans.

'I didn't think you liked all that,' he said, waving his hand around.

'Everything's already really dirty,' Benjamin said.

Leonard put the bottle back in his pocket. 'Suit yourself,' he said.

He stood up and walked to the other side of the camp where he shook the tent with his hand and leant in to look at the guy lines.

'I like your camp mate,' he said. 'You've done a good job.' He rubbed his stomach and passed his eyes over the supplies. 'You found the tins of food I packed for you then?'

Benjamin ignored him.

Forty

Benjamin walked around the camp, moving things like he was doing something important. He checked that the tins were in date and that the wood was neatly piled by the fire. He tried his best to pretend Leonard wasn't there.

'You should know, the police are definitely looking for us now,' Leonard said, to get Benjamin's attention. Leonard shook his head. 'It probably didn't help that I committed a serious road traffic offence while you were trying to steal that dog for the second time. During my latest car chase.' He tipped his head at Gary. 'We're big-time fugitives.'

Benjamin thought that seemed dramatic. He decided that going forward he would assume Leonard was fabricating unless there was obvious evidence to the contrary. Benjamin carried on stacking firewood and Gary walked over to Leonard with his tail flicking from side to side. Leonard's face lit up.

'See! He doesn't hate me,' he said.

'Dogs are very forgiving: they have kind hearts.'

'I think it's because he's a sop,' Leonard said.

Benjamin didn't laugh.

Leonard stroked the back of Gary's head. 'I'm only joking,' he said, rubbing Gary's scalp and scratching his ears while Benjamin looked around the camp, avoiding eye contact. He didn't like that Gary had let Leonard off so easily.

'I want to know why you did it?' Benjamin said.

Leonard carried on fussing the dog. He didn't look at Benjamin to answer.

'Did what mate?'

'Why did you tell them where we were?' Benjamin said.

Leonard hung his head, shook it feebly from one side to the other.

'It's probably just a symptom of my ongoing battle with depression,' he said eventually, letting his gaze creep over to Benjamin for a reaction. Benjamin thought about picking up the log. He wanted to hit Leonard again.

'I don't mean that as an excuse,' Leonard said.

Benjamin looked around at the damp ground, at a beetle dragging itself up and over some bark. 'You shouldn't lie about things like that,' he said.

Leonard contorted his face.

'It's not lies. It's wonky chemicals. I told you about my blue moods.'

Benjamin stood up and walked to the fire. He heard noises coming from Leonard that weren't words. When he turned around Leonard's eyes looked wet. He pressed the back of his hand into his eye socket.

'Are you crying?' Benjamin said.

Leonard forced himself to stop for long enough to speak.

'Is it making you feel weird because I'm a man?' he said.

'No,' Benjamin said. 'It's annoying me because this is all your fault.'

Leonard snapped a twig in his hands.

'I didn't steal a dog though, did I?'

'Neither did I,' Benjamin said, angry. 'He followed me.'

Leonard glanced at Gary, then threw the stick on the fire.

'I know how pathetic I am,' he said.

Benjamin nodded.

'But I'm going to make it up to you.'

'I don't need you to,' Benjamin said. 'We're fine. I'm going to look after him,' he said.

'I know you are. He's your spirit animal, isn't he.'

It sounded like something Camille would say.
'Did Camille tell you that?'
'She might have done,' Leonard said.

Forty-one

Leonard hung the white carrier bag on a tree and took out a can. He yanked the ring pull and shook the foam into the dirt. Benjamin saw he'd brought a change of clothes and a sleeping bag with him.

'Why did you bring that stuff?' he said.

'I never enter the bush without proper survival gear,' Leonard said.

'You're not staying,' Benjamin said.

Leonard drank some of the beer.

'Maybe we can talk about it later?' he said.

'We won't need to,' Benjamin said.

Leonard slumped down. He half-laughed. 'I said "enter" and "bush".'

Benjamin didn't smile. Even if he'd understood, he wouldn't have smiled.

'I'm only a man, Benjamin,' Leonard said eventually, swigging the beer.

'What's that got to do with anything?'

'I'm just flesh and bone. That's all.' He made a circle with his finger and thumb and put it over his eye. 'Just making sure you're viewing me through the correct lens.'

Benjamin didn't really feel like talking. He put his hand on the dog's neck and moved his fingers through the fur because he found it soothing. He felt a bump he didn't recognise.

'What's the plan, then?' Leonard said.

But Benjamin wasn't listening.

He leant in to look at the alien blob on the dog. It looked like a flesh-coloured coffee bean was attached to Gary's skin. It made him feel sick.

'There's something on him,' Benjamin said, interrupting Leonard.

'What?'

It was an insect of some kind. Benjamin looked at it closely. He couldn't even see how it was attached.

'It's stuck in his skin,' he said.

Leonard shuffled over. He eyeballed it and moved the blob around with his index.

'It's a tick,' he said.

Benjamin shook his hands and scratched the inside of his forearm.

'Get it off him,' he said.

Leonard picked up a stick and looked very earnestly at the insect. He prodded at its side, but it didn't move. Gary tried to crane his neck around to see what they were looking at.

'Hold him still,' Leonard said.

Benjamin was pacing around now.

'Why? What are you going to do?'

'Just give him a stroke,' Leonard said, taking a Swiss army knife out of his jeans pocket.

Benjamin ran over and put his hand on the pocket knife, cradling it. Leonard didn't pull it away from him.

'Don't cut it off!' Benjamin said. 'You could leave some in him. It might get infected.'

Leonard opened his hand and let Benjamin take the knife.

'I won't cut it off,' he said. 'Give it back and I'll show you.'

Benjamin worried Leonard would be clumsy and damage Gary.

'But I don't want to,' he said.

Leonard smiled. 'I'll sort it.' He put his hand out into the open space between them. Gary stood looking at them both.

'You won't just cut it off?' Benjamin said.

'Promise,' Leonard said.

Leonard knelt on the dirt and took out his lighter, balancing it on his knee. While he took a closer look, Benjamin stared at the side of his head, at his greasy hair and uneven stubble.

'Trust me,' Leonard said.

Benjamin handed him the knife.

'I could also do with that cutlery I packed in your bag?' Leonard said.

Benjamin grabbed a spoon from the duffel and passed it to Leonard, who slid the handle in under the bug and lit the lighter. He held the wobbling flame under the blade of his knife, then pressed it against the side of the insect. Holding the spoon and the penknife with the same hand, he applied pressure, gradually drawing the implements away from Gary's flesh. The more he squeezed and pulled, the closer Benjamin leant in to watch. When the tick popped out, complete but partially squashed, Leonard pressed it flat between the two sides of metal, red blood oozing out onto the steel.

'There!' he said, scooting towards Benjamin, holding up the insect for him to see. He tried to show him its bloated body and bunched-together legs, but Benjamin wasn't interested. He was too busy scrutinising Gary's skin, moving the reddened flesh around, looking for a remnant or a trace of something nasty. Leonard threw the bug into the fire.

'Is it definitely all out?' Benjamin said. 'Because they can vomit inside you.'

'As far as I can tell,' Leonard said. He laughed. 'Maybe we should have a funeral for him, though.'

'I don't want to do that,' Benjamin said. 'He was disgusting.'

Leonard tilted his head to think.

'Maybe,' he said. 'But he was alive, though, wasn't he?'

That made Benjamin feel bad.

'He might have had a family,' Leonard said, cracking a smile.

'An adoring wife. Offspring that relied on his ability to source good blood.'

Benjamin pretended not to hear. He poked the fire to get it going again, blowing on the embers and lining up twigs for kindling. He couldn't stop thinking about the bulbous insect, worrying it might have infected Gary with something invisible but terminal. He checked his own body, moving his hands around on his shins, on the bumpy flesh under the top of his socks and the bit above his waistband. He patted up and down his arms and imagined Gary dying because of an insect. He felt responsible because he'd chosen to bring the dog to the woods. He couldn't help hearing his nan again.

'Promise me you won't let them take me?' she'd said.

A tear ran down his cheek as he tucked his trousers into his socks.

'Do I look pale to you?' he said to Leonard.

'It's all good, mate,' Leonard said. 'I swear.'

Benjamin paced. He went back to Gary and checked him again, holding his legs up one by one. Gary stared at the ground while he did, allowing Benjamin to look. There was something gentle about the way he waited, like he knew Benjamin was looking after him.

When he was satisfied that nothing else was attached to Gary, Benjamin warmed another tin of beans in the fire and the dog settled on the ground. Benjamin put half on Gary's magazine, then had a mouthful himself. He handed the rest to Leonard.

'We could always heat up another one,' Leonard said, staring down at the underwhelming portion of beans in the bottom of the tin. Benjamin glanced over at his dwindling supply; the single tin that remained.

'No, you're right. We should save them,' Leonard said, tucking in with the same spoon he'd used to lever the insect off Gary. It made Benjamin want to gag. He was checking his shins again when Leonard threw the empty tin into the undergrowth.

'Do you think he needs to go to a vet?' Benjamin said.

'I'm not sure that would work out so well,' Leonard said. 'He's probably chipped.'

'You don't think he could have a blood-borne disease though, do you?'

'I'm sure he's fine.'

'But what if he's not?'

'He will be.'

Benjamin called Gary over and looked at the damaged patch of skin again. He brushed the fur away and stared at the minuscule puncture marks.

'I would go, you know,' he said.

'Where?'

'To the vets. Even if it meant I was incarcerated.'

'Even if it meant they took him off you?' Leonard said.

Benjamin thought for a second or two. About Gary being with him, or Gary being safe.

'I'd want him to be safe,' he said.

Gary moved around, and Benjamin thought about the quiet internal logic of dogs. He wondered what it is they think they're doing most of the time. He was in a kind of trance, when Leonard spat repeatedly at the ground.

'That's not a goer,' he said, clicking the lid of the sanitiser closed. 'I'd always thought this stuff was very alcoholic, but it tastes awful.'

He spat again.

'You drank it?'

'I wouldn't say drank. It's very viscous,' Leonard said, standing up and clapping his hands together. The sound echoed. After a slight delay, it seemed to carry on, even after Leonard's hands had stopped moving.

Benjamin and Leonard looked at each other.

'Is that someone else clapping?' Leonard said.

Benjamin wasn't sure. The trees seemed to do something strange to the sounds, bouncing them around. Leonard clapped again. He gritted his teeth. 'Maybe I shouldn't have done that,' he said. Then he did it again. Louder. The sound came back. 'Yeah, I definitely shouldn't have done that.'

'Stop it!' Benjamin said.

More clapping. But it was much clearer this time. Closer.

Leonard held his hand out. 'Get me the log!' he said.

'What log?' Benjamin whispered.

Leonard wiggled around frustratedly.

'You know—the intruder log! The one you hit me with.'

'I burnt it,' Benjamin said. 'In the fire.'

Leonard squinted, scrunching his face up as he tried to hear the sound. He raised his fists, assuming the traditional boxing stance, and bounced his weight from foot to foot. The clapping was incredibly close now. Benjamin was feeling overloaded. Gary licked a leaf.

'I'm going to have black eyes for the rest of my life,' Leonard said, grinning. 'Time to channel the honey badger again!' he said.

Benjamin called Gary over and prepared himself for whatever came next.

Forty-two

What came next was Camille. She was standing with her cycle helmet swinging around in her hand, beaming.

'Darlings!' she said, limping towards them.

'*JESUS* CHRIST Camille!' Leonard said, lowering his fists. 'All that clapping shit. I could have taken you out!'

'I actually thought that was very effective clap-location!' Camille said. 'I felt a bit like a dolphin.'

Leonard looked made-up; he rushed to whisper to Benjamin.

'One of only three animals that bone for pleasure!' he said. 'Along with humans and bonobos.'

Benjamin shot him a look. Leonard stuck his tongue out as Camille embraced Benjamin. When they separated, Leonard moved in. Camille tried to exit the hug and Leonard filled his lungs through his nose.

'You smell like a Nepalese ritual,' he said.

Camille blushed.

'It's just normal,' she said, flustered, the skin on her neck turning red. 'It's just my normal.'

Leonard was shaking his head at Camille.

'Well, it feels like I've just had a spiritual experience,' he said.

Camille pawed at the air.

'Oh, get off,' she said.

Camille's cheeks flushed.

'I was feeling very useless at home,' she said.

Leonard ushered Camille into the camp like a waiter showing

someone to their table. 'Take a seat, Camille,' he said, offering Benjamin's favoured sitting-stump. 'Can I get you a drink?'

He started scratching around in his plastic bag.

'I brought chamomile tea,' she said.

'I was thinking about a beer if you'll join me?' he said.

'A beer would be lovely!'

Camille hoovered the froth off from around the ring pull and went to see Gary. He stood perfectly still while she gave him a squeeze and talked to him like he was human. Leonard whispered in Benjamin's ear.

'She looks good all togged-up for the outdoors, doesn't she?'

Benjamin had a lot of respect for Camille. To him, that meant not commenting on her physical appearance. He'd also never thought about her in that way.

'He has your energy,' Camille said to Benjamin, turning to face him. 'He's beautiful.'

Benjamin smiled.

'With everything that's been happening,' Camille said, 'I've been thinking more extensively about what I said before. About reincarnation. It just feels like the timing is uncanny.'

Leonard watched Camille as though she were a mystical creature walking through the woods. She blushed.

'What do you mean?' Benjamin said.

'You know—at the supermarket? You might not recall because it was all very high-stakes at that particular time, but I was speculating about your grandfather's spiritual status shortly before we went to the dog track?'

Leonard grinned. He was clearly very impressed with what Camille had done at the track.

'Did you get banned?' he said, interrupting. 'After what you did?'

Camille looked away and Leonard took it to mean yes. He jumped in the air.

'TWINS!' he shouted. 'I'm on a lifetime ban, too.'

Camille looked genuinely embarrassed. 'I've never been banned from anywhere before,' she said.

'We're banned together, Camille. Not tethered by norms!'

Camille returned her focus to Gary. She leant in to look at the scar on Gary's chest and neck.

'Did he have any scars?' she said. 'Your granddad.'

Benjamin knew he did, from something that happened to him in the War. He didn't know if he wanted to encourage her though. He also definitely didn't want to lie.

'I think so,' he said. 'Maybe.'

'So it's possible!' Camille said. 'Imagine if he's here to help you during this very difficult time. How wonderful that would be. To guide you through it.'

Leonard was nodding. 'It does add up,' he said.

Benjamin couldn't get a read on Leonard. Not from the way he was looking at Camille. Which was like he was hypnotised. Camille shrugged.

'He found *you*, remember. Down on the beach. It can't have been easy escaping.'

That bit was true. Gary had found him. Followed him.

'I'll just leave it with you to think about,' Camille said. 'You can meditate on it.'

She closed her eyes, taking deep breaths, in and out, with both of her hands on Gary's head.

'I meant to ask you how your lip is, Benjamin? I've been worrying about your injuries.'

Benjamin hadn't forgotten about the damage to his face exactly—because it was constantly sore—but he'd stopped fiddling with it because his hands were dirty. He didn't want to make things any worse with a nasty infection.

'It's not too bad,' he said, finding a clean bit of wrist under his sleeve, using it to push on his cheek.

'I brought some special balm,' Camille said. 'It should help with the healing.'

'Thanks,' Benjamin said.

Leonard leant over her shoulder.

'I might need some of that.'

Camille held out the pot.

'Could you put it on for me?' Leonard said.

Camille laughed. 'I think you can do that for yourself,' she said. She looked back at Benjamin and stared at him for long enough that he felt uncomfortable.

'How are you?' she said.

Benjamin shrugged. She was still staring.

'Really though, Benjamin. How are you?'

For some reason the question made him want to cry, so he did. He turned away but he could feel them both watching.

'I'm fine,' he said.

Then Camille was there, hugging him again. She nodded at Leonard who held out a dirty hanky.

'The pocket-sized edition of my General-Purpose Cleaning Rag,' he said. 'No need to thank me.'

Camille pressed the hanky back towards Leonard and reached into her own pocket. She took out a small packet of tissues and handed one to Benjamin. He used it to dry his eyes. Nobody spoke for a little while. Eventually Leonard did.

'When we've had these beers,' he said. 'That entire episode has highlighted a need for better defensive measures. I felt very off guard when you were approaching, Camille. Caught with my lederhosen in the ankle position.'

Camille squeezed Benjamin tighter.

'It takes time for the oxytocin to be released,' she said.

Eventually Benjamin stepped away from her and smiled.

'What do you think we should do?' he said, looking at Leonard.

Leonard pranced forward and picked up a branch. 'I think let's start with decent sticks,' he said. 'I'd have brought my air rifle with me, but it's hard to conceal and it wouldn't be my first offence.'

'I think he's being serious, Leonard,' Camille said.

'So am I!' Leonard said. 'It's foundational.'

Benjamin pointed at his pile. 'I've already collected loads,' he said.

'No, I know. And that's top-notch foraging! But a lot of it is rotten.' Leonard stamped on a bit and broke it. 'I think it would be ineffective against an attacker?'

Leonard looked around. 'We need to roam our surroundings really,' he said.

'I'm not following you anywhere,' Benjamin said.

Leonard turned around.

'Why?'

'Because . . . last time,' Benjamin said.

Leonard looked up like he was solving a complex problem.

'He does have a point,' Camille said. She looked at Benjamin. 'Leonard appreciates your openness, Benjamin. Don't you Leonard?'

Leonard nodded. 'Yep,' he said. 'What about if you lead the way though?'

'I want to look here again first,' Benjamin said.

'Brilliant!' Camille said. 'That seems like a wonderful compromise?'

'Yeah, all right,' Leonard said. 'But I have high standards. I'm looking for an arboreal Excalibur. If we don't find anything suitable, we will have to go further afield.'

Benjamin gave Leonard a level stare.

'Let's just see how we go, shall we?' Camille said. 'Because we're finding sticks, but we're also respecting Benjamin's boundaries.'

Leonard shrugged like a reprimanded child. Then he threw himself enthusiastically into the task, looking for logs, swinging them around like a boy with a plastic sword.

When he was out of earshot, Camille leant in and whispered to Benjamin.

'Don't lose hope,' she said. 'Sometimes people can seem bad. But the bad is just a mask for a great deal of sadness. Under *that*, there is good. Someone like you can bring it out.'

Benjamin knew what she was saying, but he was still angry. He wandered around the clearing, looking for bits of wood he might have missed earlier. After a minute or so he picked up a stick with potential. It was substantial enough that it would be good for whacking, but not so chunky that the weight would make it difficult to wield. He swung it around, feeling its weight, but it wasn't as heavy as it looked. The moss got all over his hands as he performed a sequence of chopping motions until Leonard grabbed it off him and swung it around his head.

'This is the real test,' he said, whacking it on a tree. It snapped in two.

'Leonard!' Camille said. Can you please be more careful with the fruits of Benjamin's labours?

Leonard's shoulders slumped. 'Sorry,' he said. 'But this one's no good, I'm afraid. It's very rotten.'

Benjamin kicked a few more pieces of wood. He looked at Camille. 'Maybe we *could* look a bit further away,' he said.

Camille dipped her head supportively and Leonard bent at the hip, holding his arm out.

'After you,' he said.

The four of them walked out of the clearing in procession. At the front, Benjamin walked with Gary by his side. Camille and Leonard walked next to each other. Leonard was making Camille laugh by scanning the floor for animal tracks.

'You never know what you'll find out here,' he said, stumbling over a root. He pointed out potential areas to set traps or to hide if everything, in his words, 'went to shit.'

'You seem very knowledgeable about the outdoors,' Camille said.

'Lots of people assume I was in the military but I'm self-taught.

My father was a prodigious outdoorsman. Except when he was in prison. Then I guess he was an indoorsman. He was a taxidermist by trade, so we ended up in the woods fairly often. Procuring subjects.'

Benjamin was imagining glass cabinets full of awkwardly preserved animals—cross-eyed stoats with plastic eyes—until Leonard slipped down a bank and hit the deck. He made a bird-like noise.

'I think I just slipped in a human shit,' he said, lifting his own foot and pulling it close enough to smell it. 'That's definitely not an animal musk.' Leonard scanned around them through squinted eyes and jumped to his feet. He went back to looking for sticks in an attempt to mask his embarrassment. 'You don't want a feeble staff,' he said. 'If they're rotten they'll disintegrate when you hit someone. You don't want it to break like the one you hit me with.'

Benjamin resisted a smile, picking up a different, more solid-looking stick. It felt substantial in his hands.

'This seems better,' he said.

'Leonard?' Camille said.

Leonard came over to assess. He held it up to his eye and looked along it.

'This is what I'm talking about,' he said. 'Proper lumpy bit of trunk to whack someone in the bollocks with.'

Camille laughed so hard she snorted. Benjamin lifted the stick into the air and smiled. He was feeling very competent. The sensation was consuming—it pumped him up—made his muscles and his heart feel fuller.

Benjamin was celebrating by swinging it more confidently, like he imagined a medieval knight would, when a loud pulsing sound filled the sky. Gary looked around, confused, and Leonard ran towards a big tree. He pulled Camille by the hand and gestured for Benjamin to follow. They curled up at its base.

'Come here!' Camille shouted.

But Benjamin stood still while the noise above them swelled and drifted. It was hard to place.

'It's a fucking helicopter!' Leonard said, pointing skyward.

It seemed like Leonard hadn't been fabricating about the police. Benjamin ran to the tree and Gary followed. He pulled himself in close to the roots, close enough he could smell the stale cigarette smoke of Leonard's clothes mixing with the incense that Camille burnt in the office and in her flat. He held Gary tight as the thudding got closer, drumming in his ears. The dog shrank, his body trembling, as Benjamin tried to block out the sound with his hands.

As the helicopter circled and strafed—moving from one point to another then back again—they all watched the sky, waiting to see the outline. Waiting to be found.

Forty-three

Leonard's eyes met Benjamin's as the sound of the helicopter drifted off. He stood up and beat his chest, laughing, kicking at a clump of undergrowth.

'Thank Christ,' he roared. 'I thought that was us up the swanny!'

Camille had her hand on her heart, calming herself down. Benjamin was slumped, watching the newly-empty sky. After a minute or so, he put his hands on the soft earth to stand and felt something fleshy under his fingers. He'd crushed a mushroom.

'You all right?' Leonard said. 'Why are you standing with your hands out like that?'

Benjamin looked frantically around.

'I touched a wild mushroom,' he said. 'I squashed it and the juice is on my hand.'

Gary sniffed at one of the mushrooms and Benjamin jumped forward to stop his nose from making contact.

'This is all going to shit,' Benjamin said.

Leonard frowned. 'Let's have a look,' he said. He leant over Benjamin's hand, nodding. Looking at the mushroom like he'd looked at the tick.

'These ones are okay,' he said. 'I think you'd actually have to eat it to experience any ill effects.'

Leonard let his eyes roll back and stuck his tongue out like a poisoned person.

'Some you just touch,' Benjamin said, bending over to pick

up a handful of leaves, frantically wiping his hands, flapping them. Leonard walked over and grabbed him by the arms.

'I think I might feel dizzy,' Benjamin said.

'You're all right,' Leonard said.

Benjamin could smell the beer on Leonard's breath.

'But I'm dizzy. I think it's a neurotoxin.'

'It's not a neurotoxin. You're fine.'

'You really are,' Camille said, smiling.

Camille picked up a mushroom herself. Leonard rubbed it on his tongue.

'I mean I wouldn't do that,' Camille said. 'But I don't think you need to worry, love.'

Benjamin was worrying. The feelings were compounding, stacking themselves up one on top of another.

'She didn't want to go,' he blurted out, from nowhere distinct.

'Who didn't?' Leonard said. 'I thought we were talking about fungi?'

'My nan. To the hospital. She didn't want to go,' Benjamin said.

Leonard dipped his head to show he understood. Camille didn't say anything.

'Most people don't,' Leonard said.

'But if you don't go to hospital,' Benjamin said, 'you don't get better.'

'I've heard positive things about tribal medicine,' Leonard said, trying to lighten the mood. 'But yeah, I hear you.' He grimaced.

'She made me promise I wouldn't let them take her again,' Benjamin said. 'Do you think I did the right thing?'

'People don't always know what's best for them mate,' Leonard said.

'But did I do the right thing?'

Camille moved towards Benjamin.

'You did the right thing,' she said. She looked at Leonard. 'He did the right thing.'

Benjamin watched Gary for a long time without looking away. No one spoke.

'I didn't say everything I wanted to say,' Benjamin said. He was crying again. Leonard's eyes were wet, too.

'It's not always about what you say,' Camille said.

Benjamin looked up.

'Sometimes when she'd come in for her shopping, when you were on the till, we'd stand chatting by the milk fridge and she'd just look at you, smiling.'

Benjamin looked up.

'She loved you Benjamin, and she knew you felt the same. I've never been so sure about anything in my life.'

Benjamin smiled. He watched Gary licking his hand, blinking through tears.

'I'll tell you what else I'm sure of,' Camille said. 'That dog there, he's yours.'

'Do you think?' Benjamin said.

'One hundred per cent.'

Leonard held up the bottle of hand sanitiser and Benjamin grabbed it. He broke open the lid and squirted some out, rubbing it around on his hands, diluting the mud and the mushroom juice. Leonard called Gary to him, and the dog padded softly over.

'Give him a pat,' he said.

Gary was staring straight at Benjamin.

'I don't want to contaminate him.'

'You won't. Give him a pat,' Leonard said.

Benjamin crouched down beside Gary and held him.

'We're going to help you,' Leonard said, putting his hand on Benjamin's shoulder. Benjamin looked at Leonard's slim fingers and tanned forearm, blue veins bulging out like the lines on a tube map. 'I didn't get it before,' Leonard said, pointing at

Gary. 'But I get it now.' He smiled. 'I missed him,' he said. 'Old Skeletor.'

Benjamin moved his hand across the side of the dog's soft ribs. Camille squeezed Leonard's shoulder and smiled.

'We're going to help you,' she said, and Benjamin believed her.

Leonard started leading the way back to camp.

'I don't know who Skeletor is,' Benjamin said.

Leonard looked shocked. 'He was He-Man's nemesis!' he said.

Forty-four

Benjamin lay his new stick on the ground and sat down. He stared at the flames as Leonard used them to light a cigarette and opened another beer. A mound of foam pushed its way out and onto his hands. Camille accepted a drag on the cigarette and coughed.

'Classic beer,' Leonard said.

Benjamin looked at him.

'You don't think that was for us, do you?' he said.

Leonard laughed.

'What? The helicopter? Yeah, it definitely was. I didn't even think they had one of those around here. You know, because we live in a provincial wasteland.'

'It might not have been for us,' Camille said.

'All due respect Camille,' Leonard said. 'But it was.'

Camille looked Benjamin in the eyes and squinted reassuringly as he threaded his fingers together and pulled them across the front of his shins. He remembered the fear he'd felt as the loud noise of the rotors came closer.

'I don't think it was for us,' Camille mouthed, shaking her head, silently making the shapes with her mouth so Leonard didn't hear. Gary was looking at Leonard along his slender nose.

'The good thing is they clearly didn't see you,' Leonard said.

'You don't think?'

'No, course not. They'd have a SWAT team or whatever over here if they did.'

Camille winked and shook her head again.

'Maybe,' Benjamin said. He looked up. 'Do you think?'

'Definitely.'

Benjamin tried to imagine how prominent they'd have been from above, the four of them jumbled up at the foot of the tree.

'Do you think they had thermal imaging?' he said.

Leonard laughed out loud. 'This isn't *CSI*, mate.'

'You said they'd have SWAT.'

'Course they'd have SWAT. But that's police basics. Thermal imaging probably costs megabucks. They're not going to spend that around here, just so they can heat-seek doggers.'

Camille laughed.

'They wouldn't need it,' she said. 'They're all in the car park at work.'

Benjamin watched Leonard fill his lungs with smoke again. He held the cigarette out to Camille, but she didn't take it, which was good because he felt a genuine sense of dread that she might.

'I met a lady when I was at the hospital,' he said.

'I bet you did,' Leonard said, making himself laugh again.

Benjamin didn't know what was funny. 'She was called June. She's on oxygen.'

'She sounds like a catch.'

'They told her if she smokes in her room she'll explode.'

'Like a decomposing whale?' Leonard said.

'Exactly.'

Leonard stuck out his lower lip. 'Is this another anti-smoking message brought to us by Benjamin Glass?'

'I was just saying,' Benjamin said. 'About smoking. It can be very dangerous.'

Leonard chuckled. 'Okay,' he said, taking a last drag before throwing the cigarette over his shoulder. 'Enough of the propaganda. You win.'

Benjamin saw himself on the beach the day he met Gary, remembering the whale, as it was. Complete and largely undamaged.

'The whale's gone now,' he said.

Camille put her hand across her chest and pursed her lips to show she was sad about it.

'Maybe in some ways it's gone,' Leonard said.

Benjamin wondered in what ways it wasn't. Leonard seemed to sense it because he went on.

'Its body might be gone,' he said. 'But once you've sauntered about for ninety years—once you've scored your name into the trunk of The Great Oak or whatever—maybe you're never really gone. Maybe the whale is eternal,' Leonard said.

Camille had been sipping her beer, listening, but this perked her up.

'I think we're all eternal,' she said.

Leonard nodded in agreement.

'I think we've all been here before and we'll all be here again,' she said, looking straight at Benjamin. 'I think that for everyone.'

'I'm glad you think that Camille,' Leonard said. 'Because I don't feel like this is the first time we've met.'

'You don't?'

'I think we met in the desert the first time. You had a different name then: Cleopatra, I think.'

Camille hit his arm playfully.

They were both smiling. Benjamin was used to seeing Camille smile, at work. But he hadn't seen Leonard like this before.

'You're an idiot,' Camille said. She stood up. 'I think you two have some talking to do,' she said.

Benjamin's eyes flicked to the brush where the butt had gone in case it started a fire. Leonard's face turned serious.

'I do have an important question for Benjamin,' he said.

Benjamin tried to use facial expressions to communicate to Camille that he didn't want to be left alone with Leonard, but she was either oblivious or ignoring him. She smiled and walked away.

'We should stick together,' Benjamin called after her.

'I won't go far.'

'It's getting dark.'

'I'll just be over here.'

Benjamin and Leonard watched Camille walk towards the edge of the clearing. When she was about halfway there, Gary jumped to his feet and trotted after her.

'Do you think you'd eat him?' Leonard said. 'In a survival situation? Not that we're in one necessarily. But if you were?'

'Definitely not,' Benjamin said.

Leonard nodded upwards, unconvinced. He smirked.

'I think you would,' he said.

'I know I wouldn't,' Benjamin said.

'You can't know that.'

A few seconds passed.

'What do you mean?'

'You're not the version of yourself you're familiar with when you're on the edge like that,' Leonard said.

'I still wouldn't eat Gary.'

'That's the rational mind speaking. You wouldn't have a rational mind after ten days without food.'

'I wouldn't go ten days. We'd find food before then,' Benjamin said, looking over at the solitary tin he had left in the doorway of the tent. 'I'd let him eat me if it meant one of us survived,' Benjamin said.

Leonard laughed.

'He wouldn't eat you. He's wet.'

'That's why I wouldn't eat him.'

'The other thing,' Leonard said, 'is that there's not much meat on him. Maybe a bit on the thighs, but he'd probably taste rubbish.'

Benjamin was starting to get annoyed with Leonard again. He could feel it. But apparently so could Leonard because he stopped talking. The wind picked up, whistling through the trees above them. Leonard squinted at the boundaries of their camp and saw Camille with her hand on the bark of a large tree.

'Do you think I've got a chance?' he said quietly.

'A chance of what?'

'You know . . . with Camille?'

'I don't really know,' Benjamin said.

Leonard sat thinking. 'I don't know why, but I feel like something is changing,' he said.

Benjamin didn't reply. He was still thinking about Leonard and Camille while Leonard loaded up the fire with so much wood it made Benjamin's face feel dry. He picked up the bottle of boiled river water and started drinking it.

'That's from the river,' Benjamin said.

Leonard spat it out, all over the fire.

Benjamin laughed. He laughed enough that he could feel the pull of skin across his cheeks and in the tightness on his chin. Leonard laughed too.

'I probably deserved that,' he said. 'Where's it really from?'

'It's actually from the river,' Benjamin said. 'I boiled it though.'

'And you drank some?'

'No.'

Leonard smiled again. He took a huge glug of the river water, then wiped his mouth with his sleeve and smacked his lips.

'Lucky I brought some bottled water then isn't it.'

Leonard took a sealed bottle of drinking water from his plastic bag and gave it to Benjamin. Benjamin gulped half down in one go, then held the bottle out for Leonard to take it back.

'Me and Gary can stick to boiled river, mate. You keep that to yourself. Save a bit for Camille.'

Benjamin drank some more. The fire popped. Sparks fizzing out of its glowing core. Leonard gestured at the woods and at Benjamin.

'I sometimes wish I could go back to that first year we were married and exist there forever,' Leonard said. His eyes lingered on Camille as he opened up his wallet again. He slid the photo of Sally out, then unfolded it to reveal three more in a vertical strip. He was in the other pictures. In one they were both doing serious faces with big frowns. In another Leonard was sticking his tongue out and she was laughing. He looked different. Not just younger, but less tired. Not unlike the way he'd looked laughing with Camille.

'She looks kind,' Benjamin said.

'She was.'

Benjamin hesitated.

'Wait a minute. Is she—dead?'

'No, sorry. She's not dead,' Leonard said. 'I see how that sounded. She's alive. She just left me. She lives in a new-build in town somewhere, I think. With her partner.' Leonard wrinkled up his face. 'And their kids or whatever. He has a double-glazing company.'

Leonard took a closer look at the picture.

'I didn't deserve her anyway,' he said. 'She was a brilliant and radiant woman. And I'm a shithouse.'

Leonard thought himself into silence. Then he looked at Benjamin again.

'We nearly had a family,' he said. 'But it wouldn't have been the right thing, I don't think. Not really. I'm not much of a father-figure.' He half-laughed. 'Anyway, enough about my emotional baggage.' Leonard looked up. A smile crept over his face. 'About my griefcase.'

They both sat quietly, Benjamin thinking about the fair.

'I'd quite like to do the basketball thing,' he said, eventually. 'The thing where you get sixty seconds to get as many in as you can.'

That stirred Leonard from his wallowing.

'I was a master at that!' he said. 'It's better if you go with mates though.' He smiled. 'We'll go when this is all sorted out,' he said.

Benjamin looked at him for a long time.

'We'll have candyfloss and everything,' Leonard said.

'There's too much sugar in that,' Benjamin said.

When Camille came back, Benjamin and Leonard were just listening to the crackling wood as it turned to ash in front of them. Camille sat down on a log and Leonard put his sleeping bag around her shoulders. Benjamin arranged his by the fire and watched Gary's side rising and falling in the dim glow of the embers. He stared up through the gaps in the trees at the millions of stars broken up by navy blue space. Leonard threw more logs into the flames, growing them, until the clearing was glowing orange.

Benjamin shut his eyes and inhaled a lungful of air. Then he lay for a long time, feeling good about every second he'd been near the dog, feeling the parts of him existing—heat on his skin, Gary's body resting on his leg, the uneven ground beneath his back—the weight of a whole world holding him in place.

And for the first time Benjamin could remember, he felt connected to a thing much bigger than himself. To his elemental parts. To something vast and eternal.

'So, what are you going to do then? Now that you're a fugitive?'

'I'm going to stay here,' Benjamin said.

Leonard looked up.

'There are some Japanese soldiers still wandering around in the Vietnamese jungle, I suppose. I'm not sure it's a long-term plan, though,' he said.

Leonard's face was serious and a little sad. Benjamin turned away from him. He didn't want to think about that. He had Gary, and that was enough for now. Leonard stretched his arms above his head and yawned.

'Should we leave you to it, then?' he said. 'I know you said you want to do this on your own.'

Benjamin felt the rising swell of panic, skin prickling, as he remembered his and Gary's solitary night in the woods.

'You might get lost on the way back out,' he said.

'I have a keen sense of direction.'

'It's much more difficult in the dark,' Benjamin said. He had another sip of the water and waited to see what Leonard said.

'Okay. Maybe you're right. We'll hang around for tonight, if you think that makes sense? I can always head off tomorrow.'

Benjamin felt relieved but didn't reply, just focused on the warmth of the flames on his face. Felt the muscles in his shoulders relax. The dark void above them lit up with fireworks. Bursts of incandescent colour arcing through the sky, illuminating their faces.

'That's probably the fair,' Leonard said.

'Yeah, it's on at the moment.'

'I love the fair.'

'I've never been, really.'

'It's the stuff of dreams, Benjamin. I used to take Sally every year.'

Another round of fireworks pummelled the silence, streaking through the dark. Gary came running back. He was shaking, so Benjamin covered his ears with his hands to mute the sound.

Forty-five

The sounds of the birds chirping to each other woke Benjamin up. Leonard was over by the fire, prodding it with a stick, and Camille was sitting close by, on a rock just next to him. They'd fed Gary with some tins Camille brought and were watching him eat in silence. Leonard's hair was slicked back and damp-looking like he'd made an effort. He'd built a structure out of sticks to dry Benjamin's damp shoes while he slept.

'Morning Benjamin,' Camille said, turning to him. 'We didn't want to wake you up.'

Benjamin put his hand on Gary. The dog felt very warm. Leonard pointed to the saucepan on the fire.

'We made breakfast,' he said.

In the pot, a tin of mixed vegetable soup was bubbling away. Benjamin looked around for the tick spoon, for any traces that Leonard had been unhygienic. He shook his head, no.

'I used boiling water to make sure everything was sanitary,' Leonard said.

'I'm okay,' Benjamin said.

Leonard looked at Camille to back him up.

'I boiled everything, didn't I Camille?'

'He did.'

'Are you having some?' Benjamin said.

Leonard shook his head, halving it between Benjamin and Camille, but Benjamin poured some of his back into the tin and gave it to Leonard. The three of them sat in silence and ate. When they were finished, Leonard patted his belly.

'That was nice, that,' Leonard said. He rushed over to his bag, held out a little plastic orb in his hand. 'Want one of these?'

'What is it?' Benjamin said.

'It's a disposable toothbrush. Chewable,' he said. 'I found a broken vending machine at a service station that was just turfing them out. Thought they'd be useful to have in the car.' Leonard shot Camille a sideways glance. 'Not that I live in my car.'

Camille shrugged.

'I wouldn't judge you if you did. I think there's a lot of freedom in living in vehicles.'

Leonard was buoyed. 'I have a caravan as well,' he said. 'Maybe I could show you it sometime?'

Camille chuckled and took one of the toothbrushes. The inside of Benjamin's mouth felt fuzzy, so he took one too. They stood cleaning their teeth while Leonard tidied the camp, putting the clean utensils back where Benjamin had had them before. He lined up a couple of extra tins of food that Camille had brought and put the used ones in a plastic bag.

'I thought we could work on the camp today?' Leonard said. 'What do you reckon Camille?'

'Sounds like a wonderful plan.'

'I'm going to put my outdoorsman's shorts on first,' Leonard announced, making a fist and thumping his thigh. 'The nerves are all dead in there now,' he said. 'I've manually adapted them so I can wear shorts during any season.' Leonard adopted the demeanour of a knowledgeable teacher. 'I'll tell you why I like to do that.'

'You don't have to,' Benjamin said.

Leonard continued anyway.

'If you get wet, you dry quickly.'

Benjamin nodded. 'You're still wearing a jacket though?' he said.

'Yeah, unfortunately my torso hasn't had the same level of

exposure. It's more vulnerable to the elements. Camille—kindly avert your eyes!'

Leonard pulled down his jeans to reveal pasty legs covered in hairs. He was wearing white briefs. Benjamin spun his head in the opposite direction to avoid seeing too much.

'Why did you have to do that there?' Benjamin said.

'We're in the wilderness. That's just what you do in the wilderness. We don't have time to waste on societal norms, do we Camille?'

Camille spoke without turning around. 'I think it's a balance,' she said.

'I like societal norms,' Benjamin said.

Camille started by tightening up the guy lines of the tent. She made subtle adjustments to the tensions so that the inner sheet didn't touch the outer and wouldn't get wet in the night, then used extra rocks to weigh the pegs down.

'I see you've got some camping experience, Camille?' Leonard said.

Camille smiled. She was brushing her shoulders off for Leonard's benefit and looking around for more rocks when she noticed Benjamin's line of stones.

'These are wonderful,' she said, picking one up, winking at Benjamin. 'These aren't here by accident. They were expertly curated.'

Benjamin dipped his head, embarrassed.

'You have a good eye,' Camille said. She called Leonard over. 'They have very satisfying patination,' she said.

Leonard smiled. 'I think things are shaping up really well,' he said. He looked at Benjamin. 'I'm feeling very positive.'

Benjamin looked at him. 'About what?' he said.

Leonard walked over to Gary and put his hand on the dog's head.

'The whole thing. You. And him. We just need to put our

heads together and come up with a plan,' he said. 'Whatever it takes.'

Benjamin nodded. Leonard being so serious made him feel awkward. He wasn't used to it. Leonard walked over to the fire and put the last few pieces on.

Camille was still staring at the stones.

'Isn't it funny to think how these will be here long after all of us are gone,' she said.

'This version of us,' Leonard corrected. 'The same can't be said for the fire, though. We're going to need more wood if we're going to keep it going,' he said. He looked at Benjamin. 'We can go, though. Me and Camille.'

Camille looked at Benjamin. 'I'll keep an eye on him,' she said.

Leonard put his arm around Camille's shoulders and pulled her in, tilting her off balance. She blushed again.

'I'll leave my phone with you,' Leonard said, holding it out. 'If you need us just phone Camille. She's saved as Cleopatra.'

Camille laughed out loud. She was looking at Leonard and Leonard was looking at Benjamin.

'We won't be long,' she said.

Benjamin watched them as they walked towards the treeline, their bodies staying close as they walked side by side. Just before they were out of sight, Leonard turned and stopped. He shouted.

'Benjamin,' he said.

'Yeah?'

'I really am sorry, you know.'

Benjamin nodded.

'Okay,' he said.

And with that, Leonard and Camille strode away into the woods.

Benjamin filled a pot with clean water and balanced it on the fire to make coffee for when they were back. His hands were dry with mud, so he held them up to examine the dirt under his fingernails. He was thinking about using the sanitiser when Gary moved towards him. He put his hands on either side of the dog's head and used his thumbs to soft his ears. He rubbed the loose skin on his face, moving his cheeks up and scratching his muzzle. Benjamin closed his eyes and listened to the breeze moving the trees around. He held Gary's head close to his and could smell the earth and honey of Gary's fur. He reached into his pocket for the sanitiser and found Leonard's keys instead. With everything that had happened, he'd forgotten they were there. As the water started to boil, he folded the rubber keyring in his hand and felt glad he hadn't thrown it into the sea.

Benjamin was pouring the hot water into three mugs when he heard the sound of someone coming back through the woods. He turned and held the keys up in the air, smiling, but an unfamiliar voice called out to him.

Forty-six

A police officer was walking towards Benjamin with her hands held low, treading like she was on fragile ground. She was speaking into a walkie-talkie.

'Benjamin,' she said. 'Benjamin Glass?'

Gary let out a low rumbling sound.

'It's okay, Benjamin,' the woman said, talking to him now. 'We're here to help you,' she said.

Benjamin backed away. He looked for Leonard and Camille, then for his shoes. They were still balanced on sticks by the fire, too far away for him to get them.

'Just stay where you are,' she said. 'I need to let my colleagues know where we are so they can help us.'

She was speaking into the walkie-talkie again when Leonard came thundering through the trees, swinging the stick and shouting so aggressively that spit was coming from his mouth. She stumbled away from him, reaching for something on her hip. Leonard was about ten feet away when the police officer produced a bright yellow object that looked like a gun and aimed it at the middle of his chest.

'Stop,' she shouted.

But Leonard didn't.

'TASER TASER TASER,' she shouted.

And Leonard hit the deck. There was a clicking sound as the volts moved through his body, making him shake. Sharp metal conductors were lodged in his torso. He was making plosive but incomprehensible swearword-sounding groans.

Camille had caught up. She was on the edge of camp screaming his name.

When the clicking sound stopped, Leonard slumped over towards Benjamin and shouted.

'Run boy,' he said. 'Run.'

But he didn't need to shout. Benjamin was already going, flat out towards the trees, Gary hurtling along beside him.

Forty-seven

Benjamin felt himself sinking into the wet ground as it pulled at the dirty socks on his feet. The rapid beats of his heart were thumping out a rhythm in his neck that blocked out everything else and made his body feel weightless. It made him run faster and harder than he ever had in his life.

The lactic acid built in his muscles and his lungs burnt. He slowed to a stumble, turning to listen for Leonard's shouts, but he couldn't hear him any more.

Benjamin stood, replaying everything that had happened—the police finding him, Leonard charging into the clearing, Camille watching—racking his brains to work out how he could stop it, to stop everything from changing.

He didn't know what else to do but run. He moved off again along a track until he came to the edge of the woods and a field cut up by tractor marks. In the open, he heard the distant sound of a football game going on and cars screeching to a stop. He looked around. There were hi-vis jackets moving towards him from the corner of the field, so he ran faster, along a hedge and then a fence. The sounds of the game were getting louder. He sprinted around a corner and burst out onto the pitch. The people had been cheering, but gradually they stopped, all looking in Benjamin's direction.

Police officers were climbing out of their cars in the car park beside the clubhouse. They skirted the game, walking around the field towards Benjamin and Gary. Benjamin looked down at the dog.

'You'll make it if you run,' he said.

But Gary didn't run. He sat down and stared at Benjamin like he'd done that first day on the beach. A few feet away, long slow blinks like he'd just woken from a dream.

'Go on. Please,' Benjamin said, every part of him wishing that Gary would run, that he'd explode away with his ears pinned back, tongue hanging out as he belted across the field. But he didn't. He just sat there as the police closed in, moving towards them from all around.

In the distance another police car pulled into the gravel car park behind the pitch and drove straight through onto the grass. It looked like Leonard was sitting in the back, but it was hard to tell through the tears in Benjamin's eyes.

When the police officers reached him, Benjamin saw that Mike from the hospital was behind them. He was speaking, but the words were falling out of order in Benjamin's head. Mike hesitated. He tried to smile but his face was serious and pale-looking. He put his hand out to rest it on Benjamin's arm, but Benjamin backed away. Mike tried to speak but now it was him that was struggling. Benjamin could see the sadness in Mike's face, guess at the words he was trying to find. And he knew then that Mike was trying to tell him that his nan was gone.

There were hands holding him up, but Benjamin sank, the world spinning around, too heavy for all of them. His slim body was at the centre of some great rotation that seemed to be pushing him down onto the grass.

He sat, thinking about her. About her hands, covered in thin skin like bible paper and the way her collar bone poked out as she lay in the hospital bed. How she held his hands to look at the cracks from washing them too much, fine blood spreading out in the creases like tributaries in a river. He remembered how she moved hers over them, working ointment in. How she'd stepped aside in the doorway of the caravan when they'd dropped him off, the wind blowing her hair in lazy horizontals, smiling while they said he'd be staying for good this time. And about the whale, of all the days it had lived, cutting through the water, moving up through shards of light towards the surface for air.

He knew something of how it made him feel now, the whale. It made him realise that things were special because they faded, more precious because they didn't usually last. And then he lay still, cold-bright sunshine on his face, the sound of waves swelling down on the beach, rolling over the millions of pebbles there. Gary standing over him as close as he could manage.

'I love you, dog,' he said.

Acknowledgements

It's impossible to write a novel on your own. Even if you hammered it out, all in one go, padlocked in a caravan, that's still not what you'd be doing.

Everyone you know is in there. So is everyone you've met, been taught by, had a disagreement with or watched in a film. Everyone you've overheard or observed.

This book is no exception.

Since it's not particularly practical to thank everyone on that basis, below is my best attempt at the special mentions. Mentions for the people who made the book far more than it ever could have been if I'd written it without them.

Thanks first, to my wife Lucy. For opening my laptop and putting a coffee on the coaster in the early days, and for not smashing the laptop to bits towards the end. For looking after me, us, the details, the bigger picture, for paying the bills, for reading this novel more times than even I could stomache. For bailing out the water when the ship got a soaking. I could not have done this without you. I love you.

Thanks to my perfect little boy, for making me joyously happy every single day of my life, and for putting everything in perspective.

Thanks to my magical mum, for everything, and for always, always, buying me books.

Thanks to Nesie, who got me the job on the tills in Somerfields when I was at school. And for being, I think it's fair to say, my number one fan.

Thanks to Nanny Tessie, who listened patiently as I talked about the book I'd write one day, long before I was anywhere near. (I'm sorry there's a bit of swearing in here, I know you don't like it.) Thanks for the spelling tests as I fell asleep and the memories of marmalade on toast. For making the world feel safer and kinder, just by existing.

Thanks to Frannie, book dragon, for having a bookshelf I always imagined my book on.

Thanks to Dad, for being an unwavering presence, for being someone I will always look up to.

And thanks to Mark Chapman, for being the third parent, and friend, I could never be without.

Thanks to the Webbs for keeping a straight face while I told you I was going to finish the novel 'soon'. Especially Babs and Nick for all the times you looked after Arlo or mowed the lawn, or painted something, or put up shelves, while I sat in Costa struggling with the edits.

Thanks to Seth Townley, my long-standing first reader and

excellent friend. For having a brain I would trust over my own to know what works and what doesn't.

Thanks to copy desk. To Hannah Harper and Owen Nicholls for their generosity of feedback, intellect, dynamism, comradeship, power, integrity, charisma and other attributes. May the copy WhatsApp exist until society crumbles and technology fails, or the robots take over.

Thanks to everyone at the National Centre for Writing, for the help they gave me, but also the help they give countless other people. They do something very special.

Thanks to my official mentor from the NCW Escalator Programme, Ross Raisin, for his wisdom and razor-sharp insight. And for telling me what the book was actually about.

Thanks too, to my unofficial mentor, Benjamin Johncock, for breaking cover and sending me an email of encouragement I've got on the wall.

Thanks to the friends I made on the Escalator programme.

Thanks to Trezza Azzopardi for her patient guidance while I was at UEA, and to Andrew Cowan for counselling me after a run of poor attendance and bad marks. For telling me not to stress it too much, because those things often have very little to do with the writing we do.

Thanks to Hattie Grünewald, for being onboard from the beginning. For seeing what DOG might be, before anyone else. And for her patience with my irritating emails when I was fishing for news.

Thanks to Christopher Potter, for taking a punt when not many others did. Thank you for asking vital questions of the book, and for bearing with me while I finished it. Thank you for telling me that a novel is an imperfect object, which is without a doubt the most freeing and helpful guidance anyone has ever given me about writing.

A big thank you to the wonderful people at Europa. Daniela, Caro, Eva, Leonella and Michael (I particularly appreciated your keen eye) – you're all absolute diamonds. 10/10. Would recommend.

A special mention to the friends that have put up with me so far, for the generally poor contact, terrible reply speed, and lack of social appearances. Know that even if I don't make it obvious, I love you all dearly.

Thanks to James Bradley, my daytime boss and 24-hour friend, for the 'research' you helped with.

Thanks to my gym family at FitMissions, for your unwavering support, interest and love.

Thanks to the heroes of the Bakewell on-call, for letting me temporarily retire while I dealt with paying the bills and finishing the book.

Thanks to Jimmy Chase, wherever you are, for covering for me for an entire day in the shop, while I wrote the story that got me a place at UEA.

And finally, thanks to my dogs, Rhodrigo and Drew. For the love, and the details. And in the way of canines generally, for giving everything and for asking nothing in return.

Europa Editions UK

Read the World

Literary fiction, popular fiction, narrative non-fiction,
travel, memoir, world noir

Building bridges between cultures with the finest writing from around the world

Ahmet Altan, Peter Cameron, Andrea Camilleri, Catherine Chidgey,
Sandrine Collette, Christelle Dabos, Donatella Di Pietrantonio, Négar Djavadi,
Deborah Eisenberg, Elena Ferrante, Lillian Fishman, Anna Gavalda,
Saleem Haddad, James Hannaham, Jean-Claude Izzo, Maki Kashimada,
Nicola Lagioia, Alexandra Lapierre, Grant Morrison, Ondjaki, Valérie Perrin,
Christopher Prendergast, Eric-Emmanuel Schmitt, Domenico Starnone,
Esther Yi, Charles Yu

*Acts of Service, Didn't Nobody Give a Shit What Happened to Carlotta,
Ferocity, Fifteen Wild Decembers, Fresh Water for Flowers, Lambda,
Love in the Days of Rebellion, My Brilliant Friend, Remote Sympathy,
Sleeping Among Sheep Under a Starry Sky, Total Chaos, Transparent City,
What Happens at Night, A Winter's Promise*

Europa Editions was founded by Sandro Ferri and Sandra Ozzola,
the owners of the Rome-based publishing house Edizioni E/O.

Europa Editions UK is an independent trade publisher
based in London.

www.europaeditions.co.uk

Follow us at . . .
Twitter: @EuropaEdUK
Instagram: @EuropaEditionsUK
TikTok: @EuropaEditionsUK